"KAT, LISTEN TO ME," HE SAID URGENTLY. "NOBODY HAS TO BE HURT BY WHAT WE DO. WE COULD HAVE WEEKEND TRIPS. WE COULD—"

"No, Matt," she interrupted unsteadily.

"Why not?" he rapped out.

"Why?" she countered.

"We're mature people, and we want each other. Damn it, Kat, why are you denying what we both need?" he asked testily.

"Because I won't enter into a mockery of what should be mutual respect and . . . and affection. I want a caring relationship, not just an unemotional exercise."

"A fantasy? Is that what you want?" His hard, derisive tone scoffed at the idea as old-fashioned.

"Perhaps. I just know I couldn't do it your way."

"And your way is unrealistic," he muttered.

Frustration and anger overwhelmed her. "That may be, but I won't be just another itch for you to scratch! Now, get out!"

A CANDLELIGHT ECSTASY SUPREME ™

HANDLE WITH CARE

Betty Jackson

A CANDLELIGHT ECSTASY SUPREME™

Published by
Dell Publishing Co., Inc.
1 Dag Hammarskjold Plaza
New York, New York 10017

ISBN: 0-440-13424-2

Printed in the United States of America
First printing—October 1983

To Our Readers:

Candlelight Ecstasy is delighted to announce the start of a brand-new series—Ecstasy Supremes! Now you can enjoy a romance series unlike all the others—longer and more exciting, filled with more passion, adventure, and intrigue—the stories you've been waiting for.

In months to come we look forward to presenting books by many of your favorite authors and the very finest work from new authors of romantic fiction as well. As always, we are striving to present the unique, absorbing love stories that you enjoy most—the very best love has to offer.

Breathtaking and unforgettable, Ecstasy Supremes will follow in the great romantic tradition you've come to expect *only* from Candlelight Ecstasy.

Your suggestions and comments are always welcome. Please let us hear from you.

Sincerely,

The Editors
Candlelight Romances
1 Dag Hammarskjold Plaza
New York, New York 10017

HANDLE WITH CARE

CHAPTER ONE

A mild chill shivered up Katherine's spine when the cool night air penetrated the thin layers of nylon covering her. Hardly adequate protection against the April breeze, she acknowledged with a grimace. When she stepped outside to carry the trash bag to the curb, she hadn't intended being outdoors more than a moment. Her nightgown and robe had seemed sufficient covering. Now she wished she had slipped into her soft leather house shoes. At least they would have provided some protection to slim, bare feet feeling increasingly cold trudging through the damp grass.

A scattered blanketing of wispy clouds obscured the moon, limiting visibility and making the spotting of her prey more difficult than she'd first anticipated. She was ready to admit defeat when she glimpsed a blur of light color at the corner of the house.

"Marigold, is that you? Come here, you miserable animal," she whispered authoritatively, and then more coaxingly; "Please, you little beast. My feet are freezing."

And on those desperately pleading words the blur of light color became a flash of white and gold fur as the cat darted for cover amid the hedges of the neighboring house.

"Oh, dratted damn!" Katherine muttered explosively, scurrying forward to follow the cat's progress. The little devil was more trouble than she was worth! First streaking out the back door while her mistress had her hands full of plastic garbage bags and now completely ignoring the call to return! And why had Mari decided to ambush crickets or grasshoppers at the side of the Clinton man's residence? Why not in her own territory?

The sudden gleam of headlights from a passing car clearly detailed Marigold's slinking steps stalking some poor misfortunate of the insect world and also had Katherine ducking furtively behind the large trunk of a tall sycamore growing just inside the adjoining property. Good heavens, that was close! All she needed to feel like a complete fool was to be seen traipsing through the night dressed as she was. She hugged the tree until the car passed harmlessly by, then skirted it to steal closer to the area Marigold had headed for.

"Kitty! Marigold!" she whispered, hoping to call forth another glimpse of white fur, but the feline had disappeared from sight.

Katherine crept nearer the flowering Carolina jasmine growing in abundance against the gray brick of Matt Clinton's house, thinking to find the cat there. The fervently muttered vow to murder the recalcitrant pet once she caught her was abruptly curtailed, a slight, unwelcome sound penetrating her consciousness.

Oh, bother! Surely not another animal! If Mari scented another cat or a stray dog, she would be off like a shot and never come back inside tonight. Still more sound, subdued but identifiable, convinced Katherine there was no need to fear the appearance of a member of the animal kingdom. Quiet though they were, those were very definitely human footsteps disturbing the night's stillness.

Just managing to smother a loud groan of despair, she ducked quickly behind the concealing trellis of jasmine. The soft, muffled approach of the intruder filled her with cold agitation. Frantically praying she would not be seen hiding in the bushes like some guilty criminal, she pressed back against cold brick and mortar and held her breath.

A second later that suspended breath wheezed sharply from her lungs. Too petrified of immediate exposure to panic and run, she grew rigid with horror. Not two yards away, but blessedly with his back turned, stood a large male body. The obscuring darkness made accurate identification impossible, but the huge size of his shadowy form gave her a clue. Matt Clinton. Or was it?

As he paused with his head thrown back, his stance was either contemplative or watchful. Was he verifying the scents the night breeze wafted his way? Or was he tensed with an awareness of not being alone? He turned a slow half circle to face in her direction, and still Katherine couldn't discern his features. But who else could it be? In the ordinary run of things, thieves and cat burglars were a rarity in her neighborhood. *Cat burglar! How appropriate!* Her teeth clamped down hard on her lower lip to prevent a hysterical laugh from escaping. After all, she reasoned with a touch of untimely humor, wasn't it hopes of capturing a cat that had brought her to this potentially embarrassing situation?

With a heartfelt, if carefully inaudible, sigh of relief, she tensely watched the tall figure shrug almost imperceptibly and then continue on from the side of the house toward the wooden fence enclosing the Clinton backyard. The gate creaked as it swung open and shut, and although Katherine couldn't see his movements from her concealment of fragrant jasmine, she assumed the man let himself through. Only then did she sag back against the brick, closing her eyes while the tension slowly ebbed from her body.

Thank God that awful man hadn't spotted her! She couldn't have borne another confrontation with him, especially under the present circumstances. Past experience had taught her that any encounter with Matt Clinton needed to be with herself in full control of the situation—and bare feet and a nightgown were not pluses in her favor. Lord, but he was a thorn in her side! And had been since the day he moved in three months ago. Her daughter was at an impressionable age, and she was very definitely impressed with their big, good-looking neighbor, singing his praises so often that Katherine was heartily sick and tired of the merest mention of his name. And she resented like hell the encouraging attention he in turn lavished on her daughter. Laurel might look like a blossoming Hollywood starlet, but she was barely a budding, adolescent fifteen. Katherine was very conscious of her daughter's tender age even if Matt Clinton had shown less discernment and Laurel herself resented any intimation that she wasn't completely mature.

Ah, well, youth! Katherine smiled reluctantly. She could still remember that difficult age between childhood and adulthood even from her advanced, decrepit years numbering thirty-three.

Feeling comfortably certain that the awful Clinton nuisance was by then safely ensconced before his cozy hearth, Katherine brushed through the fragrant jasmine and back into the open space of lawn between the two houses. *Now, Marigold, uncover your hiding spot, you irresponsible cat!*

"Marigold!" she whispered quietly but firmly. "Here, kitty, kitty!"

There was no response. Miserable ingrate! The offer of food and a loving home was being repaid by obstinate silence. She vowed to strangle each of the nine lives from the beautiful tabby coat.

"Come on, kitty! Come on, Marigold!" she whispered urgently into the night's breeze, adding to herself: *Oh, cat, when I catch you* . . . There was something very undignified about a sedate, mature widow's being forced to traipse

14

around the lawn and bushes at eleven o'clock on a cool April night, especially if said lady was wearing the minimum of clothing, no shoes, and the damp grass under her cold feet was Clinton terrain!

Continuing to whisper an intermittent "Kitty, kitty," Katherine slunk from bush to shrub to tree, progressively nearing the high wooden fence that bordered her neighbor's backyard. Then she heard the answer to all her calls—just two small, plaintive little meows—from inside the stockade enclosure. Blast the abominable luck! Why hadn't Mari's search for insects been limited to the front and side yards?

With careful fingers and careless thought Katherine found the gate latch and examined it with a light touch, gratefully surmising it was a simple click-pull lock and all she had to do was lift the wrought-iron catch and . . . *Careful, Katherine, don't bungle it now! No need to announce your entrance into Mr. Clinton's private sanctuary.* She quietly pushed inward on the heavy wooden gate.

The moon's illumination was even dimmer once she had stepped through the gate, caused, she supposed, by the abundance of leafy trees spreading a curtain of concealment between the sky and the ground. It took a moment of squinting adjustment, but she finally spotted slanted green-glowing cat's eyes about thirty yards away in the center of the lawn. Ducking down, she slunk forward, making quiet beckoning noises to attract Marigold's attention but, she hoped, no one else's. The glowing eyes blinked twice as she approached and then disappeared completely, a flash of pure insolence speeding to the far corner of the yard and into some low flowering border plants.

"Damn, damn, damn!" Katherine muttered under her breath, extremely frustrated.

Then she froze in her bent position, a chill of fear

spreading up her spine, a sudden indefinable warning of imminent danger. She straightened abruptly, but before she could turn either to confront the menace she sensed behind her or to force her frozen limbs to run, she was manacled from behind in a hard grip of solid steel. Her arms were pinned helplessly to her sides, her body clamped tightly to another one. Instinctively she opened her mouth to issue a scream of terror, but it never emerged from her constricted throat. A firm hand covered her mouth, muffling the sound that would surely have wakened the dead.

Her attacker issued no more than a low satisfied grunt, but it sounded like a death knell to Katherine's terrified hearing. Horror mounted in leaps and bounds. Horror and a sickening realization.

Oh, God, it had been a burglar or murderer or rapist moving quietly through the darkness minutes ago! Why had she not seriously considered that possibility? Had she been so caught up in dire thoughts of Matt Clinton that she failed to sense real danger? Foolishly planting herself in harm's way?

She struggled frenziedly, kicking wildly back with her bare feet to encounter nothing but air when her attacker shifted his weight to spread his legs in a wider stance. Useless as weapons of defense, her arms were impotently pinned by one of his, but somehow she managed to twist her hands, stiffening her fingers into vicious talons to scratch the bare forearm hugging tightly under her breasts. She heard his grunt of pain with feral satisfaction and then felt the increased pressure he forced on her diaphragm in retaliation with an abrupt exhalation of air against his fingers. Then his angry, rasping breath was brushing against her ear as he bent forward to shift his position, straightening to lift her completely free of the ground.

16

Katherine moaned against his hand and tried desperately to scream, frustrated when she heard the pitifully muffled sound she managed to make. While silent shrieks of terror filled her being, only the accompaniment of her labored breathing joined the soft, stirring whistle of night air. She had never been so scared in her life! No help was forthcoming in the nightmarish situation. No cry for help was permitted. No quarter was given by the fiend who held her so securely. Her heart pounded frantically against her ribs. She fought a feeling of faintness that threatened to engulf her.

But she couldn't faint! She wouldn't! Her only hope was to outmaneuver her assailant, she realized with a resurgence of clear thinking. She would have to find some means to overpower him, to break loose, to scramble for freedom and safety.

She renewed her struggles with a vengeance, hoping to catch him off guard. Kicking back with all the force and momentum she could muster, she connected with a hard shin and hurt her heel unbearably in the process. The tingling pain shooting through her foot received only cursory consideration. The man wasted no breath on words. Once again a warning pressure was applied to her ribs, a silent but explicit order to cease struggling.

Undaunted, Katherine answered the wordless directive by biting a finger loosened almost imperceptibly against her mouth. And was immediately rewarded by his sharp howl of pain.

But, unfortunately, all of life's little rewards have to be paid for. Punishment was duly meted out for that bloodthirsty nibble. The fingers over her mouth dug painfully into her cheek and jaw. The muscled arm about her middle tightened to a suffocating pressure. Other fingers holding her arm bit painfully into the tender flesh. The excruciating combination caused tears of pain to spurt

17

from her eyes, and Katherine once again released a feeble moan of agony.

Katherine found herself slumping back against a hard expanse of muscles, her head falling near a sinew-bunched shoulder in defeat . . . for the moment. Whatever he planned doing to her, it was obvious that her present struggles were getting her nowhere. Her attacker was stronger and seemingly prepared to counteract each bid she made for freedom. Her only consolation came in knowing she hadn't made it easy for him. The harsh movement of his chest testified to his labored effort to control her. She forced herself to breathe more evenly, knowing she would need all her breath and strength if an opportunity presented itself for escape.

As if satisfied with her frail capitulation, the man moved forward, carrying her in front of him like an unwieldy parcel. She closed her eyes in dread, but when, after several long paces, he paused and removed the hand from her mouth, her eyes snapped open. Complete blackness surrounded her, and incredibly she felt herself enveloped in warmth. It took only a moment to realize it was the still warmth and silence of indoors.

When he released her completely, it was so unexpected that at first Katherine didn't know she was free. Then the deep-piled carpet under her toes and the complete lack of restriction convinced her. Her constricted throat felt frozen with fear, and she swallowed heavily, unable to make a sound. She was half afraid to move. Her assailant was at her back, and in front of her was a pitch-black room. She had no knowledge of the furnishings. A fraction of a second was all she hesitated, however, before instinct screamed that anything was better than being grabbed by a vicious lunatic again.

Darting forward, she almost immediately encountered disaster when her shins bumped painfully against some-

18

thing hard and unyielding. She felt herself falling forward, her arms flailing uselessly in the air as she fought to regain balance.

Help for her dizzying predicament came from an unwanted source. Long fingers tangled in her flying hair, jerking her back against the solid but terrifying security of a hard male body. Immediately his hands shifted to her waist, and just as quickly Katherine began twisting for freedom, determined not to be captured by his bruising strength again.

The hard, grasping hands at her waist frustrated her attempts to prize them loose, and when one slid slickly over the silky fabric of her robe and covered a breast, she became even more frantic to break free. Her sob of outrage went unheeded, and she clawed desperately at the hand intruding where she didn't want it, his continued grasp on her breast convincing her his intentions were of the basest sort. Her frantic movements and her assailant's efforts to hold on to her had them both falling to the floor, miraculously with his much larger body hitting the floor first and her slighter weight falling on top. They rolled on the carpet, bumping into furniture, twisting like two wrestling antagonists in a tangle of arms and legs until she was effectively pinned beneath a crushing weight, her arms spread wide above her head.

Through the rushing sound of blood pumping thickly to her brain, Katherine heard the man's labored breathing near her ear. As he raised his head, she felt the warm touch of his mouth brush against the hair at her temple.

"Oh, God, don't . . ." she managed to croak, her tortured lungs almost unable to draw breath.

"You crazy little wildcat! You've made this hard on yourself. Now be still, because I've damned well run out of patience!" he whispered roughly, his breath warm and moist on her averted cheek.

Katherine's frightened panic abruptly subsided, a tremendous surge of relief crowding out fear and emotional upheaval. Her attacker's voice. She knew that deep voice! Totally exhausted, she went limp suddenly, no longer fighting his dominance and wishing the room weren't pitch-black. Almost certainly the face above hers would be tauntingly familiar. Her shaky, irregular sigh of relief was issued through lips too parched to speak.

"That's better. Much more sensible not to fight a stronger force, isn't it?" he asked so ironically that Katherine had to bite her lip to keep from groaning aloud. How many times during the past three months had she been subjected to that particular nuance of Matt Clinton's deep voice?

"You've made some big mistakes tonight, and I owe you for a couple of the more physical ones," he went on in a grimmer tone, causing Katherine to wonder if she was safe after all. Her lips parted, and her breath came unevenly. Not just because of her former exertions, but because a new chill of nervousness was sweeping over her.

Unsteadily she whispered, "Let me explain. I—"

"Oh, you'll explain, all right," he interrupted with hard inflection. "Forcefully or willingly—the choice is yours. But make it good, because I'm not averse to punishing prowlers, even if they are female."

Hurriedly, her voice gasping out the words, she managed disjointedly, "Your backyard . . . crickets and grasshoppers . . . Mari . . ."

"An insect wedding?" he barked incredulously, unexpectedly loosening his grip on her wrists in his astonishment.

Immediately Katherine jerked her hands free, massaging her abused wrists to promote circulation. She glared up at him in the blackness, growling a strangled "Noooo!"

The man above her muttered something blue and unrepeatable about insects and insanity. Then, with an angry snarl, he rolled away from her and bounded to his feet.

A second later light blinded Katherine's eyes. She blinked them shut, curling to a half-sitting position, too drained by a shaky relief that he had left her to worry about her posture or possible state of undress. She could feel him standing above her and knew by his silence that he was inspecting her closely, really seeing her clearly instead of merely gaining a shadowy impression in a cloud-covered night or a pitch-black room.

Tangled honey blond hair spread down her shoulders and over her face, obscuring it from his view. One slender arm crossed protectively over the hint of her full breasts, but the almost fragile slenderness of her length was open to his scrutiny, her front-opening robe having separated during their scuffle on the floor. Both robe and gown, frosty green and delicately detailed with a silken piping, were twisted haphazardly around her slim thighs. In an effort to gain a fragment of modesty, Katherine quickly stroked the wispy fabric down past her knees, all too aware that a keen male gaze followed the nervous movement.

"Get up," he ordered quietly.

Less than steady fingers went to her face to push away the glorious tangle of her hair, and her features were revealed.

"Well, I'm damned!" Matt Clinton muttered with disgust.

Katherine's eyes focused resentfully on his size eleven and a half shod feet, her dark brown lashes darkened even further with the residue of recent tears. The delicately sculpted features of her face contorted into an indecisive frown as she mustered the equanimity to look above those large feet. The winged arch of her brow furrowed over wide-spaced gray eyes. The firm set of her chin indicated

21

a determination not to let her neighbor see how shaken she'd been by the abrupt assault in his backyard and the undignified scuffle on his den floor. Purposely she tightened her normally soft mouth into a thin, straight line of animosity and distaste—not difficult to do when she thought of the indignities this man had made her suffer tonight.

From his shoes Katherine's gaze traveled hesitantly up a long length of black corded jeans molded closely to muscular legs, powerful thighs, and trim hips. Next a kelly green expanse of lean ribs, enormous chest, and wide shoulders, the arms akimbo. In surprise she noted the deep red furrows along one arm. She concentrated on that injured arm. It was well muscled and covered with brown hair, and it came to her with something like dread that the scratches were evidence of how she had gouged him in their struggle outside. She pushed herself to a sitting position, curling her legs under her as she raised wary eyes way, way up to his face.

The grim amusement written on those rugged masculine features was a prelude for a renewal of strength that lifted her to stand. Her feet tangled clumsily on the trailing hem of her robe before she righted herself and stared, a little flushed, at the man in front of her.

Thick, rich tobacco brown hair, slightly tousled, framed a strongly molded face whose dominant features were a strong jawline and an aggressively jutting chin. Deep lines etched around the sardonic curve of a mouth most women would describe as sensual. Katherine saw it merely as tauntingly hateful. Bronzed skin stretched tightly over wide cheekbones and forehead, accenting the deep, deep green eyes, which presently gleamed with unholy mockery.

"Mr. Clinton!" she acknowledged stiffly.

"Mrs. Meadows!" he parroted with mocking emphasis,

inclining his head in a nod as insolent as the eyes raking her indignant face. "This is quite a twist on your little surprise visits—masquerading as a prowler?"

"Do you normally attack first and ask questions later? Or have you lost what little mind you possessed?" she countered, her voice a vivid representation of outraged dignity.

"Calm down, Mrs. Meadows," he ordered quietly, his own voice cool and level. "I think I should be the one with the questions. After all, *you* were skulking around in *my* yard and *my* bushes . . . uninvited." His voice had a deep, rich timbre, but Katherine wasn't in the mood to appreciate its pleasant chords.

"You nearly killed me, you big ape! And I was not skulking in your bushes!" she retorted defensively, objecting to the underhanded connotation of the word "skulking." Her hands on her hips, she glared way up from her usually sufficient five feet seven inches to his more than adequate six feet two.

"You mean that wasn't you hiding behind the jasmine a few minutes ago? And that wasn't you who came creeping through my gate moments afterward?" he asked in feigned amazement.

Katherine flushed uncomfortably. She should have known when he lingered by the jasmine that he had been aware she was hiding there. Damn! And then another thought flashed inside her brain.

"You knew it was me! Why did you use those manhandling tactics if you knew it was me?" she demanded, incensed, her face fierce with astonished anger.

"I didn't know it was you. It's too dark outside to distinguish more than shapes and shadows. And I was hardly manhandling you, Mrs. Meadows. I believe I'm the one with the bloody cat scratches on my arm and, I might add, the feline teeth marks on my hand," he pointed out with concise brusqueness, and watched her flush anew, his eyes glimmering triumphantly.

"I was defending myself against attack, Mr. Clinton!" she snapped, hating his taunting eyes.

"And I was attempting to waylay a prowler!" he shot back, his eyes narrowed in accusation.

"I was not prowling. I was looking for Marigold," she explained tersely.

"First it was bugs, and now it's flowers. Which, exactly, do you mean?" he asked dryly, clearly not believing her.

"Neither!" she snarled in exasperation.

"You just said—"

"Marigold is the cat!"

Matt stared down at her stormy features and released a huge rumble of laughter, his voice almost strangling when he muttered, "I see! The cat was after the crickets and grasshoppers, and the cool, prim Widow Meadows crept about in her nightgown, searching for the errant cat!" He seemed to be savoring mental pictures of just how undignified and unconventional her search had been.

Katherine watched him laugh, recognized his genuine enjoyment, and decided it was the last bit of indignity she would put up with. Talking to the tauntingly arrogant devil was an exercise in futility she could do without. Listening to his amusement at her expense wasn't to be borne. She turned on her heel and headed for the sliding glass doors that led to the patio, her only thought to release herself from his insufferable presence as quickly as possible.

Matt belatedly reached for her and came up with a handful of flying green nylon. Katherine balked at the new restriction and twisted, gaining her release at the expense of what little modesty she had left. The robe slipped with a smooth slither right off her shoulders and arms. Matt stared down at the garment in his hands, surprised almost as much as Katherine, then raised his amused gaze to meet shocked gray eyes.

"How . . . how dare you!" she gasped tritely.

Her intention to give him a virulent tongue-lashing that would have him cringing in abject misery was forestalled when she saw the direction his eyes were traveling—eyes darkened to a deep smoky jade. Her spate of words got lost somewhere in the realms of incredulous horror. Those alert eyes were very thoroughly undressing her—although it took little imagination to come up with every detail of her shivering flesh. The transparency of her long thin gown left little to imagine. Katherine could feel her breasts tingling, the skin tightening as goose bumps of shock and awareness spread over her bare skin and the almost bare curves so vividly portrayed by the low slashed V of the gown.

Without taking his avid gaze from her creamy, rounded flesh, Matt stepped forward, the robe in his outstretched hand evidence of his intent. Katherine obviously thought he intended something altogether different. Gasping anew, she once again bolted for the door. She reached it unharmed, only to struggle with the unfamiliar latch a second too long. Warm hands descended on her shoulders, and gentle force was exerted to turn her away from the glass panels of the door and into a massive chest. Katherine was shaking, her nose almost buried in his cotton pullover, her breath suspended to keep from screaming in useless hysteria, until the suspense of waiting for his next move had her raising a reluctant face to his.

"Hi, neighbor," he said softly, lowering his head to come closer to her face, his eyes full of purpose. The hands on her upper arms slid carefully but securely around her back, clasping her inside the warm encirclement of his arms.

"Please don't," she whispered, her eyes wide and disturbed.

"I'd never forgive myself if I didn't," he murmured near her mouth, a strong current of masculine laughter in his voice. "Consider it a belated welcome to my home, and I'll pretend you're finally welcoming me to the neighborhood."

Then he took her mouth ever so gently, brushing her lips in tantalizing little touches that surprised her by their very lack of bruising ardor. The arms at her back brought her rigid body inexorably closer so that she felt the entire length and strength of him against every part of herself and started to tremble—an undeniable mistake, she found out to her cost. His mouth instantly responded with increased urgency, and the hands at her back moved over her in gentle exploration.

When she opened her mouth to protest, she made her second mistake. His warm breath and eager tongue darted inside, a hand coming up to the back of her head to accommodate her twisting head more fully to the acquisitive needs of his mouth. The kiss was a masterpiece of devastation to Katherine's already shot nerves. Her rigidity crumbled against his easy dominance, and she felt herself sag weakly into his chest, even as every sane instinct she possessed cried out to fight against the audacious intrusion of his embrace.

This was no casual greeting. It was a full-fledged reception, complete with two honored guests, each receiving a full measure of sensuous accolade from the other.

Katherine's breath became shallow, disturbed, and her stunned senses vaguely registered the uneven tenor of Matt's breathing in the thumping beat of his heart under her hand. That heartbeat seemed to pound out a message, strong and urgent, as the kiss went on and on. Somehow her recalcitrant hands came around his back, and a tiny part of her whirling mind tried to cringe in horror when she realized she had arched her back to press even more deeply into his body. The majority of her fuddled brain registered nothing but sensory detail—the scent and taste and feel of the man holding her, kissing her, an unexpectedly powerful stimulus to her senses.

Finally it was the large, confident hand gliding down her back to cup her bottom that broke Katherine free of his power over her. It was too soon for that kind of intimacy, and when that hand pressed her firmly against his thighs, she snapped abruptly out of the sensuous dreamland where she was suspended.

She twisted out of his relaxed hold, dismayed to realize she had been responding to the undoubtedly experienced lovemaking of Matt Clinton—her hateful neighbor. He was the last man on earth she would want to be closely entwined with. God, she hated him, didn't she?

At first the huge hands reached eagerly for her, no doubt intending to haul her back to his warmth, but when green eyes caught sight of stunned, vulnerable gray eyes, the hands fell away from her. Matt ran a distracted hand over the back of his neck, desire and common sense warring in his face.

"It's been a long night," he finally offered quietly, by way of apology or perhaps excuse.

"Yes," she agreed, not looking at him, and then in a low, thready voice: "May I have my robe, please?"

Katherine was too conscious of her own participation toward the end of the last little scene to scream a reproach for his handling of her. *How very foolish, Katherine. How very uncharacteristically and foolishly you reacted,* she was silently berating herself, her mind a whirl of protests for her own behavior. *What must he be thinking of you?*

Something sleek and cool covered her shoulders: her robe. Avoiding any acknowledgment of the man who had placed it around her, she scrambled with more haste than poise into its sleeves and turned blindly for the door. Finding it already opened, she sped through it, hearing his softly voiced "Good night, Mrs. Meadows," as if he had thundered it out for the world to hear, so conscious was she of her idiotic participation in her own near seduction.

As she reached the gate, something warm and furry brushed against her legs and bounded through the gate before her. Marigold! *Now you come, you damned cat! If only you had come when I called . . .*

CHAPTER TWO

Once Katherine had finally gained the back entrance to her own home, she found the tabby primly and disdainfully waiting by the closed door, languorously cleaning a paw with the delicate strokes of a small pink tongue. Katherine opened the door, and Marigold leaped gracefully inside the warm haven of the kitchen and went immediately to her cozy basket in the corner. The green corded cushion accepted her already curling body, and the cat shut her eyes, purring contentedly.

Katherine collapsed back against the closed door and breathed a sigh of pure relief at being back inside the secure comfort of her own brightly lit, warmly welcoming green and gold kitchen.

"Katherine, my girl, you've had one hell of a night," she murmured, and then jumped in startled surprise when an adolescent tenor broke through her musings.

"Whatsa matter, Mom? You look kinda funny."

Katherine fastened her gaze on the slight, gangly body of her thirteen-year-old son, smiling wryly at his understatement. She could vividly imagine her physical state if her jumbled nerves were any parallel by which to draw a comparison.

"I've been chasing your beloved cat. She escaped into the night as I was taking out the trash—which you forgot to bag, I might add."

29

Tim ducked his head guiltily, and Katherine once again smiled, this time at how much he looked like his father when he tilted his head a certain way, the light brown hair flopping endearingly into his eyes.

"Sorry, Mom, I guess I forgot," he mumbled unnecessarily.

"What are you doing out of bed, Timmy?" she asked, noticing his grimace at the diminutive of his name. *Oh, yes—Tim,* she amended silently. *I mustn't forget how grown-up you're getting. You and Laurel both.* Sometimes she wanted to cry at how rapidly her children were growing—growing up and growing away from her. It had been hard when Barry died ten years ago to take care of mere babies of three and five. Now it was an almost impossible task constantly to adjust to the changing moods and needs of two teen-agers.

"Aw, Mom, you know tomorrow's not a school day," Tim pointed out with a look that said she wasn't thinking.

"Yes, of course," Katherine agreed, smiling wryly at both his words and his look. She had forgotten that the next day was Saturday.

"Where did you find Mari?" her son asked, squatting down to scratch the purring tabby between the ears.

"In the next yard."

"In Matt's yard?" Tim asked eagerly, his brown eyes lighting with pleasure. At his mother's nod, he continued, "Matt's real neat, Mom. He's promised to take me fishing and camping sometime. Did you know he travels all over the world? He just got back from Paraguay, where they're building bridges and roads and stuff."

"I'm sure Mr. Clinton is a regular hero," she commented with a bite, unable to prevent the scathing distaste in her voice. She regretted it instantly when her son's eyes looked troubled. "Never mind, darling, I'm tired."

"And blind," said a husky feminine voice from the

doorway leading into the hall. "I don't know what you have against Matt, Mother. He's so friendly and such a nice man," Laurel continued in a suggestively intimate drawl.

Katherine eyed her daughter through narrowed lids. At fifteen Laurel was every bit as tall as her mother, but her young figure was more lush and full. Pale, true silver blond hair was worn long and straight down her back, almost to her waist, and Laurel had a habit, gained purposely through careful practice in front of a mirror, of tossing it seductively over her shoulders with a graceful flick of her neck. Laurel's one aim in life at present was to be mature and sexy, and she was becoming increasingly successful—too successful, by Katherine's way of thinking.

"And old enough to be your father," Katherine commented tartly.

"Oh, Mother! He's only thirty-seven. That's not old! That's mature," her daughter insisted, rolling her eyes expressively.

"Thank you, Daughter. It's reassuring to know that in some instances age and maturity are so appealing to one of your tender years."

"But, Mother, it's different for a man! They age so . . . so gracefully."

"How true, O tactful one," Katherine murmured.

Katherine recognized her daughter's spiteful comment as a cross between an inherent jealousy of any female between the ages of twelve and fifty and a wish to disconcert her mother. Laurel wasn't normally a spiteful child, but the last year had been fraught with tension between mother and daughter as they entered a battleground for supremacy over Laurel's independence. At fifteen she saw no need for guidance of any sort. She was her own woman

31

and resented the interference of her mother's worry, caution, and restrictions.

"Well, in any event, it's late, and I'm tired," Katherine told her children. "I'm also filthy from wrestling with . . . with that deceitful Marigold. I'm for a shower and my bed. And I suggest you two hit the sack as well. Midnight is plenty late, even on the weekend."

She smiled as she walked to where they stood, shaking her head at their groans of repudiation of the order to bed. She hugged each child and scooted them in front of her out of the kitchen, flicking off the light switch as she left the room. As her children dutifully, albeit on dragging feet, trooped to their bedrooms, she checked each door to ensure that everything was securely locked for the night.

By the time she showered and changed into fresh nightclothes she was definitely ready for her own bed. Katherine's life was full—full of work, worry over finances, and concern for her children. Trying to keep her head aboveground financially and her children on the right course mentally and emotionally was not the stuff dreams were made of. But she had been reasonably successful for the last ten years. Keeping her home and her life from collapsing around her feet hadn't been easy when Barry died so unexpectedly, but through trials, some mistakes, and a growing belief in her own abilities, she had managed it.

The first few years she had drifted through three low-paying jobs, her lack of training a deterrent when it came to making a living. Then she'd met Charlotte Kendall— Charlie to her friends—her present employer. That had been three years ago, when financial stress had forced Katherine to consider selling her home. Charlie, head of a realty firm, had come to help sell the house and stayed to offer Katherine employment. Charlie was a dynamic woman and a beautiful friend. A lot of Katherine's present state of financial stability and sense of self-worth she owed to Charlie's advice and training. Her bank statement was out of the red, her sense of accomplishment when she collected a commission was exhilarating, and her past concern for the safety of the future was slowly ebbing as she gained more confidence in her ability to take care of home and children. Her children. Her only dream was to see them grow into responsible, self-reliant adults.

Yawning tiredly, Katherine slipped gratefully inside the welcoming sheets and then groaned as a sudden picture of taunting green eyes flashed into her mind. Matt Clinton! God, what a dreadful man! When she remembered how he had roughed her up earlier that night, all her recurrent anger rose, and she pounded her pillow into shape with unnecessary force. Insolent devil! She hoped she wouldn't have any more contact with him. Just remembering her reluctant response to his kisses and caresses had her flushing with fiery heat. What a mess the whole night had been, from creeping around in the dark to being attacked to practically being seduced. She would avoid Mr. Clinton at all costs in the future. There had been nothing but conflict in every encounter with him since they first laid eyes on each other. The first time had been on the very day he moved in—a cold January day three months ago. . . .

A friend of Laurel's was on the phone, and unlikely as the prospect might be, considering Laurel's penchant for creature comforts, Katherine stepped outside to see if her offspring could possibly be in the yard. She had searched the house without success until Tim mentioned having seen his sister in her jacket just minutes before. As she stepped through the door and out into the cold January afternoon, Katherine's gaze was already sweeping her own yard for signs of her daughter when her attention was drawn by a hearty burst of male laughter from the yard next door. Katherine and Charlie both had been stymied when they learned the neighboring house was for sale through another realtor, and for the last two months Katherine had been expecting the new owners to show up. Obviously they finally had.

In the drive stood three men, all crowded around one feminine figure perched seductively on the hood of a low-slung sports car. While Katherine vaguely registered three grinning adult males, apparently pausing in their task of moving furniture for a beer break, her concentration sharply centered on the fall of silver blond hair of their female companion. Laurel! Her heart rose in her throat in astonishment and then fell to her feet when the largest of the men calmly let Laurel take his beer to sip at it leisurely before handing it back with a sultry smile. Dear God! Was that man nuts? And her daughter! What was happening?

As she remembered it now, Katherine's stomach coiled into that same knot of tension. She shivered, huddling deeper into the bed. Every vivid detail of that horrible January encounter with her new neighbor came back to her. . . .

Katherine had been catching up on some much needed housework, and her jeans and warm flannel shirt were rather the worse for wear, as was her long honey blond hair, tied back loosely at her nape. Untidy wisps had become loose annoying tendrils about her face during the last hour of scrubbing and scouring. The January weather was freezing, and Katherine was barefoot; but the sight of her young daughter flirting so outrageously with grown men, all of whom evidently enjoyed her attentions, turned her blood first cold with alarm and then hot with righteous indignation. She stormed off her front porch, marching straight for her target, her arms swinging like a drilled recruit on parade, her eyes flashing with battle lights that would have done General George S. Patton proud. How dare those grinning idiots contribute to the delinquency of a minor? Especially *her* minor!

Laurel had seen her approach, of course, and Katherine saw more than heard the low-voiced mutter that had three male heads turning to survey her arrival. Wasting no time on civil amenities, Katherine got straight to the point, and that was to extricate her daughter immediately from what she considered an appalling situation.

"Laurel, you're wanted on the phone," Katherine informed her icily, eyeing her with a forceful look that said clearly she would hear more . . . and soon . . . and loud.

"Oh! Okay." Laurel smiled sweetly, but her brown eyes were full of an equally icy dislike of her mother's storm-trooping tactics. She scooted slowly off the car, wiggling her tightly jeaned hips as she bounded to her feet like a graceful cat. Two steps away she looked back over her shoulder with a fluttering of eyelashes and a husky " 'Bye, Matt. 'Bye, fellas," that brought three appreciatively amused chuckles for her efforts and caused Katherine's teeth to grind almost audibly together.

Katherine could cheerfully have strangled her daughter that day. There she was, freezing her buns off, while her teen-age daughter, her baby, had the audacity to flirt like a sexy temptress, a veritable Lolita, for the delight of three smiling baboons. The idiots should have known better than to encourage her in the first place, and Katherine had cheerfully considered shooting them for their participation and encouragement in the second place—or perhaps that would have been their *last* place?

Jerking upright in bed, Katherine irritably switched on the bedside lamp, disgusted anew with her daughter, Matt Clinton, and his grinning pals. Then she slumped back against her pillows, her expression a little sheepish, knowing it was more than a little possible that she had over-reacted that day. But at the time her behavior had been as natural and as outraged as fright and suspicion could make it. . . .

The largest of the men, the one free with his beer, who she later discovered was Matt Clinton, had moved considerably nearer while she tensely watched Laurel's retreating figure. That day she hadn't cared which one of the trio of lousy cretins was her new neighbor, knowing only they were equally distasteful and not to be trusted. The big one was eyeing her insolently. She turned back to glare into all three faces, her look icily scorning their idiotic male egos that could feed on the attentions of a fifteen-year-old girl. She was suspicious that any or all of them just might consider the seduction of a young teen-ager, and her eyes filled with hate—the by-product of a protective mother instinct. Two of the faces turned watchful and solemn; one remained arrogantly unaffected by her scorn, surveying her with a maddening quirk of tobacco brown eyebrows.

"Gentlemen!" She dismissed them with that one word. Her tone of voice and the expression of disdain in her freezing gray eyes indicated all her doubt that they should be so addressed. As she turned, she was totally unprepared in her grand exit for the large body suddenly standing in her path. Trembling in anger, not to mention thirty-degree weather, she threw back her head to glare up at him, her lips tightened with hostility, aversion plain on her beautiful face.

He smiled down at her tormentingly, his green eyes analytically disparaging of her appearance as they slowly raked her unmade-up face, untidy hair, and almost too slender frame covered by her oldest clothing, right down to her bare, freezing feet. Still blocking her path, he took a last pull on his beer and then crushed the empty can in one hand while wiping his mouth with the back of his other. It was all done in insultingly slow motion while the green eyes never left her face, holding her gaze with annoying ease.

"Come to offer a friendly welcome to the neighborhood, have you?" he drawled sardonically.

Katherine refused to answer him, sidestepping daintily, as if to avoid soiling herself. Her head raised at a discouraging angle, she proceeded to march back into her own yard, but not before hearing the softly voiced "Cold witch!" that put even more starch in her backbone and added length to her stride. Abominable beast! God, how she hoped he wasn't the new neighbor.

He was, of course, but fortunately she didn't encounter him again for almost a month. At least not face-to-face. Hearsay was another matter, and her children kept her inundated with glowing comments about how *wonderful* and *neat* Matt Clinton was.

With firm resolution Katherine switched off the bedside lamp. She was *not* going to dwell on any more past encounters with her big neighbor. Why should she? He was nothing to her. Her lips met in a tight line to emphasize the point.

Only to part helplessly on the remembrance of warm male lips dominating them so completely. Tonight. How could she help thinking about tonight?

Katherine buried her face in her pillow, wishing she could forget about the humiliating aspects of the evening, especially Matt Clinton's lovemaking expertise. To be caught skulking around her neighbor's yard in her nightgown was bad enough. To be manhandled and scared out of her wits was equally so. But to respond, nearly to succumb, to his undoubtedly experienced lovemaking was the ultimate in humiliation. How could she have wrapped herself around him and accepted his kisses with such senseless ardor? Senseless? No, she had been anything but senseless. In fact, her senses had been screaming out a message of total capitulation. The man was probably crowing about his success with the Widow Meadows at this very moment.

At nine o'clock the next evening Katherine was on another search—this time with Marigold trailing faithfully at her heels—as she looked through the house for her daughter. Laurel had disappeared into the back of the house shortly after the supper dishes had been done, and Katherine assumed she was holed up in her room, silently brooding over the restriction keeping her at home for the weekend. Restrictions were a crushing blow to a socially active teen-ager. And with Tim spending the night with a friend, Laurel felt doubly isolated from the world.

Walking from room to room, Katherine tried to ignore the nagging evidence of a chill that had plagued her for most of the day. At first she'd interpreted the sore muscles and tension as a by-product of her late-night excursion the evening before and the subsequent scuffle with her neighbor. The man was not a lightweight. But by late afternoon sneezing and sporadic dizziness had been added to her repertoire of virus symptoms. Now she hoped only that she would be able to locate Laurel soon and head off for bed. Early it might be, but her legs felt like lead and her head ached with explosive force.

Laurel's whereabouts remained a mystery, and Katherine paused in her search, sneezing into a crumpled Kleenex as she and the cat hovered just inside her daughter's pink and rose bedroom.

"Where could she be?" Katherine pondered aloud, and the attending Marigold answered with an unhelpful but ready purr, rubbing against Katherine's legs.

Scanning the room as if her daughter might suddenly appear from thin air, pensive gray eyes searched for clues. The stereo was going full blast, and the room was in its customary shambles of scattered makeup items, fan and fashion magazines, and discarded clothing—among which were two small scraps of pink material that constituted Laurel's bikini. Katherine frowned. That bikini. Modest by today's standards, it somehow looked very revealing on her daughter's maturing body. And in a way it was the cause of Laurel's present restriction and subsequent attack of brooding. Katherine reached for it, then settled onto the edge of the canopied bed, recalling the last time it had graced that rounded fifteen-year-old body. Just last week . . .

Early April had brought a warming trend that promoted ninety-degree readings on the thermometer—not unusual in the North Texas area—and Laurel decided she was a sun worshiper. Every afternoon after school she would don her pink bikini and lie in the sun with a radio and a magazine for company.

One such afternoon Katherine arrived home from a frustrating day with an equivocating client who wanted today's dream house at yesterday's prices. The man wasn't satisfied until he had been shown all over the Fort Worth/ Dallas metroplex. He complained about economics in general and in such stentorian tones that Katherine had acquired a nasty headache during the last two hours of inflation and dollar philosophy, wanting nothing more than to have a long, relaxing soak in a warm tub.

The first thing she saw on parking her ten-year-old Chevy station wagon in the drive was her bikini-clad, smooth-skinned, voluptuously endowed Lolita again perched on the hood of a vehicle in the Clinton drive—this time a large four-wheel-drive pickup. And standing indolently to the side of Laurel, leaning a hip against the front fender, was the insolent ape who, unfortunately, was also her neighbor.

It was an alarming scene for a mother to witness, especially when a tanned large hand reached out and tousled the silver blond hair and a rich masculine chuckle traveled across the space that separated the two drives to attack Katherine's hearing with another piercing pain to her head. The suggested intimacy of the situation brought out all her suspicious instincts. Her dismay with Laurel was tempered by the realization that her daughter was trying her wings as a woman, prematurely but nevertheless naturally. But she saw no excuse whatsoever for Matt Clinton's behavior. This was not the first time she'd seen him treating Laurel as if she were mature enough to handle a grown man's attention. Anger had simmered at what she considered the man's total lack of scruples.

The purring Marigold, rubbing gently against Katherine's arm, broke into her frowning reminiscence. She stroked the tabby's head, murmuring, "Who was wrong that day, Mari? Laurel, for wanting to be mature and yet immaturely spinning a web of lies to gain an adult male's attention? Matt Clinton, for unquestioningly swallowing those lies and then compounding his mistakes by boldly offering advice on a parent-child relationship? Or myself? Did I make more of the situation than it would normally have warranted? Did I behave rationally, or did I react with instinctive dislike to a man who'd shown me nothing but insolence since the day we met?"

She sighed pensively, tossing the bikini to the side. It all had seemed so cut-and-dried that day. Matt Clinton was the villain of the piece, and Katherine had heroically taken him to task. . . .

After reaching Matt's cement drive that day, Katherine had immediately dismissed Laurel—a rather chagrined fifteen-year-old in a woman's body, whose brown eyes had flickered guiltily before she'd scampered on winged feet toward home. Then Katherine had turned her scathing attention to the large man waiting negligently for the fireworks reflected in narrowed gray eyes to spark. He hadn't a long wait.

Hating the touch of watchful contempt in his green eyes, Katherine had said simply and coldly, "Stay away from my daughter!"

He encompassed each aspect of her very slim but still feminine figure in its three-piece celery green suit with bold appraisal. Then, duly noting the look of strain around her eyes and mouth, Matt had come back with a dryly voiced "Jealous? Of her youth and beauty?"

"Hardly!" For a moment her gray eyes bristled with outrage, before surveying him with cool hauteur. "I'm proud of my daughter's looks, Mr. Clinton, but I'll not have some lecherous fool old enough to be her father licking his chops over her!"

He hadn't liked that comment, any more than she had the one about being jealous of Laurel's looks. But other than a flaring brilliance in his green eyes, he'd remained cool, offering a controlled "A young woman almost twenty is bound to rebel against the strict control you're subjecting Laurel to." And then he noted with satisfaction Katherine's stunned reaction to his words.

Oh, yes, he'd thought he'd scored a point for Laurel that day. *Or, more likely, a point against me,* Katherine thought disgruntledly. The man took each opportunity presented to him to get under her skin.

On a feline whim Marigold jumped out of her mistress's lap, and Katherine slowly stood from Laurel's bed, her fingers rubbing gently to ease the tension in her temple. With a rueful attempt at a smile, she wondered if the present degree of pain in her head was due to a cold or to the memory of Matt offering advice on child rearing that day. Looking back on it, she acknowledged that the man had been basing his arguments on the intricate pack of lies

Laurel had woven to gain his notice, but at the time she hadn't appreciated his comments. Anything but . . .

She had stared up at him mutely, wondering where on earth he'd found a figure of twenty for Laurel's age. Her fast-working brain and the knowledge of her daughter had already told her how when he continued politely. "Mrs. Meadows, you and your husband—"

Automatically she murmured, "I'm a widow."

For just a moment he seemed disconcerted, a new light entering the green eyes. Then he pressed on. "A woman your age should be able to remember—"

"A woman my age?" A niggling interest at what he'd been told that was had her interrupting him.

"Any woman past forty begins to feel a little older, a little threatened. It's understandable." He was searching her features, seemingly making an effort to state it gently.

"I'm thirty-three."

"My God!" He was clearly astonished but as yet unaware of how he had been hoodwinked by a slip of a girl less than half his age. "How old were you when you had her?"

"Eighteen, Mr. Clinton. A very young eighteen, I grant you, but nevertheless eighteen," she answered crisply, fed up with Laurel's chicanery and Matt Clinton's brainless ineptitude. "And before it boggles your brain to do the sums, Laurel is fifteen—just turned fifteen at the first of the year. So I'll tell you once again, because I've decided that any man as lacking in perception and intelligence as you, bears being repeated to. Stay away from my daughter. If you in any way encourage her to be an adolescent salve to your faltering ego, there'll be trouble. I believe in cases such as this the law is on my side."

Katherine could still see the absolutely stupefied expression on those rugged features as the context of her words had penetrated his brain. And unwillingly she could still hear his "The little witch!" uttered in such patently amused tones that she'd known he was referring to Laurel, not to herself.

Katherine's next sneeze punctuated her irritated thoughts. *Period. No more thoughts of Matt Clinton. They're bad for the health.* She stepped over to the mirror over Laurel's dresser, surveying her wan appearance. Her gray eyes were watery and sunken, her complexion was pallid, and her poor nose was as pink as Laurel's bikini. If she didn't take some aspirin soon and crawl under the tempting covers of her bed, she was going to collapse. Damned inconvenient cold! All winter she'd stayed healthy, not a germ in sight. Now that spring was here with warm days and cool nights, she had contracted some ridiculous virus. She couldn't afford to be sick. Her bankbook might be out of the red, but fat it was not.

Deciding the lure of the April night might have called to a bored teen-ager, Katherine grabbed a handful of Kleenex from the box on the dresser top and headed out of Laurel's bedroom. At the front door she pushed the trailing tabby gently back inside the house, admonishing softly, "Oh, no, you little beast. You had your turn last night."

The front porch and yard were unoccupied. She traipsed leadenly to the backyard in hope of finding her rebellious teen-ager curled up in the comfortable hammock that often lured Katherine herself during the spring and summer months. It was empty. She plopped heavily on its edge, wishing she weren't feeling so light-headed and silly. Stuffing the loose tissues into the pocket of her comfortable chino jogging pants, she wrapped her arms tightly across her chest, shivering with a sudden chill. With a vague frown she heard the soft, sensuous beat of guitar strains drifting her way on the night air. Wondering if Laurel was in some corner of the yard with her portable radio, she diligently searched the shadows but found nothing.

Laurel might have walked down to Lisa Webb's house at the end of the block. A remote possibility suggested she could have taken Tim's bike for a turn or two around the block. In the normal run of things Laurel would have asked permission to do either, but guilt and defiance had colored most of her actions this past week. She hadn't liked being caught in her lies to Matt. She had definitely thought the weekend punishment was an unjust one, pointing out airily that it was no big deal telling Matt she was twenty. Regardless of whether she was fifteen or twenty, a man like Matt could be interested in her—she wasn't a child after all. Each word she said, and the defiant way she said them, only underlined the fact that she wasn't as mature as she pretended.

Deciding her search was a complete dead end, Katherine moved away from the hammock, retracing her route, only to stop in her tracks on a sudden thought. Where would a defiant girl go for mature comfort when her mother didn't understand her? Why, to an adult who showed her the kind of attention she craved, of course! Oh, God! Matt Clinton!

Heartbeats racing in time with an overworking brain, trembling legs carried Katherine swiftly in the direction of the gray-bricked residence next door. The sharp memory of herself, in a nightgown, being held intimately close to her neighbor's warm, pulsing body brought her up short not far from the sweet-smelling Carolina jasmine at the side of the house.

Surely he wouldn't be callous enough to entertain the idea of seducing a young teen-ager, no matter how she might press for his attentions? Shaking all over, Katherine swayed on her feet, knowing with firsthand certainty that his seductive prowess couldn't be faulted. But she was a grown woman, able to take care of herself. Laurel was just an inexperienced girl, yearning for maturity and with a crush on Matt. . . .

The intent to march straight for Matt's front door and demand to know if Laurel was with him was spoiled by a wave of nausea. Katherine sank weakly to the grass, her head bent between her raised knees. Her mind reeled with sickening conjecture; her stomach rolled with sickening reality. When she raised her head a moment later, it was to focus slowly on a lighted window just beyond the spread of jasmine. Silhouetted against that window was an embracing couple.

They seemed to drift before her eyes, swaying in an odd pattern, their movements partly syncopated to the lilting chords of guitar music and partly accented by Katherine's woozy vision. Shadows. Shapes. No positive images. Was it Laurel with him? Low masculine laughter drifted out with the music, joining it, accenting the beat, filling Katherine with dread. She forced herself to stand, swaying unsteadily, her head as light as a helium-filled balloon, her feet as heavy as a ship's anchor.

Her cold legs refused to work free of her numbed apathy until the dictates of her anxious heart and her swimming mind urged them into a trembling antipathy. The sound of another masculine laugh increased her shivering from fear. She hated the infirmity that made her movements jerky, uncoordinated. She despaired of making it to Matt's front door without falling. She didn't want to be sick at this moment; she couldn't let herself be sick. A silly thought intruded into her churning mind. Maybe she could ask her neighbor for a couple of aspirin . . . right before she punched him out.

On her enemy's front porch Katherine leaned drunkenly against the doorframe, trying desperately to still the debilitating tremors in her legs. One shaky but determined finger pressed into the doorbell and stayed there with obstinate purpose. *Answer the door!* Regardless of how unwelcome her appearance might be, she had to find out if Laurel was here. *Answer the door, damn you, or I'll break the blasted thing down!*

Gruff, impatient cursing came from inside the house a second before the door was thrown open. Her enemy glared menacingly down at her, the normally attractive features of his face contorted into a fierce scowl of annoyance that slowly changed into a frown of wary concern. Each of her pale, stricken features was inspected carefully. She lurched feebly through the door, stumbling almost to a fall before a brawny arm came out to right her.

"What's wrong?" Matt asked with hoarse urgency. The seductive quality of his raspy voice had her frantically twisting away from him, her eyes a sick grayish green as she turned in horror and hate to face him.

"Don't touch me!" she croaked, seething anger giving her the momentary strength to stand straight and stiff, challenging contempt in every line of her slender length. She demanded hoarsely, "Where is she?"

That shocked him. In fact, he looked strangely stunned, staring down at her in amazement and speculation. Katherine wondered if he was feeling guilty because he'd been caught. Then he laughed—a low, deep sound of genuine humor and not a little smug pleasure that had Katherine gulping back another wave of nausea and fighting an urge to collapse ignominiously at his feet. His green eyes skimmed over her length, examining and assessing her. Through her anger came the dismayed awareness that he liked what he saw.

"What business is that of yours?" he taunted lazily.

"Are you insane? I warned you!" she managed in a

46

shaky voice, trying to focus on what appeared to be twin images of her neighbor. Both were distastefully large and equally repugnant at that moment and finally merged to form one terrifically annoyed man.

"What the devil are you talking about now, you crazy female?" he thundered explosively, green eyes suddenly narrowed and threatening.

"You're obviously less intelligent than even I gave you credit for! You'll have to go through me to get her!" she warned him with scratchy-toned vehemence.

Those words were barely out of her mouth before he grabbed her, hauling her up against his long, hard body so forcefully that the breath left her body in a hissing whoosh on impact. His eyes flared with anger. His hard fingers bit through the soft cotton of her sweater and dug into her arms. He growled, "Lady, you've got some screws loose yourself! Either that or you're as frustrated as hell!"

Frustrated! With a strength born of anger, Katherine jerked out of his arms so violently that she had no time to regain her equilibrium. She landed against a small table in the foyer, the edge digging sharply into her ribs before she came down hard on one knee. The painful jolt brought tears to her eyes, and for a moment she didn't move. But when large hands swept inside her pain-clouded line of vision, reaching to help her from the floor, she twisted away from them and stood up.

Matt's gaze narrowed when she moved away from his helping hands, and he let them fall loosely to his sides. He watched her get to her feet, his mouth grim at the sight of her swimming gray eyes and blanched complexion. But when she turned those eyes up to face him and he saw the contempt in their depths, his whole manner hardened, his body tensing as if to spring.

Katherine ran her tongue over her dry mouth, gathering courage into words. Then a slight noise to her left had her turning to focus on a stunning brunette in tight jeans and a clinging pink sweater. The girl—woman—sauntered into the foyer and gave Katherine her curious attention, her bright blue eyes filled with a mixture of humor and sympathy. As she neared, Katherine's eyes widened and then blinked with horrible dismay. This was a mistake . . . *her* mistake. . . .

"Hi!" the brunette said cheerfully, and then; "You in some kind of trouble, honey? Are you sick?"

"You're not Laurel," Katherine whispered stupidly, an unsteady hand going to her trembling mouth. She leaned weakly back against the foyer wall for support.

The woman eyed her with a funny smile. " 'Fraid not, honey. Just li'l' ol' Bibbi, the gal Matt left behind," she explained flippantly, her baby blue eyes opened innocently wide, a hint of laughter in her throaty voice.

Matt's low, growling curse had Katherine's stunned gaze swinging to meet his. For a moment they just stared at each other, her eyes full of dismay and a kind of mute apology, his filled with anger and disgust that were directed as much at himself as they were at her.

"I'm not after your kid," he muttered tightly.

And then the doorbell rang. With a mumbled expletive Matt flung the door wide, and there stood the source, the issue, the bottom line, looking her age, for once. Her face was freshly scrubbed, her silvery hair tied back at her nape with a frilly strip of lace, and her brown eyes were swimming with anxiety. Her fingers were nervously twisting together, accentuating her distress.

"Matt, my mother's disappeared! I've searched everywhere and can't find her. The car's still in the garage and . . . and . . . I'm so worried!"

Matt's obvious bulk blocked Laurel's view of the inside

of the foyer. She couldn't see her mother, ghostly white with shock and pain, leaning against the wall.

"No need to worry, Laurie, she's here. Everything's cool!" He spoke reassuringly at the same time that Katherine whispered an unsteady "Laurel!" and Bibbi screeched, "God, Matt, she's going down for the count!"

Matt turned just in time to see Katherine glide down the wall and meet the floor in a dead faint.

CHAPTER THREE

Strain and the effects of the flu collapsed under exhaustion and medication so that Katherine slept around the clock, not wakening until midnight Sunday night. When she finally roused, groggy and disoriented, she was completely unaware she had lost twenty-four hours. It wasn't until after going to the bathroom, splashing cold water over her face, and brushing her teeth that a few coherent thoughts trickled into her bleary mind. Not quite awake even after her ablutions, she tried to remember what was nagging at the back of her brain. Laurel! Where was Laurel?

She hurried to her daughter's bedroom on surprisingly wobbly legs, vaguely disturbed by the stiffness of her knees but not pondering the cause as she rushed on. From the light in the hallway she peeked in to see Laurel's sleeping form in the middle of her canopied bed. At the bedside she looked down at the childishly innocent face sleep produced. *Oh, darling, why are you in such a hurry to grow up? Why can't you stay my little girl, all innocent and uncomplicated?* She bent to kiss the smooth forehead lightly before quietly tiptoeing from the room, closing the door noiselessly behind her. Leaning back against it, she breathed a deep sigh of relief. Laurel was safe.

At Tim's door she halted abruptly, surprised to see it shut. On opening it, she was disconcerted to see another sleeping teen-ager. At his bedside she ran a loving hand

50

over his tousled brown hair, tucking an errant foot back inside the sheets. Tim immediately groaned and turned over, kicking the foot free of the bed sheets. *Okay, okay! You're not five years old anymore and unable to keep warm during the night!* Her mouth curved into a sweet, wry smile.

Tim was home, safe and sound, but when had he returned? Her fingertips stroked her temple; she tried to remember. He should have been at Chad Carlson's for the night, and the last thing she remembered clearly was searching for Laurel. Matt Clinton! A sudden vision of angry green eyes glaring into hers had her hand going to her mouth to stifle a loud hiss of breath. Now she remembered! She had gone in search of Laurel only to find Matt with a woman called Bibbi. And to discover a very angry man—understandably so, she realized now. She had acted like a total fool. The last thing she recalled clearly was the floor of Matt's foyer coming up toward her. She must have fainted. How she got home was a mystery, but at the moment she felt too fuzzy to unravel it.

Padding out of Tim's room, she headed for the kitchen, hoping a cup of coffee would clear her thought processes. Marigold slitted one eye as she neared the corner basket, and Katherine bent to scratch her ears, feeling a sudden twinge of pain in her ribs as she did so.

"Mari"—she addressed the tabby softly—"I had another fantastic night, didn't I? It's a wonder the man didn't throw me out on my suspicious fanny. I accused him of all sorts of foul deeds. Two nights in a row tangling with that big bruiser are enough to make me find a way to get along with him. Much healthier that way."

The faintest of sounds answered her dry comments, and she glanced toward the darkened hallway, seeing nothing there from the spill of light in the kitchen to cause concern. Shrugging, she turned back to the uninterested Mari-

51

gold and, with a final pat, straightened and filled the kettle with water for instant coffee.

Feeling chilled in her thin gauzy white nightgown, she hugged her arms about her, waiting for the water to boil. A sudden memory of an unfamiliar male voice, mellowed and reassuring, urging her to lift her arms out of her sweater, caused her hands to stop abruptly from filling her cup. Then the whispery remembrance of Laurel, saying softly, "It's okay, Dr. Thompson, I'll undress her," had her shakily completing the task. Who was Dr. Thompson? A figment of a crazy dream? She stirred dried coffee crystals into the cup, her frown pensively confused.

Moments later, as she lay huddled in bed and gratefully sipped the coffee, her thoughts dwelt once again on her neighbor. The night's episode had proved she was wrong about his designs on Laurel, but he had been unnecessarily crude in his assessment of the situation. A vivid memory of a growling voice calling her frustrated had her shuddering with distaste. Had he really thought she had come clamoring to his door to fight for a place in his arms like some jealous female? The man had a high opinion of his attractions.

When a yawn broke through her musings, she laid the mug on the bedside table and clicked out the lamp. She snuggled into the covers, only to be disturbed by vague, insubstantial snatches of conversation drifting in and out of her mind. It was difficult to sort facts from the fantasies of a dream, but she definitely recalled Laurel's tearful whispers telling someone she could count on Charlie to help. Help with what? And then, clear and definite, came a voice she would rather not recall, and it was saying, "Don't call Charlie, Laurie; I'll handle it." Handle what? Why would Laurel want to call Charlie? And why would Matt Clinton interfere?

Sleep enveloped her moments later, but Katherine's last

clear vision was of emerald green eyes, not glaring in anger or gleaming with mockery but warm with gentle concern. A husky voice seemed to murmur her name. An illusory figure hovered just beyond her consciousness, and reason, even the dreaming variety, pulled away from a caressing hand. As she turned over, her frowning face was smothered into the pillow.

The first thing Katherine noticed, after having showered and dressed in trim cream slacks and a long-sleeved rose blouse the next morning, was the quiet. Sunday mornings usually were heralded by the loud tones of her children's stereo and television. She wondered if Laurel and Tim had overslept, but when she checked their rooms, she found them empty and both beds made. Curiouser and curiouser. Weekends found beds unmade as late as noon, her teen-agers lazing about until direct orders were made to get busy. As she neared the kitchen, the rich aroma of freshly brewed coffee and frying bacon hit her nostrils and caused her to groan, hunger pains attacking her stomach with ferocious growls. Prepared to enter the kitchen and praise her children for their uncustomary ambition, she stood in stunned silence at the sight meeting her eyes once she cleared the doorway.

Clad in well-worn, faded jeans and an equally faded western shirt, the sleeves rolled to mid-forearm, his large feet inside boots that were shined but not new, and turning bacon strips with deft economy, was the last person Katherine expected or wanted to see. Her wary gaze drifted up to his head. She half expected to see a Stetson perched there to complete the picture of a tall, rangy cowpoke, but the thick tobacco brown hair was neatly combed and uncovered. Matt's back was turned to her, but she recognized him nonetheless. Who else did she know had that

53

powerful physique? And who else could make her hackles rise on sight?

"What are you doing here?" Her voice sounded faint when she intended it to be forceful and demanding. She watched with rounded eyes as he twisted his head to look over his shoulder. His alert eyes took their time as they traveled from her head to her bare feet and slowly back to her astonished face. Under that unnerving gaze, Katherine was unreasonably grateful that the reflection in the bathroom mirror after her shower had shown clear gray eyes and a touch of healthy color in her cheeks.

"Fixing breakfast," Matt replied laconically, turning back to remove the last of the bacon from the frying pan. "How many eggs and what kind?" was tossed negligently over his shoulder.

"Wait a minute! You haven't answered me!" she yelped quickly.

After calmly switching off the burner, he turned to face her, folding his arms across his broad chest. Bracing his hips against the kitchen counter, he spread his long legs out in front of him, indolently crossing one booted foot over the other.

"Sure I did. But I think you must mean *why* am I here. Is that right?" He favored her with a singularly sweet smile.

"Yes, yes. Why?" she retorted impatiently, not at all impressed by that maddening smile. Any thought she might have of seeking friendlier footing with the man was being swiftly pushed to the back of her mind by his tauntingly self-assured manner.

"To take care of you for a couple of days."

"I don't need taking care of and especially not by you," Katherine informed him stiffly.

"That's where you're wrong," Matt contradicted mild-

54

ly, observing her surprised blink at his quietly confident answer with a deepening of the grooves around his mouth.

"Where are my children?" That was asked suspiciously.

He glanced at his watch and then back to her face. "I imagine they're halfway through their first-period classes by now."

"What?" she shot out quickly.

"I imagine they're halfway through—"

"I heard you!" she interrupted crossly. "I meant, what do you mean by that? Today's Sunday and—"

"Today's Monday," he corrected smoothly.

"What?"

"Today's Monday. I think your cold bug must have affected your hearing. Your ears seem a little stopped up this morning." He eyed her closely, seemingly waiting for her eyes to snap fire. He wasn't disappointed when they did just that, narrowing to peer at him truculently, obviously not liking the touch of smug humor on his face.

"It can't be Monday," she whispered finally. "Why, I couldn't lose . . . You can't be . . . Laurel wouldn't have . . . But Timmy was in bed last night," she finished flatly; then faintly: "I have lost a whole day, haven't I?" Matt merely inclined his head in agreement while her head spun wearily. Then she abruptly sprang for the kitchen wall phone, yelping an agitated "My job! Oh, good grief! Charlie!"

Her hand grabbed the receiver, and she punched the series of numbers that would reach Charlie Kendall, intending to explain her absence from work. Just as her shaking finger stabbed at the last digit, a big hand reached calmly over her shoulder, easily took the receiver from her unsuspecting grasp, and hung it back in place on the wall. Katherine was too surprised to put up a struggle, but she did turn to send him a glare that should have withered him on the spot. Instead of withering, however, Matt seemed to glow, his eyes like bright polished emeralds and his mouth spread into a wide smile of enjoyment. Tantalizing devil!

With a last, almost challenging quirk of a dark eyebrow, he turned back to the stove, and Katherine defiantly lifted the receiver again. This time when Matt relieved her of the instrument, he maneuvered his big body between her and the phone, so that she stumbled back to stay out of his immediate reach. They silently took each other's measure, gray eyes stormy, green ones assessing. Then he advanced as she retreated until the calves of her legs bumped into something solid and she abruptly plopped down onto a kitchen chair. Their eyes locked in silent battle.

"Stubborn little wench, aren't you? Now sit still while I finish cooking breakfast," he ordered with soft menace, straightening to walk back to the range.

"Listen, you oversized bully!" she stormed when he was far enough away to be less intimidating, starting to rise from the chair.

"Sit!" he barked without looking back at her, and surprisingly she did, dropping back into the chair with alacrity.

"Look, Mr. Clinton, you've got to understand that—"

"Matt," he interrupted.

"Mr. Clinton, would you stop this!" *This* was exasperating!

"Matt," he repeated patiently, breaking eggs into the heated skillet.

"Matt!" she bit out furiously, and then tacked on sarcastically, "Satisfied?" And was a little disconcerted by his husky chuckle.

"I think I could be. Fried eggs okay with you?"

"Dammit, Mr. . . . Matt! Forget the eggs! You've got to understand . . . what are you doing?" she squeaked, her eyes widening with shock as he walked slowly toward her.

Then he bent down at eye level to glare into her face—every inch of his more than considerable inches a threat, an ominous, intimidating threat.

"Let's get one thing straight, Katherine Meadows," he said softly but spacing each word with forceful clarity. "I want you to shut up until after breakfast. No more questions, no more sass, no more spitfire behavior until I've cooked the damned eggs and we've eaten them. You got that? At the rate you're going, we'll both develop ulcers in the next half hour."

Katherine blinked, surprise and alarm uppermost in the expressions flitting across her face. Granted, she was still angry, irritated and resentful, but alarm won out. She bit her bottom lip and nodded, her eyes held by his until he once again straightened and walked back to the stove. Her small sigh of relief was heard, and she caught a fleeting glimpse of his grin. How very rewarding to be a bully!

Eyeing his broad back resentfully, Katherine thought that if he was always so abrasively dictatorial, he probably had no close friends. But he did. She'd seen them the first time the day he moved in next door and again a month later on a cold, windy February night. That night she hadn't known Matt by sight, only by name and reputation via her children, but before the night was over, she, unfortunately, had a clear physical identification of the wonderful and neat Matt Clinton her children lauded so often and so fervently. . . .

Sleep had been impossible that night. After a full hour of hearing nothing but the growling, popping noises of an intermittently and loudly revved car engine from next door, Katherine exhaustedly read the dial on her bedroom clock. What in the name of heaven was that miserable man doing at eleven thirty at night? Getting ready for the Indianapolis Five Hundred? That horrendous noise had kept her tossing and turning until she was convinced one more revving would have her finding a gun and charging over there to shoot a large hole in the pistons, or engine, or exhaust, or whatever was causing the racket. And on that thought, sure enough, another loud rumble sounded forth from next door.

Jumping out of bed in a frenzy of irritation, she jerked on jeans and a pullover sweater, hastily stuffing her flimsy pink nightgown under the knitted white wool of the top. As she marched over the expanse of their combined lawns, barefoot once again in her haste, she found out the hard way that the ground was icy cold. But frostbitten toes were her last concern at that moment. All she could think of was screaming at her neighbor for his inconsiderate behavior.

Matt Clinton's garage doors were open, and bright overhead lighting was streaming down onto the opened hood of a cherry red sports car parked inside. The two men slowly straightening from their bent positions under the hood of the vehicle Katherine had easily placed as the same two who had been with the big insolent devil that day in January.

With a nervous frown Katherine glanced at the man cooking her breakfast. He worked unselfconsciously, and she was relieved he didn't know the turn of her thoughts. With a pensive sigh she realized she'd been relieved that February night, too. At least at first. Relieved that he hadn't been with his friends. Relieved that she wouldn't have her teeth set on edge by his well-remembered insolence . . .

Stopping just inside the neatly laid out three-car garage and grateful to be out of the cold, biting February draft, Katherine had glared at the two men with angry annoyance.

"Hi!" The taller of the two, a thin thirtyish redhead,

greeted her cheerfully, either ignoring or not acknowledging her stormy expression.

"Are you Mr. Clinton?" Katherine demanded frostily.

"Nope, just a friend with a sick car" was the laconic reply, a funny smile lighting his otherwise steady-looking features.

"Are you Mr. Clinton?" Katherine addressed the shorter, stockier, dark-haired man with boyish features.

"Never been mistaken for Matt before" was the laughing rejoinder.

"Well, are you two *gentlemen*"—she paused, deliberately stressing the title—"aware that it is after eleven o'clock and that most people are trying to sleep? Or that your . . . ah . . . *sick* car is an unusually loud one, especially when the motor is continuously revved?"

"Sorry, lady," apologized the shorter one, his friendly brown eyes surveying her warily, while his companion muttered something under his breath and kicked one foot against the front tire of the car.

"Would you please inform Mr. Clinton that Mrs. Meadows would appreciate it if he would try being more considerate of his neighbors in the future, and could he possibly remember the normal sleeping habits of most decent, working people?" Her voice had been as chilling as the icy February breeze freezing her back and nipping at her toes.

Those same toes curled around the bottom rung of the kitchen chair in agitated recall of that cold night. Glancing up, Katherine saw Matt take eggs from the skillet and deftly slide them onto two plates. Seconds later he was serving her an appetizing meal of bacon and eggs and toast and coffee. With a polite thank-you, she started eating, thirty-six hours without food telling in her voracious appetite. Matt did justice to his meal as well, she noticed, his portions about twice what hers were.

Sipping a second cup of coffee, she reflected ironically that six feet two inches of well-toned muscle probably put a big dent in somebody's grocery allowance. Her eyes went to the dark head bent in concentration over his meal. That thick swath of tobacco brown hair was the first thing she'd seen that February night when Matt had rolled out from under the car in his garage. . . .

His sudden appearance had flustered her. Not because she wouldn't have said the same things to his face that she'd said to his friends, but because of the fact that she hadn't been aware of his presence. To have it revealed so quickly and in such an unexpected way had her swallowing heavily on an annoying gasp of alarm, her eyes widening warily. He stood lazily to his feet, wiping greasy hands on an already soiled towel as he walked toward her. Katherine resisted the impulse to retreat like a coward as he advanced with a slow, calculated stride until he stood towering over her.

"Want me for something, Mrs. Meadows?" he asked, bold eyes taking in every aspect of her appearance.

His very size up close was intimidating, but Katherine held her ground, glaring up at him courageously.

"Only to tell you what I'm sure you've already heard. But if you would like me to repeat it, I'll be more than glad to speak slowly and precisely so that possibly even your mind can retain my message," she informed him overpolitely, her eyes telling him how she detested his impertinent manner.

There was a muffled sound from behind him, and she had to force herself not to look around the bulk of his body to glare at his laughing cohorts. Mr. Clinton obviously heard the same telltale sound, for he frowned at the noise and then smiled with cryptic amusement, continuing to survey her.

"I'm sure that won't be necessary," he answered with

equal politeness. "But there is one thing I'd like to say before you take your . . . ah . . . refreshing presence off my doorstep." A hint of smug laughter was in his tone, and the very devil shone out of those too green eyes.

"And that is?" she inquired, meeting his eyes with an outward show of icy dislike but with an inward feeling of trepidation. He was just too insufferably smug, and she was wary of the cause.

"That your"—he paused, a large hand reaching near her waist to give a gentle tug—"nightgown is lovely. Does this mean you want an invitation to stay?"

Quite naturally that was the telling end to their little verbal exchange. With a deep embarrassed flush Katherine had turned on her heels and exited his garage with his husky, taunting chuckle following her out into the night.

Annoyed with her memories, Katherine gulped down the last of the coffee in her cup. She wondered if Matt was as prone to these recollections of their encounters as she was. If so, he probably had a lot to smile about. One way or another he always seemed to find them very entertaining.

Matt swallowed his last bite of toast dripping with creamy egg yolk and leaned back in his chair, surveying Katherine's empty plate with a wide smile of approval. That smile almost undid Katherine's calm resolve to be a cool, collected woman who takes charge of the situation. Those white teeth flashing a contrast with his bronzed, rugged face, the crinkling humor lines around his too green eyes were something of a revelation. There was no mockery or taunting in his face; only open friendliness. Attractive brute! There were probably countless ladies clamoring for a place in line. She found herself wondering if he and Bibbi shared a special relationship and then chided herself for being curious about a man she purportedly detested. But under his smile, her foolish heartbeat sped up, and she was sure her lips were parted in open-mouthed appreciation. In fact, as she watched his friendly eyes narrow, she made a conscious effort to snap her gaping mouth shut.

"I'm ready for your questions now," he informed her brusquely, sitting forward to rest his elbows on the table and his jutting chin on his clenched fists.

"Thank you," she responded tightly, managing to sound as if she'd rather throttle the breath from his body. "First of all, I'm going to call work. Charlie will be worried," she said assertively.

"No need. Laurie called Charlie before she left for school this morning. Everything's squared away." His smile was benign.

"Oh!" His smooth announcement took the wind out of her sails—but not for long. Impatiently she snapped, "Why didn't you explain that a few minutes ago instead of letting me worry about it?"

"You needed food more than you needed answers. You're a little peaked, and you're way too skinny," he replied with a lack of tact that seemed deliberate.

"Why, thank you . . . Matt. I don't know when I've had a more complimentary tribute," she murmured sweetly, but her teeth were tightly clenched.

"It wasn't meant to be a compliment," he assured her easily, adding informatively, "Truth seldom is."

"You overgrown ox, not everyone has to weigh a blasted ton!" she flared, piqued at being considered skinny. "Skinny" sounded so unattractive and unappealing. Why couldn't he have called her slender? "Slender" had more likable connotations.

"Yep! You're right there, but most women need a little meat on their bones to keep their youthful appeal. You're not getting any younger," he pointed out amiably.

"You arrogant ba— Oh, forget it. I don't want to talk about my looks!"

"Okay by me," he agreed. "I don't blame you. Anyone in your shape . . . well, I'm sure you do the best you can in the circumstances," he finished kindly, smiling sweet reassurance, which would have been appreciated if his eyes hadn't been glittering with oblique amusement.

A sudden stab of pain in her temple had Katherine closing her eyes and swallowing back a moan. The man was actually giving her a headache! Why was he here, in her home, tormenting her? He seemed more bent on harassment than caring, as he'd claimed was his reason for being there. An urgent sense of frustration had her realizing she was neither as calm nor as refreshed by sleep as she should have been. Lingering traces of her illness were making themselves felt. She wished he would leave, just disappear before she said or did something to betray her loss of composure. When she opened her eyes, it was to find his gaze fastened on her face before dropping to the nervous clenching and unclenching of her slender fingers in her lap. She was making a conscious effort to relax her hands when he reached inside his shirt pocket and extracted a plastic container, which he opened to shake out two white tablets into the palm of his hand.

"Here. Take these," he ordered quietly, offering them to her.

"No, thank you. I don't have that particular habit," she informed him crisply, a scorching look of distrust undisguised in her eyes.

"Is that a fact?" he asked, slowly grinning. "Well, there's always a first time. Here," he repeated, proffering the pills once again.

Katherine was feeling shaky but not incompetent, and she wasn't about to take illicit drugs. Her fingers gripped tightly over the edge of the table. She was almost at the end of her emotional tether.

"I said no! Take your beastly drugs and get out of my house and leave me alone!"

"Such suspicion," he muttered, half to himself. Then, oh so quietly, he advised, "They're not *my* beastly drugs, and you'd better sit down before you fall down, lady." His narrowed gaze made a thorough study of her agitation: the pain in her eyes, the strained look of her tightly set mouth, the pale features, and the slight trembling of her slender length.

"Go to blazes, Mr. Clinton!" Katherine shouted, beyond seeing the swift tensing threat of his body. She was fed up with his bullying, his sarcasm, and his presence. "And take the fastest route you can find as long as the first step takes you out of my house!"

"Lady, you're about to buy some trouble," he warned mildly. Seemingly at ease, he laid the pills on the table and replaced the container in his pocket, snapping the pocket tab shut while his eyes never left her face.

The chair scooted back on the tiled floor with an unpleasant screech as Katherine jerked to her feet. Rapidly scanning the contents of the table, she grabbed the first thing that could be used as a weapon, a heavy pewter pepper mill. It was a treasured part of a set Barry had given her for their sixth anniversary, and it always remained in the center of the table. Approximately twelve inches long, it was solidly weighty, and she presently wielded it like a war club.

"No, you've bought the trouble. Now get out of here before I bash your brainless skull in!" she threatened. She was breathing shallowly in her extreme agitation and became even more provoked when his mouth spread in a slow, lazy smile.

"You know, Kat, I really think you'll feel better if you calm down and stop all this hell-raising."

The easy intimacy of the "Kat" disconcerted her for a moment, but his smile—no, more than a smile, a laugh—gave her a renewed sense of purpose. How dare that big ape laugh at her! She swallowed an angry shriek and forced herself to speak with quiet warning.

"Ah, but you don't know me, Matt. I assure you nothing would give me more pleasure than to knock you winding."

Her intent was serious. She couldn't remember ever feeling so ruffled, at least not to the point of physical violence. But this man positively encouraged her to violence by taunting, by taking charge when she didn't need him, by not heeding the direct order to leave, by laughing. Oh, yes, definitely by laughing!

"Do you think you can manage that?" he asked skeptically, eyeing her slender form quizzically. "Appears to me you don't have the muscle for that particular job."

Katherine was silently agreeing with him, watching the muscles in his forearm flex when he laid it casually over the back of the chair. Then he eased the chair back, twisting it slightly to the side; but he didn't spring up and grab her, and that thwarted the tensing spring of her stance. She had drawn the pepper mill over her shoulder to gain leverage for the quelling blow she fully intended striking, but her hand trembled almost uncontrollably.

"I may be skin and bones in your considered opinion, you huge buzzard"—she reinforced herself with words—"but I've got an equalizer, and you'll soon wish you'd left when I told you to." Despite the shaky sound of her voice, Katherine believed everything she said.

Matt stood up slowly, lazily, indolently, and faced her, his legs spread in a relaxed, easy stance and his arms hanging loosely at his sides. He never lost his smile. It was almost friendly.

"Put it down, Katherine. I'm sure it's getting too heavy for you."

Katherine's shaking arm testified to the truth of his words, but she refused to back down. "No! I'm warning you!"

"And I'm telling you. Either you put it down or I take it, and you might not like the way I do it," he informed her quietly.

That did it. She stepped forward and swung all in the same movement, aiming for his grinning face. Her cudgeling blow didn't connect. The only things that did were fingers of steel around her forearm when Matt's long arm shot up, proving he wasn't indolent after all. Another set of deft fingers removed the pepper mill from her loosened hold and placed the would-be weapon back on the table, coming immediately up to catch her other arm swinging in a wild arc for his face. Now both hands were trapped impotently above her head. But Katherine was not yet ready to admit defeat, so she swung a bare foot and finally made a connection, smartly bending her toes on his hard boot-protected shin. Even as she cried out from the stinging pain, she was pondering the only other line of attack left to her. She hesitated briefly before trying it. Whether Matt read her intent or her pause was too long, the resulting attempt was a failure, too. When she sharply raised her knee, he adroitly sidestepped, and she once again missed her target.

"Naughty, naughty," he scolded, laughing.

"Let go of me!" she ordered in a breathless croak, trying to twist out of the firm hold of his lean fingers and managing only to tire herself with the fruitless efforts.

"Uhh-uhh, you plucky little fighter. You might find another weapon, and I'm not crazy enough to allow you

66

to kill me. Now calm down, and maybe we can negotiate a truce." Matt inspected her flushed, agitated features with laughter prominent in his eyes, but also with a hint of reluctant admiration Katherine was too incensed to interpret.

"You're going to regret this, Matt Clinton," she warned, glaring at him defiantly.

His eyes glittered, reflecting complacent knowledge of his superior male strength. He easily pulled her arms behind her back, urging her stiffly held body slowly closer until they were just brushing, breast to chest and thigh to thigh. He taunted softly, "I don't see how, Katherine Meadows."

Without a conscious thought of the possible consequences of her action, but with a great deal of satisfaction, she twisted her head quickly to the side. She clamped onto a portion of his upper arm with all the tenacity she could muster from small, white, even teeth. Matt yelped and lost his grip on her arms when he jerked in astonished reaction to the sharp, painful wound.

At the first lessening of his grasp Katherine was free, running for cover straight out of the kitchen, directly through the house, and swiftly into her bedroom, terrifyingly conscious that pursuit was hot on her heels.

The door to her bedroom slammed shut with a bang, and with a gasping groan Katherine belatedly remembered it had no lock to keep Matt at bay. As she heard the door crash open behind her, she frantically grabbed the first thing her hands could reach. Unfortunately she wasn't able to be as discriminating or as lucky as she'd been with the pepper mill, and naturally a bed pillow didn't intimidate Matt. When she hoisted it before her, he just grinned like a Cheshire cat and languidly advanced into the room. Katherine stumblingly retreated until she ran out of space, effectively backed into a corner between an étagère and a nightstand. Her arm dropped, the pillow hanging loosely in her hand for a moment before it plopped to the floor with a soft poof. One more long step brought her pursuer in front of her, his hands braced on the wall at either side of her head to give him leverage. He lowered his face level with hers. Her eyes were enormous, and his noted that telltale sign of wary alarm with a glimmer of triumph.

"You bit me," he accused softly.

"I—I w-warned you," she stammered shakily. She pressed her back against the wall in an effort to shrink away from his too disturbing nearness.

"And I told you," he retorted in concise reminder, adding softly, "Are you ready to take your medicine?"

"I shouldn't have bitten you," she whispered. "But . . ."

"Where would you like it, Kat?"

"Why are you doing this? Why can't you leave me alone? Are you going to punish me for biting you?" The questions rushed quickly forth, her eyes pleading for respite.

"What a lot of questions," he scoffed. "I offered to negotiate before you bit me, remember?" At her reluctant nod, he added, "If I offer again, will you consider it or are you determined to do me bodily injury?"

"Yes" was a whispered capitulation, but as his face loomed a fraction of an inch closer, she quickly expanded it: "Yes, I'll negotiate!"

"You just bought yourself a reprieve," he murmured softly, tucking a loose strand of honey gold behind her ear, his warm palm lingering to caress her neck. Then he straightened away from the wall and drawled, "After you, ma'am."

Katherine kind of sidled past him, not trusting him completely, and scurried out of the bedroom. A quick look over her shoulder found his eyes fastened on her trim hips and effectively sped her steps. Once in the kitchen she was directed to a chair while he filled a water glass, handed it to her, and pushed the pills he had laid on the table in her direction.

"What are they?" she wanted to know, looking at him askance.

"My friend Rob's prescription for what ails you. And before you start balking again"—he paused, removing the bottle of tablets from his shirt pocket and holding it out for her inspection—"they're yours, little skeptic. When you passed out at my place the other night, I called Rob over to look at you."

"Oh! Well, you could have said so earlier," she reproached him, but with a flush of embarrassment at her earlier assumption of illicit drugs. "Is Rob one of the men who flirted with Lau—who works on sick cars?"

"The tall one with red hair. Rob Thompson. He specializes in obstetrics and gynecology, but bruised ribs and kneecaps and viruses aren't beyond his ken. Katherine?" His voice turned from lazy to serious on her name, and he stooped down in front of her chair. "Katherine, the other night . . . what happened . . . I never intended hurting you. I want you to know that."

And then incredibly, the hard, taunting Matt Clinton claimed her hands and carried first one and then the other to his mouth, placing a warm kiss in her palms. Katherine didn't have difficulty recognizing the quiet sincerity of his words. It was in his eyes searching her features for understanding. The realization that she owed him an explanation for her behavior that night, perhaps an apology as well, had her trying to explain.

"I was hysterical . . . and sick, I suppose. I thought Laurel was with you," she told him quietly. "Matt? . . . Laurel's so young, and I know she's beautiful and looks much older; but please don't . . ." She hesitated at the look of pain in his eyes.

"I always knew Laurie was a baby, even when I swallowed that lie about her age, but Kat, I wasn't attracted to her. Not the way you thought. My friends and I indulged her that first day because she's cute and can sweetly ply the tools of her sex. John Rogers, my other friend, has a twelve-year-old daughter who tries much the same thing. Believe me, Laurie was never under any threat from us." He smiled to offer reassurance.

And that's when Katherine broke down. She twisted her hands free to cover her face and broke into big gulping sobs of relief. She cried as she hadn't in years, cried as she hadn't since those terrible months after Barry's death. She believed Matt. He was too sincere and plausible not to believe. But for months she had harbored the dread that he was a threat to her young daughter, and the relief of knowing he wasn't, coupled with the tense emotional scenes of the last few days, produced a flood of feeling, feeling that had built to a point where it needed release and Katherine could no longer contain it.

For a while Matt let her cry, gruffly patting her knees from time to time but for the most part just watching her with impatient frustration. But as Katherine's sobbing continued, her face hidden behind her hands so he couldn't see the extent of her pain, only the rivulets of tears running down to drench her wrists and dampen the cuffs of her blouse, he began a stream of soft cursing.

Into Katherine's consciousness came a soft "Hell's bells, Katherine, stop it." Then a gruff, "Dammit, woman, you're making yourself sick!" Then a palm holding two pills and another holding a glass of water were replacing her hands covering her face. She was forced to swallow the tablets, strangling when the water was sloshed down her throat a little too hurriedly. Her choked coughing was answered by a forceful pounding on her back, his easy strength pushing her toward the floor and his quick arm about her waist pulling her roughly back.

And then he lifted her like a child, carried her into the den, and cradled her warmly and securely against his chest when he sat back on the sofa. He stroked her face and hair and back with gentle fingers, patiently waiting for her to calm. When she did, she looked up at him with drowsy, red-rimmed eyes.

"You okay now?" he whispered gruffly. His eyes seemed more than a little wary as they inspected the ravages weeping had stamped on her face.

"Just sleepy. I'm sorry for the weeping fit. I don't normally succumb to that sort of display."

"That's good," he commented, sounding relieved. "I've never comforted a crying woman before."

"Your mother never cried?" she questioned softly.

"Not to my knowledge, but she died when I was two, so I couldn't say for sure."

"No sisters, aunts, grandmothers?"

"Nope. Just a contrary old grandfather and a bullheaded father, both as tough as they come," he reflected wryly.

"Well"—she yawned—"they must have instilled a little gentleness in you along with the contrariness and bullheadedness."

"Can't say they did. Ol' Dad and Ol' Granddad taught me a lot, but sissy emotions weren't part of it. Besides"— he grinned—"I'm an ex-marine and the marines—"

"Build men. Well, you're that all right," she murmured into his chest, her head feeling unusually heavy and in need of a resting place. "The most tormenting man I've ever met" was a fuzzy addition that tickled the hair at the open neck of his shirt.

Matt's next comment was muffled in her hair. "You need your bed, Kat."

"Mmmm" was neither yes nor no but very, very contented.

His "Oh, lady," was very, very amused as he effortlessly lifted her with him and carried her toward her bedroom. But when he tried to lay her on the bed, soft clinging arms tightened their hold on his neck.

Her mumbled "Don't leave me" had him awkwardly half lying, half sitting beside her.

"Hold a minute, Kat," came to her in a husky whisper before he eased away and she heard the sound of two soft thuds on the carpeted floor. Then hard warmth came back to her, and she was enclosed inside the circle of his arms. His hands made slow, soothing sweeps over her back and shoulders, lifting her just enough onto his chest to take the majority of her weight.

Too sleepy to realize she snuggled closer, she only half heard his wryly muttered "Ol' Dad and Granddad failed to tell me about skinny widows," which drifted into the spilled tresses of her blond hair across his chest.

Wednesday morning Katherine was sitting at her desk in the Kendall Realty office, studying a sales contract point by point.

Matt had overruled all protests about returning to work on Tuesday, again bunking down on her den floor Monday night in a custom-made sleeping bag that accommodated his length more easily than her small Victorian sofa. And the truth was Katherine had possessed very little energy with which to fight his directive, antibiotics and tranquilizers keeping her in a low-energy state. But Tuesday evening she had slept her fill and very assertively assured him she was feeling fantastic and was going to work the next day. The aid of cosmetics and a determinedly bright expression helped convince him, although not without a certain amount of skepticism.

As she rolled the sales contract into a typewriter for a quick correction, Charlie came through the office with brisk, sure strides, her stylishly short hair bouncing attractively with each step. She stopped at Katherine's desk and eyed her friend critically.

"You'll do. Laurel had me worried when she called, but I can see you look more rested. Who in heaven's name is Matt?" A delicately arched eyebrow added insinuation to the question.

Katherine laughed. How like Charlie to pounce immediately on the possibility of a man on the horizon of Katherine's *dull existence*—Charlie's words. How often had she heard them over the three years she'd worked at Kendall Realty?

"I should do, Charlie. I've done nothing but sleep for three days. Sorry about not coming in Monday and Tuesday."

"Katherine Meadows, who's Matt?"

"My neighbor. He was a big help with the kids," she explained. She was unable to prevent the revealing blush coloring her cheeks when she recalled waking up Monday afternoon to focus on two big boots on the floor by her bed. Matt hadn't explained. She hadn't asked. But there had been a wicked gleam in his eyes when he'd brought her a mug of hot soup and caught her astounded absorption of his discarded boots. After handing her the mug, he had blithely sat on the edge of her bed, calmly tugging the boots onto his stockinged feet. The very nonchalance of his movements and attitude caused her to burn her tongue on a quick sip of tomato soup and then smother a small sound of pain as her mind frantically searched for recall. Fortunately Marigold had chosen that moment to pounce lithely on the bed, saving Katherine from facing Matt's speculative appraisal as she buried her face in the tabby's furry coat.

"And?" Charlie was insistent.

"And that's about it, dear Abby. Nothing more to recount."

"Laurel rather likes him. What does he look like?"

"A man—big, brawny, sure of himself. Want an introduction?" Katherine snapped sarcastically.

Charlie's husky laugh was deliciously amused. Her friend Katherine was covering up. "No, honey. I've got enough on my plate right now with Russell. I think I'll make him husband number four," she confided, laughing again as Katherine rolled her eyes.

Charlotte Kendall was a vivacious blonde of forty-two years, who looked thirty-five on her best days and who didn't have worst days. She was a bright, energetic, forceful woman who ran her realty firm with clever skill and her personal life with a little less insight. She had been divorced three times, and Russell Malone, another realtor, was her present marital target. Charlie considered men much as she would pieces of real estate: as investments. Buy, maintain, and enjoy, then sell when the market offered something better, and in between each contractual arrangement, scout all the possibilities for future reference. She and Katherine were as far apart in that respect as the North and South poles. But childless herself, Charlie had a deep love for children and had won Katherine as a loyal friend by showing an honest interest in Tim and Laurel.

As Charlie excused herself to phone a client, Katherine silently wished her well with Russell and reflected on her own love life. There wasn't all that much to reflect upon. Over the last five years there had been several dates, a few uninteresting kisses. But between Barry's death and the five years just past she'd managed to make three drastic mistakes in the name of romance.

Two years after becoming a widow she had met Mike.

He was an up-and-coming lawyer, and Katherine had been searching for lost security. But the first time she asked him home for dinner, she discovered his major flaw. He didn't like children. He hated the sticky little beasts. He wanted Katherine, but he wanted boarding schools and paid nursery help. She told him good-bye without a qualm.

A couple of years later it was Bill she had allowed to enter a corner of her life. Bill was fun, and Katherine had needed some fun during those days. He also liked children. What he didn't like was responsibility. He wanted a live-in arrangement that would allow him access to the amenities of Katherine's home and bed without emotional encumbrances. Katherine advised him to drift out of her life, and he did with a moue of regret for her old-fashioned ideals.

Then a year later Jerry had rushed her defenses. Smooth-talking, handsome Jerry, who, with the insight of a scoundrel, wanted to invest in a few properties, but with Katherine's capital or, more explicitly, the capital left over from Barry's insurance proceeds and a few investments he'd wisely made during their brief years of marriage. At first Katherine had seen nothing but Jerry's ardent attention, an ardency she realized much later that carefully was held in check when he sensed her reluctance to settle for less than commitment and security. Their relationship ran smoothly until the afternoon Katherine walked into his apartment with the proceeds of a cashed bond and found him and a luscious brunette so passionately involved in a torrid love scene that her shocked gasp almost went unnoticed. One look at her tightly scornful expression convinced Jerry to bow out gracefully. He never called her again. Katherine never missed him.

And during the last five years Katherine had learned to draw on her own resources. The money Barry had provided through insurance and investments went into trust funds for Laurel and Tim, and their mother stopped searching for security in the form of the opposite sex. She had learned the hard way that men, most men, weren't worth the trouble. As a widow with two growing children she had too many considerations to complicate her life with the clutter of the male sex. Perhaps subconsciously she was searching for another Barry. That was Charlie's theory. Maybe she was right.

She and Barry had been high school sweethearts, marrying when Katherine was seventeen and Barry twenty-one. Their six years together had been blissful, only to come to a horrible, unexpected halt when Barry collapsed from a heart attack at the age of twenty-seven. Such a wonderfully loving man he had been, something of a poet, definitely a romantic. He had inundated Katherine with love poems, letters, tributes that she'd kept as mementos, stored away now in an old shoe box in her bedroom closet, indelibly etched into her heart. If only . . .

A picture of another man swam before her eyes, intruding into her thoughts, and she shook her head to dispel it. But the taunting grin she was beginning to know so well and the hooded assessing look from emerald eyes refused to be dispelled.

Don't even think it, Katherine. If there's one thing you've learned in the last few years, it is to recognize a confirmed bachelor and womanizer. Didn't Bill and Jerry teach you that much?

She briskly forced herself back to the work at hand—the contract that just might bring a much needed commission.

CHAPTER FOUR

It wasn't until the following weekend that Katherine saw Matt again, and it wasn't in circumstances she would have preferred. But then, would any circumstances be desirable? As yet, each encounter with her neighbor was somehow disastrous.

Dressed in old cutoff jeans, a short-sleeved cotton pullover shrunk barely to cover her midriff, and sneakers that had definitely seen better days, Katherine was industriously clearing the flower bed fronting her house. Laurel was supposedly similarly occupied in the back, and Tim was mowing the back lawn. Although Katherine was confident Tim would diligently finish his chore, she wasn't so positive Laurel would work with the same degree of persistence. Laurel hated *dirty* work, and messing up her manicure was the height of indignity. In exasperation at her complaints, Katherine had shoved her own pair of gardening gloves into the well-kept hands, deciding a few thorns and a little dirt were a better bargain than a barrage of sullen gripes.

After uprooting one particularly stubborn weed, Katherine took a swipe at a loose strand of hair tickling over her cheek, dirty fingers leaving a smudge of soil on her face. Her hair was tied back loosely at her nape, but the pyracantha had already snagged several wispy strands into untidy disarray, so that what wasn't standing on end was clinging to her perspiring face. In addition to her soiled face, hands, and clothing, her arms were scored with myriad scratches, the precious gift of a vicious holly bush.

Down on her hands and knees, she was trying to reach the back of the flower bed, where a wild clover weed flourished. Her head and chest were lowered and hidden from view through the bushes, the main purpose being not to again court disaster with the sharp, prickly holly. From the waist down she was plainly in sight, her derriere up because it was more comfortable than snaking over the lawn and earth on her stomach and bare thighs. If she had thought about it, she might have decided the clover was welcome to its domain in the rich soil at the back of the flower bed. But in her anxiety to make a good job of clearing out the weeds and dead leaves, the potentially embarrassing aspects of her posture hadn't crossed her mind. Just as she wrapped triumphant fingers around the base of the clover, she heard a sound from behind her. Believing it to be the interfering Marigold, she spoke a sharp warning.

"Get away from here, you blasted pest! This is my territory today. Go chase butterflies or crickets some-where else!" Then she wriggled her bottom in an effort to gain leverage for pulling the clover free of the ground.

"But the view is so . . . stimulating from here," answered an amused masculine voice. "Are you sure I couldn't catch a little of the action right here?"

Katherine stiffened at Matt's first word, loosening her hold on the weed before abruptly lowering her hips and raising her head—both unwise moves. Her hair tangled in the holly, and the thinly worn cutoffs snagged on a broken branch of pyracantha.

"Damn!" she muttered angrily. She tried to free herself from the tenacious hold of spiky holly leaves, her dirty fingers only making a tangle of her hair as they worked with imprecise haste. When she felt warm, sure hands near her bare thighs, she twisted sharply. And heard a rending tear ripping her shorts just below the back pocket. She groaned in dismay.

"Be still, woman!" was ordered in a deep voice shaking with laughter. "I'm trying to free this end, and you've only made things worse by wriggling. You've torn your shorts."

"I'm aware of that!" she informed him with icy sharpness. She jumped when she felt those large competent hands at the back of her cutoffs. She closed her eyes, counting to ten, gratefully thinking how fortunate it was that Matt couldn't see her flushed, embarrassed face. Then the thought of what he *could* see sent another rush of hot color to stain her face and neck.

"Then stop squirming till I get you loose," he directed gruffly, and there was no mistaking the hateful amusement that threaded his voice.

She tried to be patient, but it seemed he was taking an inordinate amount of time to unsnag her. Finally the limb was broken free of its hold on her shorts. At the same moment a large, warm palm gently squeezed the roundness of her backside, and Katherine practically strangled on a shriek of pure outrage. How she would love to wrap her soiled fingers around his muscle-corded neck and choke the life slowly out of his insolent body! Damn his impudence!

"Everything looks great here. How's it going on your end?" Matt asked blithely, removing his hands with one last, softly stroking movement along her thighs.

"Just great!" she gritted out so sarcastically that Matt's hearty laughter rang out loud and clear.

Determined not to scream abuse at him until she could do so from a less embarrassing position, Katherine quickly untangled her hair. Using more jerky speed than careful caution, she came away with a dozen or more prickly leaves buried in her honeyed tresses.

Clenching her jaw, she knew that if she didn't want to become ensnarled again, she would have to raise her posterior to scoot backward. She had no choice but to resume her former position. Awareness of all-seeing green eyes had her quickly lowering her head and raising that part of her anatomy as she gingerly bustled back. Before she could accomplish her objective, however, his very willing hands came back to help, high on her hips, the fingers curling over her sensitive hipbones as Matt hauled her free. The impetus of his tugging strength, together with her efforts to bullet away from his touch, had Katherine sprawling on top of Matt on the grass, her shoulder blades digging sharply into his flat belly when she struggled to get up.

"You big blockhead! Why did you pull so hard?" she rasped out heavily, disgusted with her inelegant spraddle.

His long fingers firmed along her hipbones, warmly caressing, and Katherine found a new reason for her labored breathing. She renewed her efforts to squirm up and away from him, overwhelmingly conscious of his disturbing touch. It infuriated her, as did the fact that for all her frantic struggling he could hold her to him so easily.

At last he sat up, bringing her, stiffly resistant, between his legs, the tremors in his chest and belly evidence of his silent laughter. Warm breath tickled the sensitive flesh at her neck when he bent forward.

"I didn't catch a cricket or a butterfly. I caught a katydid," he whispered with gruff impudence, a hand moving to her stomach and another to her waist, holding her securely.

"Let me up, you laughing oaf!" she ordered through

80

clenched teeth, her voice sounding more breathless than imperative.

"Must I?" he asked plaintively, not duly impressed by her command, his hands slow to loosen their grip.

When she felt herself less restricted, she threw two sharp elbows into his stomach, hearing Matt's grunt of surprise with an emotion kin to exhilaration. She bounded to her feet. Two steps away she whirled back around, belatedly remembering the tear at her seat. The grin on Matt's face as he rose lazily to his feet punctuated her embarrassment. Her grubby hands went back to cover the seat of her pants to discover the extent of the damage. The tear was much larger than she'd thought, covering almost a three-inch triangular area. Her eyes went wide with the acknowledgment of how much he had seen.

She was already uncomfortably aware of how scruffy she must look, and his crinkling eyes thoroughly surveying her figure made her even more so. His alert gaze started a lingering appraisal at her grubby sneakers, traveled appreciatively up the slender length of her bare legs and thighs, and paused at her waistline, evidently finding something of interest at that point. The slant of his mouth and the lift of his eyebrow spoke volumes. Katherine reluctantly looked down to find the cause of his unwarranted interest and groaned in dismay. Her hands quickly twitched her shirt down over her bared midriff. And then she was more dismayed. Her rough tug had caused the scooped neckline of her T-shirt to dip low, baring the beige lace of her bra. She gasped in alarm, but before she could straighten her error, his eager fingers were there ahead of her, delicately easing the cotton pullover to a more modest level, lingering to brush the tops of her breasts softly. She was flustered by the intimate contact but not incapable of action. With a shocked screech she slapped his hands away, glaring at him ferociously.

"Now, Kat!" he appealed, backing away and pretending alarm. As he held his palms up placatingly, his pleading stance did little to hide his aura of supreme self-confidence. He offered soothingly, "I was only trying to help." He seemed to enjoy the stormy glare tossed his way, and Katherine realized he was having hilarious fun . . . at her expense.

"Help?" she yelped fractiously, clearly not believing him. "You've been nothing but a hindrance since the day you moved in!" Her soiled face was flushed with annoyance and discomfiture, and she had no idea how desirable she looked with bright, flashing eyes, bare, slender legs, and a T-shirt one size too small. She only knew that Matt's gaze seemed equally fascinated by the clinging fit of her top and the leggy expanse below the frayed hem of her shorts.

"Peace?" he offered solemnly, a trace of wicked humor in his eyes capturing hers. He formally extended his hand.

He looked so repentant, so falsely contrite that a reluctant smile transformed Katherine's stormy look. Fighting him was becoming increasingly impossible. She lost too much in the way of dignity and self-possession each time. Besides, in his present mood Matt was somehow very appealing. She offered her own soiled hand in return.

"You're feeling better, I take it, than you did last weekend," he commented, lifting leaves from the ruffled strands of her hair, concentrating on her unexpected smile.

"But then I never was really sick," she informed him pertly.

Matt's expression was skeptical. He lifted the last holly leaf from her hair and tossed it to the ground. When her hands came up automatically to smooth the tangled tresses into a semblance of order, the grooves at the sides

82

of his mouth deepened, his gaze narrowing over the tight fit of the T-shirt across her breasts.

"Yeah! I remember your strength when you were supposed to be puny," he attested wryly, gingerly touching the place on his arm that still held teeth marks. "It was almost as ferocious as your strength when you were well." He held out his other arm, inspecting the lingering scratch marks from the night she had wandered into his backyard in search of Marigold. Katherine flushed an uncomfortable shade of scarlet, and he laughed. "That's okay, Katherine, I'll have my revenge yet," he informed her very seriously.

"Oh, no, you don't! I consider us quite even. Those scratches were in direct retaliation for squeezing the air from my lungs and scaring me witless, and the bite was for . . . was for . . ." She searched her mind for a feasible reason.

"Was for taking your cute little equalizer away from you?" he jeered softly, referring to the pepper mill. Her guilty face was eyed with intense satisfaction. "That won't wash! If your hasty aim was any indication, I believe you intended crashing that little toy into my mouth. Rest assured, Kat, you owe me for my past restraint. If you hadn't been sick that day, you'd have already felt my retaliation."

"I thought you offered peace a moment ago," she said with a pretty, coaxing smile, hoping to change the subject.

"So I did," he drawled slowly, his gaze narrowing on her dimple. He muttered something under his breath and reaching inside his hip pocket, extracted an envelope, which he handed to her with a sudden frown. "The mailman dropped it in the wrong box. I thought it might be important."

The return address was Big Spring, Texas, and the writing was boldly masculine.

"Oh, it's from Peter!" she exclaimed with a delighted smile, slitting open the envelope and eagerly scanning the contents of the letter. Her smile softened as she read, and she glanced up to find Matt leaving. She called softly, "Matt?"

He turned back with a glowering look and rapped out a terse "Yes?"

Katherine's soft smile wavered uncertainly. He suddenly looked fierce, but she politely proceeded, determined to offer her thanks. "Thanks for bringing it over. Laurel and Timmy will be so pleased. They've been invited to spend their summer vacation on their grandparents' farm." She flapped the letter to indicate it was the invitation.

"Grandparents?" he asked sharply.

"Peter and Martha Meadows, their paternal grandparents. They have the children out most summers. My offspring adore it, especially Timmy. He loves outdoor living. I think Laurel just likes the pampering they lavish on her. Anyway, thanks for the letter," she finished lamely, not understanding the funny twist to his mouth. Maybe she was boring him with details of her family life. With one last wavering smile she turned and walked toward her house.

It was the muffled laugh behind her that abruptly halted her steps. She glanced over her shoulder to find an interested gaze on the seat of her pants. Whirling sharply about, her hands flying belatedly to cover the tear, she backed away until the steps leading up to her porch forced her to a halt. Her dismayed eyes never left Matt's amused face as he slowly followed in her wake.

"How are you planning to negotiate those steps?" he wanted to know, grinning like a devil, his thumbs hooked negligently inside a couple of belt loops on his jeans.

"Easily, if you'll be kind enough to turn your head," she informed him primly, tossing him a reproachful look.

"Why, when I've already seen? I was there, remember?" he taunted, and watched her freezing gray eyes try to turn him into a block of ice.

"I should have remembered you're no gentleman!" she muttered, shaking her head in frustration.

"Oh, but I am!" he assured her, reaching into a pocket and coming out with a folded handkerchief. He flourished it with a snap of his wrist and stepped just close enough to alter Katherine's breathing.

"What are you doing?" she asked warily, wishing she could back a couple of inches away.

"Providing you with some modesty." He grinned and leaned over to tuck a corner of the handkerchief into her back pocket, working around her covering hands.

In that position Katherine's nose was practically buried in his shoulder, and she had to force herself to stand rigidly still, her nostrils flaring as she breathed in his clean male scent. All too aware of her increased pulse rate, she felt him carefully arrange the loose folds of the handkerchief over her hands. Then he repositioned those stalwartly covering hands to hang loosely at her sides. He gave the handkerchief one final, perhaps unnecessary adjustment, and Katherine bit her lip, fast losing her desire to escape his nearness. When he straightened, there was a roguish glint in his eyes.

"Say thank you, Katherine," he urged softly.

"Thank you!" She obeyed tartly and watched his teeth flash in smiling appreciation at her tone.

"Come on, Kat, you can do better than that," he admonished softly, bending down to favor her with a seductive gleam.

"Take it or leave it!" she retorted flippantly, determined not to be taken in by his wily charm.

85

His large hands snaked out and lifted her by the waist to set her gently on the porch, bringing their eyes level. Retaining his hold on her waist, he leaned forward, his breath a warm caress on her face.

"Katherine Meadows, you're one stubborn woman," he whispered huskily, the gravelly thread in his voice making it sound like a lover's tribute. "Your face is dirty, and your hair is a mess." Green fire caressed those areas. "But I want a thank-you, nicely given, or I'll take it my way and remove my handkerchief at the same time," he threatened softly.

Katherine didn't consider for a moment it was an idle warning. She lowered her eyes from the disturbing glitter of his, afraid he might somehow determine how affected she was by his proximity. Extremely tempted to take her chances and ignore his threat, she also wondered why she was finding an unexpected delight in his teasing. Raising her eyes from their contemplation of his cowboy boots, she gazed at him with limpid eyes. Her hands crept slowly to his broad shoulders, then to the back of his neck to curl into the rich brown hair at his nape. She pitched her voice to a deliberately husky, seductive whisper that even Laurel would have envied.

"Thank you so much, Matt, for all your . . . ah . . . gracious help today," she said invitingly, batting her eyelashes in slow, seductive sweeps. "What would I have done without you?" A slender finger trailed over the outline of his jaw and then to his ear; she held back an impish urge to tweak his earlobe sharply when his smug mouth curled in satisfaction. Abruptly she straightened and twisted away, adding over her shoulder with softly biting sarcasm, "Does that suit you, you self-complacent oaf?"

His hand reaching out and snagging the handkerchief from her hip pocket was a prelude to his big body bounding the steps in one easy stride. As she ran, shrieking, through the front door of her house, another large hand snagged a handful of T-shirt, and then she was in his arms. Backed against the wall of the foyer, his muscled thighs and massive chest pinned her motionless. He grasped a warm hold on her neck and head, his thumbs gently exploring her jawline.

"Don't say I didn't warn you, Kat," was breathed against her mouth just before he took warm possession.

Thorough, expert, the kiss was a sensual invasion, his warm tongue teasing her lips apart to take the sweetness of her mouth in leisurely pleasure. He found her hands and placed them around his neck, then lifted her closer, pressing her breasts flat against his chest with the pressure of the embrace. An exploring hand went to the pocket of her shorts, near the jagged tear. When her arms tightened invitingly around his neck and she released a soft moan of pleasure, he lifted his mouth and stared down at her slitted eyelids, his smile curving attractively.

"Kat?" he whispered huskily.

"Yes?" she said weakly, having difficulty fully opening her eyes.

"I was wrong. You're not too skinny." The hand on her hip pocket lowered to press her closer. "You're round in some very nice places."

And then he was kissing her again, with hungry demand, and Katherine was responding, thoroughly caught up in the unexpected pleasure of the moment. The urgency with which his mouth slanted over hers was met by the eager parting of her lips, his tongue stroking inside her mouth having no need to plunder what was offered so freely.

The slamming of the back door broke them apart. Matt groaned as he released her, and Katherine scrambled away from him to back weakly against the opposite wall just as Laurel came through the hall and spotted them.

87

"Oh, hi, Matt," she said in greeting him.

" 'Lo, Laurie," Matt managed to say, his voice surprisingly pitched at a normal level.

"I've cleared the flower bed, Mother. May I take a shower now?" she asked, looking at her soiled clothing with ill-disguised displeasure.

"Sure, honey. Is Timmy through mowing?" Katherine hated the husky sound of her voice, but there was nothing she could do about it. Laurel sent her a funny look, nodding her answer, and then turned to Matt.

"By the way, Matt, there's someone looking for you," she informed him, a mischievous twinkle in her brown eyes.

"Who's that?" he asked lazily, eyeing Katherine.

"Dunno," Laurel drawled, shrugging. "But she looks upset. And by the color of her hair, I'd say you might be in for some trouble."

"Stacy," Matt murmured, smiling slowly.

"You should know." Laurel smiled nonchalantly and waltzed buoyantly to her bedroom.

Katherine was stunned. Her eyes were big pools of confusion. She stared at the man who had just completed a passionate onslaught on her senses. First Bibbi; now Stacy? And next . . . Katherine Meadows?

Matt's stance was relaxed, his hands tucked into his back pockets, but he was carefully watching the expressions chasing across Katherine's face. At the hint of hurt bewilderment in her eyes, he seemed almost satisfied.

"Guess I'd better go, Kat. Laurel's right. Stacy doesn't like waiting." He reached over and flicked the dirty smudge on her cheek. "Better take care of that face," he murmured, bending down to give her a parting kiss. She moved aside just in time, and his mouth hit nothing but air. Seemingly unaffected by her aversion, he casually straightened and offered a soft "See you" as he turned for the door.

The sweet, serene smile that curved her mouth was dredged up from an inner source of calm. She reached over to open the door for him, curtailing the impulse to help him out the door with a hefty shove in the small of his back. As she watched him saunter through the door, she even found enough insouciance to murmur pleasantly, "Not if I see you first."

Satisfaction came when his back went rigid right before she softly closed the door behind him. Then strength and indifference flagged, and she wilted back against the door. But she meant what she'd said. Katherine Meadows was nobody's fool. She might find Matt Clinton unbearably irresistible while he was kissing her, but she valued her peaceful existence too much to let it be undermined by his particular brand of heartache. She sighed feebly, raising unseeing eyes to the ceiling. Tears threatened, and she irritably blinked them away.

Don't be more of a fool than you've already been, Katherine. You're not hurt. You're angry. Angry at that big devil for thinking he had another prospect all lined up for his string of bed partners. And angry at yourself for letting him break down your defenses. If there's one thing you don't need, it's a man like him messing up your life. Oh, blast, Katherine, you've known from the beginning what a nasty sort he was. Why, oh, why did you let him kiss you? Why, oh, why did you respond?

She pretended that the big tear that plopped onto the front of her soiled T-shirt didn't exist.

The next Saturday Katherine drove into her driveway and immediately spotted her big neighbor and his two cronies hovering over the insides of yet another sports car in Matt's drive. This model was brand-new and sleek and powerful. A cursory glance relieved her mind over worry about Laurel. The three men were alone.

As she smoothed the lightweight skirt of her leaf green dress over her knees and swung her slender legs out of the opened car door, she became aware of a sudden cessation of comradely laughter across the lawns. A quick, hooded glance found three pairs of masculine eyes seemingly very interested in ten-year-old Chevy station wagons, not just spanking-new sports cars. Refusing to acknowledge their gazes, she left the car and walked to the back, which she unlocked to remove two sacks of groceries. With each arm clutching a bag, she started for the house, out of the corner of her eye catching a glimpse of a moving figure. That startled her into hesitating, and she turned to see Matt's redheaded friend loping across the lawn in her direction.

The man smiled as he approached and then relieved her of one of the bags. "We've never been formally introduced, Katherine Meadows, and I believe it's time to alter that mistake. I'm Rob Thompson."

"Yes, of course, the doctor. I've wanted to thank you for your help a couple of weeks ago," Katherine told him politely.

"A cup of coffee would be nice," he suggested so appealingly that Katherine laughed and invited him inside.

Ten minutes later Tim traipsed into the kitchen with another guest, and Katherine found herself greeting Matt's other friend.

"John Rogers" was offered with a boyish smile, a friendly hand outstretched. "I couldn't let ol' Rob have all the fun."

"How nice to see you in these circumstances," Katherine commented. "I've always felt I owed the two of you an apology for my grumpy behavior that night in February."

"Apology accepted and discarded as being unnecessary," John told her with a wide grin.

"What did you do with Matt?" Rob wanted to know, sitting at ease at the kitchen table.

Katherine handed John a cup of coffee and offered him cream and sugar before seating herself at one end of the table with John and Rob on either side.

"Left him scowling at your new Porsche," John replied with a wink at his friend.

"That's strange," Rob commented dryly, eyeing Katherine obliquely. "I could have sworn that racy engine had him completely fascinated."

Katherine smiled politely, but she wasn't all that knowledgeable about cars, so she remained silent.

"I don't know if he thinks it's fascinating or not, but he was glaring down at it like it was a big wheel with pedals and muttering dire expletives when I left," John said innocently, but he, too, sent Katherine a glance that was full of subdued laughter.

The two men exchanged knowing grins and quickly changed the subject, for which Katherine was thankful. She didn't want to talk about Matt, and she couldn't add much to a conversation about cars. When the talk turned to real estate and economics, she relaxed and joined in with a smile. Matt's friends were nice. Too bad some of their urbanity hadn't rubbed off on him.

Fifteen minutes later Tim brought yet another visitor into the kitchen, and this one Katherine neither smiled at nor greeted with a polite welcome. She just stared at him silently, leaving all the exuberance to her son.

"Hey, Mom, Matt's here. Isn't that great? I told him you'd want him to have coffee, too," Tim explained with a wide smile, innocently unaware of his mother's tension.

While Katherine wondered at her son's lack of perception, Matt sent her an ironic smile, one dark brow lifted

91

almost challengingly. She met his look with one of cold disdain. Three times over the last week Matt had dropped over for one reason or another, and each time Katherine had been otherwise occupied. The first time she was conveniently in the shower, the second occasion unfortunately on the phone, and the third regrettably in bed.

"Mom, you do have coffee for Matt, don't you?" Tim's young voice was pointedly reminding her of her duties as a hostess, a frown on his thin face.

"Of course. Mr. Clinton, would you care for some coffee?" Her words were stiffly polite.

"Thank you . . . Mrs. Meadows. I believe I do," he answered just as stiltedly, but his eyes were anything but formal, sweeping intimately over her length.

He hooked a chair with a booted foot, turned it to face away from the table, then straddled the seat with his arms laid over the back. He peered up through lowered lids to send his friends a censuring frown. At their openly grinning answers, a faint twitch teased the corners of his mouth. Then he punched the waiting Tim playfully on the arm, and the boy bounded, laughing, out of the room.

The steaming mug was placed in front of him with a sharp little bang that sloshed coffee over the sides. Matt sent his hostess a glittering look that spelled danger and disapproval of her coldly hostile manner. Katherine's unintimidated answer was to raise her delicately arched eyebrows inquiringly and scornfully. John broke the tension by asking about her pewter saltshaker and pepper mill, admiring the line and weight.

"My wife collects pewter pieces. Our house is full of them. These are nice."

"Yes, I've always been fond of them."

"Because they're such heavy equalizers . . . er, equipment, and they're sturdy enough to bruise . . . er, use everyday?" Matt asked innocently, but with a mocking lilt that was meant to disconcert her if his deliberately stumbling phraseology didn't manage to do so.

Katherine favored him with a haughty frown, but she answered the question seriously and quietly. "Because they were a gift from someone special." Then she turned back to John. "They're antique. Barry found them in an out-of-the-way shop, tucked into a dusty corner. But the stamp on the underside is the mark of a famous nineteenth-century craftsman. Does your wife collect antiques?" She didn't miss Matt's disgusted scowl at the mention of Barry's name but was still unprepared for his snide comment interrupting John's reply.

"Barry sounds like a regular gem!" he muttered, the tone of his voice making the comment an indictment instead of a compliment.

Laurel, who had entered the room unheard, crossed to her mother's chair and for once sent Matt as fierce a frown as that presently being shot at him by Katherine.

"We think so, Matt. Mother kept several things he gave her. She says Daddy would want me to have some of them when I get married. Isn't that right, Mother?"

Katherine nodded her agreement, for once speechless, her face a study of perplexity. Why in the world would Matt disparage Barry?

"Barry was your husband?" Rob inserted quietly.

"Yes," she murmured.

"Well, he had fine taste," John commented gallantly. "In all things. You'll have to come over and see Maggie's collection of pewter. I'm not sure whether or not there are any antiques in the lot, but she has some nice pieces."

Katherine murmured a polite answer, feeling green eyes fixed on her with such deep intensity that she finally raised her own gaze to meet them. There was no anger in those eyes, and no apology either, but they were burning over her face with concentrated avidity. She felt mesmerized.

His look was possessive, proprietary, causing a shiver of apprehension to trail up her spine. His blazing look seemed to stamp her as his, and she felt herself enthralled to the point of not having a mind of her own to dispute his claim.

Neither Matt nor Katherine seemed aware that John and Rob were tactfully occupying Laurel with questions about school and rock music, and it was several long seconds before the spell of their gaze was broken. It was Tim who managed it, suddenly bursting through the back door in a breathless rush of excitement.

"Mom, can I ride my bike down to the high school and watch the track meet?" he asked eagerly.

Katherine faced her son, the physical reminder of Barry with those chocolate-colored eyes and light brown hair. Laurel had the same eyes, but Laurel looked more like Katherine. Tim was growing straight and tall, and his thin face, with its wide forehead and ears just a little too big, was almost an exact replica of Barry.

"When will you be home?" she asked.

"When it's over," he answered with maddening logic.

"How long, Timmy?" Her exasperation was tempered by a fond smile.

"Couple of hours, Mom. Can I?" He was fidgeting from one foot to the other, impatiently waiting for the yes he knew would be coming.

"Okay, buster, two hours. You be home by four thirty, or I'll send the home guard after you."

"Thanks, Mom!" was thrown over his shoulder as he bounded back through the door, all long legs and enthusiasm.

Laurel gained her attention next. "Mother, I'm going down to Lisa's to listen to her new tape. I'll be back when Tim gets back. Okay?"

Katherine smilingly nodded an affirmative. Tapes and

94

Lisa were so much easier to contend with than too much makeup and practiced sensuality. As Laurel left the room, Katherine turned back to her guests, only to find to her dismay that two of them were rising from their chairs in preparation to leave.

"Thanks for the coffee, Katherine." John was the first to speak, his pleasant face stretched into a broad smile.

"You're welcome, John," she replied with a sincere smile, rising to bid them good-bye.

"Katherine." Rob took her hand. "I'm glad we had a chance to talk. I was worried about you the last time I saw you. No more ill effects?" With his tall, lean body, with the curly abundance of carroty hair and freckles so thick he appeared deeply tanned from a distance, he looked the antithesis of a doctor; but his voice was deep and well modulated, and his blue eyes inspired confidence.

"Nothing I can't handle," she assured him with a double meaning that surprisingly wasn't lost on Dr. Rob Thompson. He grinned, shooting a quick glance at Matt.

"Well, so long, Katherine Meadows. Perhaps we'll meet again soon," he said, looking over her shoulder at Matt and reading something there that had him grinning again.

And then there were two.

Katherine busied herself collecting cups and rinsing them at the sink while Matt watched her movements with hooded eyes, idly playing with the pepper mill. That is until, on her last trip to the table, Katherine snatched it out of his hand and placed it in its proper place, glaring annoyance into his eyes before she once again walked to the sink. When she heard his chair scraping under the table, she turned, wiping her wet hands on a towel.

"Good-bye, Matt." She smiled, but it was a travesty of good manners.

"I'm not leaving," he stated quietly, unequivocally.

"Yes, you are!" she retorted, just as surely but with a little more vehemence.

"Nope."

She tried to stare him down and then decided on another tactic. A furtive glance at the refrigerator assured her the car keys were still where she'd laid them. If he wouldn't leave, she would. Common sense made her unwilling to subject herself to any more of his company. Common sense—and the erratic betrayal of her heartbeat.

"Suit yourself," she said calmly.

The towel was tossed onto the counter, and she reached for the keys from the top of the refrigerator. His large hand was there before hers, adroitly palming the keys.

"And you're not leaving either," he stated in a quietly positive voice, tossing the keys from one hand to the other.

"Whatever gave you that idea?" she pretended astonishment, reaching for her purse on the counter. "I was going to put my keys away so I wouldn't forget where I placed them," she said in quick invention, trying not to show her surprise . . . or dismay.

He handed her the keys, and she plopped them into her handbag, which she snapped shut with an irritated flick of her fingers. He smiled when she tossed it onto the cabinet next to the discarded towel—smiled like a crafty crocodile.

"Excuse me, Matt, but I'd like to change into more comfortable clothing," she said sweetly, clenching her fingers behind her back. She was desperate to get away from him.

"That dress looks cool and comfortable to me. Such a pretty green." His fingers were toying with the short sleeves, lightly brushing the skin of her upper arms.

"Thank you, Matt. It is a nice cover-up for my skinny bag of bones," she retorted with a soft bite, and then wished the words unsaid when he grinned. *That was dumb, Katherine. Now he thinks you worry about his opinion.*

"A very nice cover-up," he agreed, his grin spreading with wicked enjoyment.

"Whatever," she muttered, gazing at a point somewhere past his left shoulder. "In any event, it's Saturday afternoon, and I'm bushed, so I'm changing out of my working clothes and into something more casual. Have another cup of coffee, Matt," she said as an afterthought, calmly turning away from him.

She forced herself to use slow, sedate steps to walk to her bedroom when she really felt like galloping in frustration and panic. Her thoughts were equally discordant. Mr. Clinton felt in need of female companionship, did he? And the Widow Meadows was close at hand? Wonderful! Her scowl was fierce. She had been considered something more complimentary than *handy* in her lifetime, and it was time some woman told Matt a big fat no anyway. He was just too sure of himself. And what was more, he seemed too sure of her.

The bedroom door was shut with a soft little snap, and she turned toward her closet. Her fingers flicked irritably through her clothes, finally jerking jeans and a soft chambray tunic from their hangers. Unbelting the waist of her dress and then unzipping the back, she turned from the closet, her change of clothes clutched in front of her. Three steps away from the interior of the walk-in closet, she froze.

Leaning casually against the doorjamb of the opened bedroom door was a giant threat to her fraying composure —big and powerful and dangerous in the form of Matt Clinton. Or was that just a figment of her overactive imagination and overwrought nerves? His facial expression was only mildly pleasant, and his eyes weren't even focused on her. They seemed to be scanning the furnishings of her bedroom.

"Have you had lunch, Katherine?" he asked unexpectedly.

"I wasn't planning on lunch today," she answered coolly.

"Why not?" was his almost unconcerned reply, his eyes lighting on something behind her. He seemed to find the room's decor surprisingly interesting.

"I'm not hungry. I don't eat lunch every day."

"Dieting?" he asked with derogatory emphasis, his gaze flickering over her slender length with a less than complimentary summing-up.

"No!" she answered shortly, hating him for again reminding her that he thought her too thin.

She was also uncomfortably aware that she was partially undressed, the cool air on her bared back a reminder of the unzipped dress and the lack of a bra. The dress was full-bodied and opaque, and wearing a bra was unnecessary. But as she stood in rigid stillness, the loosened dress shifted, and she had to clutch it tighter to her breasts to keep from losing its concealing folds altogether.

"Well, no reason why you shouldn't eat today. I've got a couple of steaks," he said as if it were all settled. His eyes shifted from her to return to the wall at her back, this time with a strange glitter, as if the flowered wallpaper were revealing an unexpected delight. "Change into your jeans, and we'll go to my place."

"No, thank you, I'm not hungry," she insisted, and immediately her stomach unleashed a voracious growl. She flushed a guilty pink, and Matt's eyes came back to her face, a sardonic lifting of one brow telling her he had heard.

"Change, Kat. I'll turn my back," he offered in resignedly bored tones, clearly indicating it wouldn't matter one way or the other. After all, skinny bones weren't all that appealing.

"Oh, all right!" She capitulated less than gracefully.

She hated his disparagement, was fed up with his dictatorial manner, was frustrated with her inability to stay sane and cool in his presence, and was all too aware that her dignity was in danger of slipping along with her loosened dress. Even now the gaping back was making her skin goose bump. The only thing keeping her poise intact was his unawareness of her predicament.

With one last long appraisal of the fascinating wallpaper Matt turned and leaned indolently against the doorjamb, facing the hall. Katherine tartly thought of offering him the name of a good interior decorator since he was so interested in wallpaper. Matt's terse voice broke through her spiteful musings.

"Hop to it, Katherine. I'm hungry even if you're not."

Katherine stared malevolently at his broad shoulders, wishing she had the strength to toss him out on his ear. Then she sighed resignedly and began changing. After laying her jeans and tunic on the bed, she peeled down her pantyhose and slipped out of her half-slip while still in her dress. Then she wriggled into her jeans, a smug smile curving her mouth at how efficiently and modestly she had managed the transfer. Removing the dress and pulling on the tunic was a different matter. There was nothing for it but to let the dress fall to her ankles and quickly duck inside the blouse. That accomplished, she turned and bent to pick up her discarded clothing, eyeing her flushed features in the floor-length mirror as she patted a stray strand of hair back in place. Something niggled in the back of her consciousness as she eyed her reflection, but she shrugged and turned.

"I'm ready," she told him.

Matt turned and gave her a quick but thorough scan,

said, "Good," as if he couldn't care less, and then slowly gave the wall at her back another appreciative look.

And that's when it hit her. The mirror! The perfect, somewhat bored gentleman who had turned his back while she dressed had been eyeing her all but naked back in the wall mirror while he talked her into having lunch with him! She closed her eyes and groaned audibly at her stupidity, snapping them open to shoot darts of ice at him for his audacity.

"You were . . . were . . . !" she muttered incoherently.

"Looking," he confessed easily. "You really should eat more. Your ribs show."

While Katherine floundered, searching for the proper words to set him back on his booted heels, he reached out, relieved her of her bundle of clothing, and tossed it carelessly on the bed. He grasped her arm in firm fingers to guide her from the room, his green eyes crinkled at the corners with wicked laughter.

"I ought to belt you one," she stated direly.

"Do that, Kat. One of those muscle-packed fists of yours is bound to lay me low. Besides, it might help release some of that prissy frustration." He chuckled.

"Laugh away, Mr. Clinton, laugh away," she said wryly, her mouth curving with reluctant amusement. She really had been a little stupid not to remember her own wall mirror. And despite the fact that she would like to deny it, her outraged reaction to his perfidy had sounded prissy.

And of course, he did laugh, heartily, as he pulled her along beside him at a swift pace. She was practically forced to run to keep up with his long strides.

"Matt, slow down! I don't have my shoes on," she complained, balking against his hold on her arm.

"Don't try telling me those feet of yours are tender because I won't believe you. I've seen you barefoot more often than not. If I remember correctly, the first time was in thirty-degree weather," he retorted, not breaking his stride.

"Well, I wasn't running that day!" she managed acidly.

"No, you were marching." He grinned.

"There were extenuating circumstances," she reminded him, gasping breathlessly as she ran alongside him.

"Yeah, the lioness was protecting her cub."

"There's nothing to scorn in that!"

"I agree."

"You do?"

"You'd be surprised at what we see eye to eye on, Katherine. Your handling of your children is just one thing."

She didn't answer, glancing up at him, surprised. But she was pleased by his comment.

CHAPTER FIVE

Despite Katherine's earlier reluctance, lunch was surprisingly pleasant. Matt's kitchen was ultra-modern with fixtures of chrome and smoky glass, black and white tiling, and all the modern timesaving devices Katherine would have cherished on nights when cooking was another chore in a day of tasks and running. In addition to a dishwasher, disposal, range, oven, and microwave, there were a trash compacter, a built-in food processor, and an electric griddle laid into the counter tiling—everything arranged for easy fingertip control.

Matt popped potatoes into the microwave and started on the steaks, instructing Katherine to throw a salad together after directing her to the butcher block counter in the middle of the room and producing tomatoes, lettuce, and greens for her to work with. She busily chopped and shredded while he grilled two good-size T-bones over the hot electric griddle. The appetizing aroma of sizzling beef wafted her way. Her purported nonexistent hunger insistently grabbed at her insides so that she was occasionally tempted to pop a piece of celery or cucumber or tomato into her mouth to forestall her ever-increasing appetite. By the time she tossed a spicy vinegar and oil mixture over the bowl of greens Matt was turning the steaks onto two dinner plates.

He smiled when she closed her eyes and murmured,

"Mmmm!" And frowned when her nose wrinkled in aversion to the filled glass of red wine set by each plate.

"What is it, Kat? Don't you have this habit either?" he asked in mild annoyance, holding the bottle aloft.

"Not exactly," she answered crisply, more to his tone than to his actual question.

"Which means?" he prompted with raised eyebrows.

"Which means I don't normally drink very much, and I seldom have wine with meals. Therefore, it's not a habit, but I don't disapprove. So you can take that disparaging look off your face," she answered sweetly. "Actually it makes me sleepy. Charlie says wine is a waste on me anyway. I have no palate." The wry smile curving her mouth was directed at her low alcohol consumption level.

"Charlie could be wrong. Try a little. It's very good, and my steaks taste better with a good wine," he informed her, edging a glass filled to the brim closer to her plate. "It might increase your appetite."

The last comment brought him a reproachful frown, but she disdained answering except with a small lift of her chin. Raising her knife and fork to cut into the succulent piece of meat, she was certain her tastebuds were already tempted sufficiently without the aid of wine. The first bite was delicious, and she eagerly cut a second. She was soon enjoying the steak and potato and salad with hungry fervor.

Matt started in on his own meal, idly conversing about Rob's new Porsche, unaware or uncaring that Katherine didn't understand or appreciate the intricacies of a turbocharged engine or the possibilities of five forward gears. While she ate and nodded her responses, he topped her wineglass from time to time, ignoring her faint protests completely. With outward urbanity and only the faintest glimmer of appreciation in his eyes, Matt watched her gradual relaxation and dimpling smile, and somewhere in

Katherine's mind came the conviction that her host could be charming when he set his mind to it.

"You're fascinated by engines, aren't you?" she commented. He had just finished a rather lengthy dissertation on the increased density of the Porsche's engine charge and the atmospheric pressure that created more efficient combustion. It was all like a foreign language to Katherine, but she could tell Matt knew the subject well.

"Oh, sorry. Was I boring you?" But his grin was unabashed.

"No, of course not. I understand the male interest in all things mechanical. Timmy has studied my Chevy from the inside out."

"Tim's an observant boy. He told me you would never think to change the oil in your car if he didn't remind you."

"Well, that's true enough," Katherine admitted in some amusement. "I never can remember to do more than put gas in the tank."

"Why don't you get a newer car, Katherine? That old heap of yours will someday leave you stranded on the side of the road." He sounded truly worried about her welfare.

"New cars, Mr. Clinton, cost money, and I've got a mortgage and two teen-agers," she explained with an easy smile that was supposed to imply she wasn't worried about the situation. "Besides, I use the company car when I'm showing property. Charlie insists." She watched Matt frown as if he disapproved. "And my old Chevy is not an old heap. It's an old friend. And it's good enough to get me to work and back." At his skeptical expression, she veered the conversation back to him. "Where did you gain your knowledge of cars, Matt?"

His laugh was wry and abrupt. "Ol' Dad. When I was sixteen he had this beautiful Corvette, but he wouldn't let me near it. He said Corvettes and other luxuries came to men who earned them. I hadn't. My earnings at the time totaled seventy-five dollars, every dime of which went for an old beat-up Dodge with a sputtering engine and no spare tire. When the engine blew, Dad said if I couldn't afford to have the repairs done, I'd better learn to do them myself. A man who can't take care of what he has is a lazy man."

"So you learned how to repair the Dodge."

"Nope." He grinned. "I borrowed Dad's Corvette one night and wrapped it around a tree."

Katherine's eyes widened as she realized that Matt had borrowed the Corvette without his father's knowledge. "Were you hurt?"

"Not seriously. But then, Ol' Granddad wouldn't let Dad kill me. He said even a foolish man could learn from his mistakes. After that evenings and weekends were spent at a repair garage, earning money to replace a wrecked Corvette. I learned while I earned. And Dad took my Dodge, had it repaired and fixed up, and drove it himself. He made a vintage classic out of that old heap."

Katherine was trying not to laugh. "Did you ever get a Corvette of your own?"

The affirmative nod of his dark head was accompanied by an attractively crooked smile. "Three years after I graduated from A&M. I drove it home that first day, high as a kite because I'd finally earned the luxury I'd coveted for years, and Granddad borrowed it that same night to visit a friend. He left my new beauty on a steep hill outside his friend's home, the gearshift in neutral. It wound up at the bottom of the hill, totaled."

"Oh, Matt!" Katherine burst out laughing. "You paid for two Corvettes and drove them only twice?"

"Yep! After that I lost my taste for Corvettes. I decided a pickup was a sturdy vehicle, more economical, more reliable, and more sensible in the long run than all the fast, beautiful cars on the market. I still admire sleek sports models, but only from a distance."

"Very sensible," she said teasingly, her relaxed smile full of appreciation for his reminiscence.

His laughing green eyes fixed on her mouth and became warm and dark. "Oh, I'm a sensible man, Kat. Now, when I see something beautiful and sleek and want it urgently, I remember those two Corvettes and . . ."

"And deny yourself stoically," she finished for him, her eyes sparkling.

"No. I carefully weigh all the advantages and all the drawbacks. I don't deny myself unnecessarily. I just make sure that what I covet is going to be worth the price and the effort expended."

Something in his eyes told her he was no longer talking about cars or material possessions, and she felt a feathering of apprehension tickle along her spine. To hide her disconcertedness, she drank deeply of her wine and then asked brightly, "I understand from Tim that you're an engineer, Matt. Have you completed your project in Paraguay?"

His smile was filled with the knowledge of her deliberate change of subject, and he answered slowly. "No, progress has been temporarily suspended because of a mix-up with one of the supply firms. But after a passel of phone calls and long-distance communication, I've been assured that everything will be straightened out by the first of next week." He sat forward in his chair, his eyes intent. "Kat, I tried three times this week to see—"

"What kind of project is it?" she interrupted quickly, not sure she wanted to hear the reason he'd tried three times to see her.

Matt showed his annoyance with a frown, and Katherine held out her empty wineglass for a refill, smiling a little stiffly. The shrug of his wide shoulders seemed to dispel an infinitesimal tension, and he obligingly tipped the bottle over her glass. Then he sat back in his chair, once again concentrating on his meal.

"Your project in Paraguay, Matt. You didn't say what it was."

"A much needed road from a minor agricultural district to a major marketing district. The plans were drawn up and agreed upon back in January. We started construction the last of February, and if there aren't any more unforeseen delays, we should be finished sometime this fall." He forked a piece of steak and brought it to his mouth, and Katherine caught the wry smile as he popped it into his mouth.

Her own fork chased down a piece of celery from her salad bowl. For a bachelor and an ofttimes traveling one at that, it seemed strange that Matt would buy a large suburban house. She heard herself ask, a little wonderingly, "Why did you buy this house?"

"Ah, Kat, would you believe I wanted a home?" His smile was slow and ironic.

"I believe you wanted to live in comfortable surroundings." Her eyes swept the comfort and convenience of the large modern kitchen and dining alcove. "But I don't believe you were looking for a home, not in the traditional sense of the word, unless . . ." A sudden thought halted her words. What if Matt were married? What if, somewhere, there were a wife and kids waiting to join him in this spacious house? Good Lord! She'd never even thought of that! He'd told her there were no mother, sisters, aunts, grandmothers, but she never thought to inquire about a wife. Her eyes were enormous as she whispered, "Are you married?"

He almost strangled on his wine, her question voiced just as he'd taken a long sip. He gulped it down abruptly before rasping out a choked "No!"

The relief that swept through her was just as abruptly washed away by a feeling of irritation. His no had sounded like a denial of a fate worse than death.

"Would you like some water?" she asked, sweetly solicitous when he had to clear his throat, but her eyes held a new conviction. She couldn't have received the message more explicitly if he'd spelled it out. Marriage was at the bottom of his list of priorities.

Matt eyed her through hooded lids as she widened her smile to a saccharine curve. He said, "Ol' Dad and Granddad brought me up in apartments. I never really liked it when I was growing up. I bought this house because I liked the neighborhood."

"Did you? It is rather a nice neighborhood, isn't it? Charlie says it's one of the better suburban sections of the city. Property value is higher, and crime rates are lower. And the neighbors are very big on keeping it that way, very careful. We put up fences to keep out stray . . . tomcats and such. And we use locks on our doors to discourage undesirable elements from walking in uninvited." And with that oblique warning delivered in light conversational tones, she scooped the last forkful of fluffy potato out of its jacket.

"How commendable," he said very dryly, not missing her indirect warning. "Back in February an *element* drifted into my garage on a cold north wind, although it wasn't necessarily an undesirable element," he murmured with a warm appraisal of her chambray-covered breasts and her delicately defined features. But before she could decide to be flattered, he added, "And just a couple of weeks ago a scrawny little female cat wandered stealthily into my backyard."

"Very funny," she muttered, stabbing a cube of cucumber and bringing it to her mouth, a faint wash of color

108

spreading over her face. She had left herself wide open for his little sally, and she wasn't feeling too bright.

Conversation ceased on his low, satisfied laugh, and Katherine concentrated on finishing her meal. When there was nothing left in her salad bowl but a drop or two of the spicy dressing and the steak was no more than a stripped bone, she sipped the last of her wine.

"That was very good. My compliments." She saluted him with her raised wineglass.

"Thank you, ma'am. Care for some more wine?" Matt asked solicitously.

"Just a little," she said, dimpling. "It's very good, but if I fall asleep, you won't have any help with the dishes."

Matt's slow smile was full of warm amusement. He filled her glass to the top, his gaze seemingly fascinated by the dimple in her flushed cheek.

"How long have you been a widow, Katherine?" he asked idly, leaning comfortably back in the large captain's chair that fitted his bulk like a glove.

"Almost ten years," she answered easily, mellowed by the wine into total relaxation.

"Any serious relationships from then to now?"

"One or two . . . almost," she admitted, sipping from the stemmed glass.

"Which means?"

"Let's see." She pondered, her eyes screwed up in concentration for a moment before she suddenly laughed. "Mike maligned motherhood, Bill believed in beds, and Jerry was a jerk."

Matt chuckled low in his throat, enjoying her little alliterative joke, but he still pressed on. "Which means?"

"Just what I said. Mike wanted me but not Laurel and Timmy. Bill wanted a bedroom arrangement without any strings. Jerry was a jerk—a smooth-talking, double-dealing conniver who already had a luscious girl friend but needed some cash, Barry's insurance cash, to be exact, which I've since put into trust for the kids. I wasn't a very good judge of character, I guess. That's what Charlie says anyway." She finished a trifle glumly, vaguely wondering what had caused Matt's sudden scowl.

"Charlie's opinion means one hell of a lot, I guess," he bit out sarcastically, but Katherine responded to the words, not the tone, too relaxed to put much emphasis on the tone.

"Well, Charlie's pretty bright about most things, and in this instance I would have to agree. I haven't judged men well since Barry. But it's been five years since the last error in judgment, and I'm a wiser woman now." And with that last cutting phrase meant just for him, accompanied as it was by a look of contemptuous scorn, she polished off her wine.

Matt seemed undaunted by her scornful contempt, but possibly that was because the wine had relaxed her facial muscles into a perpetual smile, making her appear nothing worse than drowsy.

"Is Charlie thinking of marriage?"

"As a matter of fact, yes! How did you know that?"

"Lucky guess," he muttered. "Will you agree?"

"To what?" she asked, puzzled.

"To whom," he corrected, and then more explicitly: "To Charlie!"

"You mean, do I approve? Well, it's Charlie's decision, and it's hardly my place to offer an opinion," she said with a snicker of faint amusement.

"Boy, you really are a stupid female, aren't you? No wonder you had bad judgment with those three creeps. You can't even make up your own mind!" he barked, suddenly furious. Then he muttered something under his breath about Charlie and a pompous ass.

Katherine's mouth dropped open in astonishment at

110

such abrupt and infuriated anger, wondering what had triggered his display of temper. Obviously the state of matrimony was a very touchy subject with Matt. Earlier he had practically strangled himself when she'd asked if he was married, and now, just because she wouldn't offer an opinion on Charlie's decision to marry, he was absolutely livid with anger. Shaking her head in ironic disgust, she rose to her feet, leaning against the table for support when her head started whirling. When the spinning stopped, she glared at him with open dislike, but bewilderment shone out of her eyes as well.

"You know something, Matt Clinton? I'm sick of you. I'm sick of your contempt and your interference, and I'm sick of your condescension. But most of all, I'm sick of your friendliness one minute and your hostility the next. Go to the devil and stay out of my life!"

After her carefully enunciated little speech she lurched away from the table and, on completion of a funny little spin, stumbled toward the door. But she wasn't very cautious in her disgusted anger or her mild inebriation, for as she walked right past him or, rather, as she intended walking right past him, something went wrong.

It wasn't necessary for Matt to strain a muscle to stop her. As she came abreast of him, he didn't even look at her but stared stonily ahead. Only, just as she would have passed his chair with stiff dignity, a long arm shot out and hooked her waist. She was in his lap before she could blink, sitting awkwardly on his knees and slightly swaying from the effect of his swift grab and more wine than she should have imbibed.

When he turned her abruptly to face him, her hands came up to his shoulders in an effort to steady her spinning world. Instinctively she stiffened her elbows to keep him at a distance while she reasoned that once her head had

111

stopped whirling, she would rise disdainfully from his lap and make a dignified exit.

"How sick of me are you, Kat? I've had the impression a couple of times that you're anything but sick of me. Shall we test it?" he said tauntingly with hard inflection, his gaze narrowed on her face in an equally hard threat. The pressure he applied to her back had her elbows sagging, but she valiantly braced her forearms against his chest and managed to keep his warm mouth just a tantalizing breath from her own. Then, seemingly in a deliberate attempt to provoke her, he asked softly, "Lost your voice? Or was it your nerve, you bombastic little hypocrite?"

That title provoked her. One of her hands flew back and then arced forward. It hit. Unfortunately for Katherine it didn't hit his taunting mouth. Matt held his wine better than some, and his reflexes were fast and accurate. His head reared back, and her wildly swinging palm stung against her other arm, knocking it off his chest and herself off-balance. With maddening ease, he now had them breast to chest and was tugging her straining arms behind her.

But Katherine found her voice. It was muffled somewhere near his throat, but she did find it and began to use it . . . vehemently!

"You hulking, pea-brained bully! Let me up! If you think I'm going to sit here and calmly let you manhandle me, you're out of your slipshod skull. If you had to rely on brain instead of brawn, you'd—"

"Shut up, Kat. You're only digging a bigger hole."

"Don't order me to shut up, you great a . . . Oh! What are you doing?" The last was said a little shakily, because he'd bound both her hands in one of his and was using his other to bring up her chin.

"Just a little preliminary testing, Kat. Don't let it interfere with your screeching." His grim smile was a maddening confirmation of her inability to combat him with anything but words. It also acknowledged the new element of alarm entering her eyes.

"Let me up!" she ordered on a thready whisper, and helplessly watched his smile until it disappeared somewhere near her temple. Her flushed, agitated features were traced with evocative deliberation. His arousing lips first saluted her suddenly throbbing temple, then moved to close her flickering eyelids. Skimming over the tip of her nose, they brushed softly across her quivering mouth, eliciting a soft gasp of perturbance from Katherine's throat. Then, at her throat, she felt his tongue test the wildly beating pulse and knew her stiffly held body was going limp. But still she ordered, with breathy insistence, "Stop that!"

"You stop me, Katherine," he said challengingly at the corner of her mouth, his voice low and husky. She parted her lips to answer that challenge, intending to issue a virulent demand. He caught her lower lip gently in his teeth, nibbling sensually, murmuring, "Charlie should worry less about your palate and more about your pledges."

Katherine wasn't given time to ponder that enigmatic remark. As his lips moved over hers, hungrily, she could only groan a soft protest and then meet the demands of his mouth with her own awakened need. Her hands were released and found their way to his head, her fingers tangling in his dark hair, while Matt's hands began a rousing caress from her hip to the underside of her straining breast.

When he stood, cradling her against his chest, she blinked open heavy eyes, locking into a smoldering green gaze. Then her languid gray eyes were effectively shut, a smiling kiss going to each eyelid. He began walking, and her head fell weakly to his shoulder. She was floating, and it was a pleasant drifting sensation compounded of wine-induced judgment and passion-induced senses. When she felt the firm support of something cool and solid beneath her, her slumberous eyes lifted to find Matt standing above her, smoky eyes narrowed over her recumbent form. He was tugging off his boots, and then he calmly began pulling his shirt free of his jeans, his movements unhurried.

A prickling of awareness brought Katherine to her elbows, her eyes widening when they beheld the darkly masculine bedroom and the large bed on which she lay. Her mouth formed a soft circle; her mind formed a return of reason. When the mattress dipped with the weight of Matt's knee, she released a funny little moan, scrambled for the far side of the bed, and gained the floor with all the agility of a drunken acrobat.

A moment later they faced each other across the width of the bed. He saw slight, confused feminity, poised warily and breathing in shallow agitation, long honey blond hair curled in a riot of dishevelment about her tense shoulders and watchful face—a face flushed to emphasize large, astonished gray eyes. She saw danger—six feet, two inches of solid muscle in a wide-legged stance, sinewed arms extended, his big head thrust aggressively forward as he peered at her through irritated green slits, his mouth a hard line of determination.

Horrified, Katherine stood immobile. How could she have blindly allowed Matt to seduce her into his bedroom? Where was her common sense? Her normal self-control? She closed her eyes, trying to block out the realization that just a few well-executed kisses had melted her from anger into submission. She was a fool, and Matt was an exploiter of fools. And idiotically she had almost let herself become just another woman for his manipulative, outsize ego. Recurring anger firmed her mouth: anger directed at her witlessness; at his presumption.

114

Her eyes snapped open to find the presumptuous male of her thoughts rounding the end of the bed, his stockinged feet on the carpeted floor silencing his approach. His shirt was unbuttoned, and for a moment all she could concentrate on was the bared muscular expanse of his chest, drawing nearer. The covering of dark hair over those hard sinews received her unwilling admiration. A vivid knowledge of what his chest would feel like under the touch of her hands had her fingers digging punishingly into her palms. Then his large hand snagged her nape, forcing her eyes up to his.

"Change your mind?" One dark eyebrow lifted to emphasize the jeer in his voice, and his mouth formed its habitual sardonic curve. His fingers massaged her tense neck muscles, their warm touch insidiously undermining the anger she was striving hard to maintain. "What was it, Kat? A natural aversion to being human, to giving in to human desires? Or did you suddenly remember a reason for not giving yourself to *me*?"

"Get your hand off me, Matt!" she gritted stoutly, fervently nurturing her waning anger. She hated him for making her sound prissy and uptight when it was his despicable character that was in question. After all, who had seduced whom? Then, as if she were in a position to give orders, she added volatilely, "And button your shirt!"

Matt's eyes filled with strange glittering lights, and his mouth quirked into a genuine smile, wide and full of appreciation of her undaunted state.

"Lady, you're something else!" He chuckled after a suspenseful moment, but he was stepping back from her as he said it.

Eyeing him warily as he moved away from her, afraid her victory had been too easy, Katherine slowly inched forward, nonetheless eager to take advantage of her reprieve. The bed was given a haughty frown; the man it belonged to, an icy glare. Then she turned her back on both, moving for the door.

Dismay and surprise were equal parts of the shriek she uttered as his large hand reached out and grabbed hold of the back of her tunic, tugging hard enough to bring her tumbling back against his warm chest. Some deft maneuvers—and the unfair advantage of muscular strength pitted against feeble defiance—had Matt falling back to the bed, Katherine landing right smack on top of the broad, hairy chest she had admired just moments before. Encircling her within the secure cage of his arms, Matt effectively pinned her own to her sides.

"Gotcha!" he growled, laughter imminent.

"Let go of me!" she panted furiously, her mouth smothered in the dark tuft of hair below his throat.

"No, you haven't taken the test yet," he informed her with infuriating calm, then curiously: "Did you really think all you had to do was order me to get my hand off you and I would obey like a good little boy?"

Katherine actually groaned at the "good little boy." There was nothing either good or little or boyish about the wicked tone of his voice or the huge body beneath her or the virility stamped along his entire length. She raised her head to glare resentful fury in his face, jerking away from his hand, gently smoothing ruffled strands of hair from her neck and face, agonizingly conscious that she had once again foolishly underestimated Matt's determination to win the encounter.

"What test?" she hissed.

"The one where you try convincing me I make you sick."

"Well, that's easy," she managed to say tartly, although her nerves were screaming a denial of his disturbing effect on her. "You make me si—"

The word was abruptly smothered inside her mouth as

116

his face came up and hers came down from the pressure exerted by his hand at the back of her head. Katherine made a last-ditch effort to free her mouth, straining away, but Matt was having none of that, his finger and thumb stretching from her nape to the base of her jawline, firming their hold while his mouth gently and sensuously undermined her resistance.

And with her most potent defense busily engaged by his warm, seductive mouth, she slumped her tensed body into his, hearing his low growl of approval with a heightened sense of awareness. He shifted their weight to roll her underneath him, and in that position Katherine could neither think nor act with firm resolve. She simply responded. Her ability to cope against his effect on her and her own soaring senses was nil. Finding her arms freed, she raised them to encircle his neck, capitulating with the total lack of caution that underscored every close encounter with Matt—every embrace they shared, every kiss they experienced. Her fingertips teased his neck, curled into his thick tobacco brown hair, and spread lovingly over the broad shoulders. All the while she gave back as much as she received with her lips and tongue, softly savoring his mouth, warmly offering her own.

Before long she was drowning in a pleasure she had denied just moments before, the pleasure of his warm, giving mouth and gently stroking hands adding tenfold to her delicious enjoyment of the moment. His bold hand reaching under her tunic to stroke her midriff was a part of that enjoyment, and she quivered with a giddy helplessness. When his mouth glided moistly to her slender throat, it arched toward him. What the wine hadn't done to her rationality, Matt finished off with his own brand of intoxication. She could feel his smile against her flesh before he raised his head. His eyes took satisfied inventory of her

117

haze-filled eyes, her softly parted mouth, and her lips, rosy from his kisses, were warm and inviting.

"Ah, Katherine, nice and rounded in all the right places," he murmured huskily, carefully watching her reaction when his hand openly claimed her breast. He smiled at the startled sensuality in her eyes. "Are you still sick of me, Kat?"

Too languorous to offer a protest, she stopped his smile with a low, appealing "Matt?"

His darkened eyes probed hers, and she heard him catch his breath before his mouth firmed with desire. His hand at her breast shifted so that his thumb could abrade lightly over her peak, the sensation it aroused causing Katherine to inhale sharply. She curled her fingers invitingly around his bronzed shoulders, arching closer and dragging a groan from Matt's throat.

And this time his kiss was demanding, taking more than teasing, insistently anxious for satisfaction. And she gave and gave, but he seemed to want more, plundering her mouth hungrily, his hand at her breast suddenly warmer, more urgent, the one moving to her hip holding her closer, more insistently, arching her softness to meet his hardness. And still the kiss went on and on until Katherine moaned and surged against him, inviting him to more than her mouth, offering herself for his pleasure and her own, raking the smooth taut flesh of his back with impatient demand.

Then it was over. Suddenly. With ragged breath, Matt tore his mouth from hers, grappled with her frantic hands, and pulled them away to pin them by her head. He held her still with the weight of one powerful thigh as he shifted to the side, denying her the appeasement of a hunger he had deliberately seduced her to feel. Her eyes opened in confusion and searched his face for clues, his eyes for reasons.

And saw the taunting curve of his mouth with a sick feeling of dread, read the hard glitter in his eyes with a coiled knot of tension in the pit of her stomach, heard the satisfied tone of his voice with the painful knowledge that she had only herself to blame. He hadn't had to wrench a response from an unwilling woman. She had offered it uninhibitedly.

"Mrs. Meadows, you're not sick of me. I'd be more inclined to believe you want me. You respond like a lady with a very big need."

Katherine gained total sobriety with his words. Her eyes closed to shut out the sight of his mocking face, absorbing his deliberate cruelty into every inch of her tensing body, flailing herself for the dreadful mistake of letting herself be seduced into senseless ardency not once but twice. She wasn't just a fool. She was a mindless one. It took a moment to gain enough courage and equanimity to face him, and when she finally did, her eyes were cold with outrage at him, but mostly at herself.

"Nothing to say?" he gibed softly.

"I think you've said and done enough for both of us," she answered solemnly, wondering how she managed such a matter-of-fact, uncaring tone when her throat was blocked with strangling words of fury.

With a short snort of derision Matt released her arms and rolled to his feet, moving away from the bed to button his shirt. Katherine sat up slowly, turning toward the opposite side of the bed. She arranged her clothing with coldly trembling fingers and ran unsteady hands over the disarray of her hair. Then she edged off the bed, knowing she must get out of his room, out of his house, before she could give vent to the trembling self-disgust threatening to overwhelm her.

Her face was stark white as she neared the door, only

119

to blanch still further at the sight of his broad frame taking up almost every inch of the doorway.

"There is one more thing, Katherine. Have you considered how unwise it is to marry one man while wanting another?" Matt's smile was hard.

"What do you mean?" She eyed him with complete bafflement.

"Don't play dumb, Kat!" he growled, losing his smile. "From today's performance, I doubt the depth of your commitment to Charlie!"

It clicked. Incredibly it all clicked into place on those last words. The seduction scene, his taunting, his whole attitude—he thought Charlie was a man; furthermore, a man she was contemplating marrying. She started to deny it, wanting to hurl the truth at him in anger and disgust, but the smug curve to his mouth stopped her. Glorious color spread over her face, her hands tightening into fists at her sides. Couldn't his enormous ego stand for a woman to prefer another man to himself? Was that what had prompted his despicable attempt to seduce her, just to reject her?

"You understand now, don't you, Kat?" he asked quietly, his eyes trying to read the changing expressions chasing over her face.

"Almost perfectly," she replied with a tight smile, fighting back an urge to scream abuse and another to crash her fists against his pompous skull.

"You can't marry Charlie when you respond so strongly to me," he said almost gently, but blatant triumph was stamped into every line of his strong features.

Katherine smothered a hysterical laugh. *Oh, God, what an arrogant devil!* "Yes, I know, but if I don't marry, what then?"

"I want you, Kat."

"Why?"

"Because that scrawny little body of yours turns me on," he answered crookedly, but something about the determined set of his jaw said it was a truthful response.

"But—"

"You want me, too. Don't deny it. We could be very good together."

"You want to take me to bed," she stated baldly.

"More than that, Katherine," he insisted, a glimmer of unease in his eyes when he noted the fringe of trouble in hers.

"A quick, illicit night, then, in an out-of-the-way motel, where we satisfy our lust for one another. Does that explain it better?" Storm clouds were gathering in the gray depths of her eyes to belie the even tenor of her words.

He reached for her then; hard fingers bit into her shoulders as he shook her once, roughly. "That's not what I meant!"

"Then perhaps you'd better explain what you do mean!"

"Dammit, woman! You make it sound like some cheap little scene from an X-rated movie!"

"And you wanted some cheap little episode of your own making!"

"Katherine!" He practically roared her name in his exasperation. But he got her full attention, and the cold storm of her anger momentarily abated under the heated turbulence of his. "Why do you always jump to the worst possible conclusion? I want more than one night with you!"

"How much more? An affair?"

"If you have to label it, then, yes, an affair."

"How, Matt? My children are not toddlers. They're growing adolescents. How am I supposed to justify a brief sexual liaison with you when I'm telling them sexual promiscuity is wrong?"

"Hell, Katherine, we want each other! We could work it out. I can't give you instant solutions to all your little fears."

Little fears? Laurel and Tim? "My little fears, Matt, my two kids, have been the mainspring of my life for ten years, the reason for everything I've done, everything I've striven and worked for. And you want me to risk my relationship with them in order to appease a physical craving for you? I think I'll be better off with my original plans," she finished with finality, thinking of her well-ordered existence before this man had erupted into her life. She tried to shrug out of his hold.

"You can't marry Charlie!" he rasped explosively.

"I never intended to, you blind buzzard! Charlie Kendall is a woman! Now let go of me!" she ordered tightly, fed up with the whole scene, wanting only to get away from Matt and retreat to her own safe and cozy home.

"Why didn't you say so before?" he ground out savagely, his grip tightening until she winced.

"Because it wasn't until after your little planned seduction that I realized you thought she was a man!" Her voice was scornful, but it still conveyed a touch of bitterness and hurt.

Anger was slow to leave his body, and his features were grim with it. Then he smiled. She didn't like his smile. It was a slow, satisfied tiger's smile that stated as clearly as words that she was the tender game he saw within easy reach.

"You still want me," he pointed out, the fingers on her arms easing to stroke caressingly.

"Well, I'll just have to suffer, won't I?" she said bitingly, shrugging out of his grasp.

"Neither of us has to suffer. Come to me now, Katherine, and I'll show you what we have is worth a few risks." He coaxed her huskily. His hands reached out to clasp her neck gently, the long fingers tunneling through the thick honeyed tresses.

"But the risks are all mine. You don't risk anything, Matt. You never intended to," she told him with a precision she was sure of.

"That's not true," he denied, narrowing his gaze.

"I risk my relationship with my kids and my self-respect. As far as I can figure, you risk nothing. Perhaps it would even enhance your virile image, having the poor *frustrated* widow panting at your door?"

"There would be compensations," he insisted, annoyed by her lack of capitulation.

"Oh, God, you're unbelievable, you know that? What compensations? Your respect and trust? Your affection? Your friendship? Your caring and understanding? What, damn you?" she stormed shakily, hating his single-minded determination that could overlook all the things so important to her. His fingers tightened in her hair so that she released a soft moan. Straining against the pain in her scalp, she whispered, "And your gentleness."

Her whispered words seemed to bring Matt to the realization that he was hurting her, and he abruptly released her. He turned away to brace his arm against the doorframe and lowered his head on that arm in an obvious effort to control his anger and his thickened breathing.

Katherine felt shattered. Not by the tingling pain in her scalp. That was mild to what was torturing her insides. The sudden, horrifying realization that her list of compensations was exactly what she wanted from Matt had her feeling panicky and nauseated. She couldn't want those things! Not from Matt! That list, when added up, formed emotional commitment . . . love. An awful, empty devastation of feeling was swamping her mind and heart and body. Emotional commitment wasn't what Matt was implying. Love was far from what he felt. He wanted the shell of her, her *scrawny little body.* Succinctly he wanted a sexual affair.

Matt turned to face her, eyeing her pale features with a gentling of his own. "Kat, listen to me," he said urgently. "Nobody has to be hurt by what we do. We could find a way to be together without involving your children. We could have weekend trips, just the two of us. We could—"

"No, Matt," she interrupted unsteadily but clearly nonetheless. *No, Matt, don't offer me an affair based on nothing but sex. Offer me something with more depth of feeling.*

"Why not?" he rapped out, frustrated, slightly angry again.

"Why?" she countered. *Say you care about me. At least say you care about building a relationship with me.*

"We're mature people, and we want each other. Dammit, Kat, why are you denying what we both need?" he asked testily, exasperation surfacing with a bang.

"Because I won't enter into a mockery of what should be mutual respect and . . . and affection. An affair, strictly for the motive you've given, is just a glorified one-night stand. And I want a caring relationship, not just an unemotional exercise in sexuality." Her eyes pleaded with him to understand and filled with dismay at the incredulity entering his.

"An idealistic romance, is that what you want?" His hard, derisive tone scoffed at the idea as old-fashioned.

"Perhaps. I just know I couldn't do it your way."

"And your way is unrealistic," he muttered tensely. He leaned back against the doorjamb, his strong body seemingly relaxed, his grim smile indicating the opposite. Then, with equally hard realism, he advised patiently, "Be reasonable, Katherine. Be honest. Affairs don't have to be labeled by romance or prefaced with love in order to be fulfilling. Your expectations are too high."

"I don't expect anything from you, Matt," she stated adamantly. But she did. She expected him to see her as something more than just another woman to hop in and out of bed with. She expected him to realize her need to be loved, respected, cared about.

Unbelieving, he said, "Don't you, Katherine?"

Frustration and anger had her shouting. "No! But I won't be just another itch for you to scratch! And I won't . . . Oh, forget it. This whole conversation is pointless."

Matt's expression went grimmer at the finality he read in hers, his body stiffening. He seemed to be gearing himself to say something else when the doorbell rang. His eyes filled with an echo of the angry frustration Katherine was feeling, and the bell pealed again, insistently. With a low-voiced mutter that made her wince, he stalked out of the bedroom.

Katherine hesitated only briefly before following him, wanting to leave without any more coercion on Matt's part or any more words on her own, frightened either that he would physically persuade her or that she would verbally reveal her own need of him. She reached the front entrance right behind him and heard his strained welcome to his visitor a moment before a husky feminine voice spoke from the other side of the threshold.

"I'm sorry I'm late, Matt, but I couldn't get away any sooner."

"No problem, Stacy. I wasn't in that big a hurry," Matt told the woman stepping into the foyer.

Stacy's sensual beauty came as no surprise to Katherine. It matched the husky voice and Laurel's detailed inventory of the redhead's physical attributes given that day a week before. What surprised Katherine, or perhaps disconcerted her, was the woman's obvious chic. Her subtle glamour in an expensive ivory linen suit made Katherine feel dowdy and unkempt in her old jeans, tunic, and bare feet. If Stacy and Matt hadn't been standing in the doorway, she would have bolted through the door in embarrassment. As it was, she straightened her spine and dreaded the moment when his eyes would compare Stacy's sensual elegance to Katherine's understated attractiveness.

"You're going to love me when I tell you what happened right before I left." Stacy laughed.

"Look, Stacy, why don't you go on into the den? I've got someone here and—"

"No need for that, Matt. I was just leaving," Katherine inserted, coming out of her ridiculous immobility with the decision that it was time for her departure. More than time.

The two in the doorway turned in surprise to face her, Stacy with an inquiring expression on her beautiful face and Matt with a visible tensing of his body.

Fighting down both tears and anger, Katherine murmured, "If you'll excuse me."

Her gesture to the blocked doorway had Stacy sidestepping gracefully to allow her through. Matt didn't budge, however, his eyes commanding Katherine to look at him. With difficulty she forced her features into a blank mask of calm and met his gaze, only to find it roving her face, searching for something, a frown drawing his eyebrows together.

"I need to leave, Matt," she insisted quietly when he didn't speak.

"Katherine, I haven't finished talking to you."

"Timmy and Laurel will be home and wondering where I am," she excused herself, inwardly screaming: *You've said all I needed to know and failed to say all I wanted to hear.*

"All right, Kat, but I'll talk to you later," he muttered, and the way he said it made it sound like a threat.

126

Katherine raised the delicate arch of her brows in inquiry, slanting a quick, meaningful glance at the waiting Stacy. "You'll probably be busy."

"Later, Kat!" he growled under his breath; but he finally stepped aside, and she was free to leave.

She didn't answer him; she didn't acknowledge hearing him; she didn't even look at him again. She just left, with as much dignity and at the same time with as much haste as possible.

CHAPTER SIX

Katherine never waited around for Matt's talk. As soon as her children were home, she loaded them in the car and headed for a theater. Tim and Laurel were delighted with the unexpected treat of a movie and then a meal out and afterward a carefree hour at the Water Garden in downtown Fort Worth. While her teen-agers sat enthralled through the latest sci-fi thriller, chattered over pizza, and trekked through the concrete-terraced Water Garden, enjoying the spectacular water effects, Katherine brooded over her afternoon with Matt and the resulting acknowledgments she'd had to face.

How had she come to care for that hard, tormenting, arrogant man? How had she allowed him to become important to her? He wouldn't know a tender emotion if it hit him in the face. His approach to having an affair proved that. *"We want each other . . . we could be very good together,"* he had said, meaning physically. And then later, scoffing at her emotional needs as outdated romantic ideals, *"Your way is unrealistic. . . . Your expectations are too high."* Not a token of love or affection, not even a desire for a close relationship and the resulting companionship. An affair with Matt? She would be insane even to contemplate it, considering his motives.

Matt didn't want an affair, not in any romantic or emotional sense. He wanted a sexual liaison. He wanted a willing bedmate. Self-sufficient by nature and impassive to emotional needs, he was interested only in fulfilling his physical desires. He selfishly expected her to forsake everything she thought important to a relationship and hop eagerly into his bed. And while the thought of giving in to the force of his passion filled her senses with a heady excitement, the thought of doing it his way touched off cold abhorrence in Katherine's heart. That in turn triggered a recurring anger at his insensitive attitude. An affair should mean more than sexual satisfaction. There was nothing old-fashioned or wrong in wanting and expecting affection and respect and love to be incorporated into a relationship. Her life with Barry had taught her that.

Anger tempered into wistfulness when she thought of that long-ago life. As a young bride she had been all dreams and starry-eyed emotion, and Barry had been a tender lover, sweetly worshiping her into fulfillment. Somewhat sadly she forced herself to acknowledge that not only was Barry gone, but so was the sweet, gentle young woman she had been all those years ago. Life and circumstances had toughened her—not to the extent of hard cynicism but to the extent of practical realism. She had learned to depend solely on herself and to lay aside starry-eyed dreams of romance and happily-ever-afters. Dormant for years, all those romantic sentiments she'd packed away like fragile crystal in tissue paper had been tucked into a far corner of her heart, waiting to be reawakened. Why did it have to be an ungentle, untender, unromantic, tormenting man who ripped them into life again? And then scoffingly stomped them into shattered hopes beneath his unsentimental boots . . .

Needing to dispel a growing feeling of melancholy, Katherine forced herself away from thoughts of Matt . . . or tried to. Inside the terraced grounds of the Water

Garden she walked to the edge of a lighted pool. Her gaze sought out diamond drops of water from the fountain, watching them separate from the jettison of spray shooting skyward, following their graceful, free-floating dives back into the circular pool at the base of the fountain. The soft April breeze caught some of the finer sprinkles and carried them to her face. She was reminded that the night was cool, and the hour late, and she would soon have to round up her teen-agers and head for home. Pensively she sighed, knowing the afternoon and evening with Laurel and Tim had been just a temporary reprieve from Matt. Sooner or later he would demand they finish their talk. Fiercely she frowned, determined not to let an aggressive, single-minded man undermine what she knew was right for her.

"Hey, Mom, you're missing a great time. Even old lazy Laurel is having fun skipping over the stepping-stones at the big pool."

Tim stood in front of her, a fine mist from the spraying fountains and waterfall effect of the largest Water Garden's exhibit sprinkled onto his hair. He was eager and energetic and happy. Katherine smiled at his exuberance and the reference to old lazy Laurel.

"This is a lovely place, isn't it?"

"Come on, Mom, you come down with us," Tim coaxed, referring to the group of stone slabs leading stair-like down to a large pool. "You'll have fun."

Katherine smiled again and walked with him toward the pool. Laurel was at the bottom, standing on one huge block of graveled concrete, shouting something that was lost over the rushing sound of water. With a smile more carefree than she felt, Katherine joined her children in their enjoyment.

"The first one falling and bloodying an elbow or a knee

gets abandoned to his pain and injury," she threatened playfully.

Both children laughed in response to her remark, knowing their mother's aversion to blood all too well. Katherine couldn't stomach the sight of blood. It actually made her sick. More than once Laurel had been made the reluctant nurse in the family.

"My mother, the healing saint!" Laurel teased her, laughing, bounding up two stone slabs to meet Katherine's descent.

"Yeah," Tim gibed from directly behind her. "Last time I needed a couple of puny stitches in my arm, I almost died from loss of blood before Laurel could get me to the hospital, my brave mom having collapsed on the floor."

"Okay, okay, I stand accused and convicted, but I repeat—anyone falling and coming away bloodied gets abandoned."

The phone call came a week later, and without sight or word of Matt in those long seven days, Katherine was surprised to hear the deep, pleasant timbre of his voice. When she groped for the receiver on the stand by the bed, a squinting glance at the illuminated clock told her it was after midnight. She'd been asleep only about forty-five minutes.

"H'lo," she mumbled into the receiver.

"Mrs. Katherine Meadows?" asked an unfamiliar voice.

"Yes," she answered sleepily, her loud yawn smothering the flurry of voices coming through the line.

"Katherine?"

"Yes," she managed to say again, this time clearly, knowing immediately whom that voice belonged to.

"You in bed?" Matt's voice sounded distant.

"Yes, of course. It's late."

131

"And you're tired," he acknowledged wryly, then accusingly: "You didn't stay around for our talk last week."

"Judging by the last seven days, I imagine it wasn't all that important whether I did or not," she offered with soft irony.

"It's important. I have a lot to say to you."

"At midnight?" she asked skeptically.

"Or after three A.M." he laughed softly.

"I'll hardly be talking to you at that time."

"You are talking to me at that time."

"Are you drunk?" she asked suspiciously.

"No, I'm tired. And lonely."

"I'm certain you could change that easily enough," she informed him coolly. "Just look inside your little—or is that large?—black book. But don't add my phone number to your list. I don't appreciate senseless calls in the middle of the night. I sleep during those hours and leave the playing and nonsense to those of a more frivolous and pleasure-seeking nature. And furthermore—"

"Whew, Kat, you sure do get wound up!" Matt interrupted sardonically. "I'll bet those gray eyes look like silver bullets. It's a good thing I'm not in your target range, or I'd be a dead man for sure."

Katherine fell silent, dropping back against her pillows and rolling her eyes heavenward. *Silver bullets, indeed!* The man's mockery was limitless! But then, she thought with reluctant amusement, she had sounded lethally dismissive. And he, damn him, was amused. She could almost see the ironic quirk of his strong mouth and the taunting look of devilment in those green eyes.

"You still there, Katherine?"

"I shouldn't be," she admitted, the divertissement in her voice all too evident.

"I wish I were there with you." His deep voice was low, sexy, suggestive, and a feathering of awareness tickled along her flesh, causing her to shiver. She wondered where he was. A slight background noise or interference over the line indicated he wasn't at home or perhaps not alone.

"Where are you?"

"Paraguay. A lonely hotel room." The pause was fractional. "Your face woke me up. I had to hear your voice."

It was as if he had touched her, caressed her. Katherine melted back into the sheets, feeling warm and light-headed. Paraguay. That's what he'd meant by 3:00 A.M.

"In my dreams I was holding you, Katherine."

The knowledge that he was deliberately making verbal love to her didn't check her response. The picture his words conjured caused her stomach to coil in tension and her voice to lower to a husky level as she whispered softly, "Oh, Matt."

In her ear his groan was low, almost tortured, but he said nothing. Katherine felt speechless as well and curiously tense, clutching the receiver tightly in her fingers.

"I'll call again, Kat," he muttered hoarsely.

He didn't give her a chance to reply or say good-bye, and the loud crackle in her ear convinced her he'd hung up. She slowly replaced the receiver in its cradle, lying back against the pillows, feeling weak and disoriented. He had been dreaming of her, wanting to talk to her. Did that mean he felt something special for her?

Oh, stop trying to rationalize each word the man says to fit the dictates of your own heart, Katherine. You need more than wanting. And Matt just wants you. Period.

Her pillow received an extra pounding, and it was late into the night before she drifted into restless sleep.

Two evenings later Katherine was in an unsettled mood. An unexpected bout with a stuttering car and a weak battery had her juggling her checkbook to meet the expense of a new battery, and the mechanic's warning that the tread on her tires was worn to a dangerous level hadn't helped her disposition.

Then there was a rather disturbing call from a man she hadn't heard from in almost eight years. Mike Hudson, the young lawyer who hadn't wanted the responsibility of Tim and Laurel years before, was now a well-established lawyer with a huge tool company and quick to inform Katherine he had two young children of his own. He sounded proud of them, and Katherine allowed herself a rueful smile at his change of heart. Mike was also eager to convey that he was divorced, remembered Katherine well and fondly, and would like to see her again. Politely, but evasively, she implied she was unavailable. She didn't need any more complications in her life, especially those of the male sex.

And added to worry about the upkeep of her Chevy and mild annoyance over Mike's call were disturbed thoughts of Matt and his late phone call two nights before. One moment she was buoyed with hope, remembering the husky tenor of his voice hinting of need and desire, and the next moment she was despondent, realizing nothing had changed. Wanting wasn't loving.

The phone rang just as she was turning out the lights in the kitchen for the night, thoughts of a warm, soothing bath in her head. Leaning against the kitchen counter, she reached for the wall phone, her quiet hello into the receiver answered by an accented voice asking her name and phone number. Then Matt's voice, deep and achingly familiar, tripped like a rough caress along her spine.

"Katherine?"

"Of course."

"Of course," he echoed dryly, picking up on her cool tones. "I've reached the aloof and disdainful widow tonight, I see, even after making special efforts to call early enough in the evening to ensure reaching a more receptive woman."

Katherine's mouth tightened at the deliberate taunt. Aloof and disdainful? Is that how she came across? Somehow she felt rattled and out of sorts, and her whole body was suffused with heat just from hearing his voice.

"You'd better say something, lady, or I'll think you've lost your cool self-possession to my killing charm."

Killing charm? Well, he had that all right, she admitted with a sense of despair. Rough, ungentle, tormenting, he had slain her composure more often than she wanted to admit. He was trying to do it now.

"Why is it that when you call me lady, I get the impression it's less than a complimentary title?" she asked levelly. *Why, indeed?* she jeered inwardly. Had he ever once given her a compliment?

Matt's laugh sounded incredibly sexy over the wire, low and sensual and filled with delight. It infused Katherine with the same warm emotion, sweet and heady.

"You're a hard woman to please, Kat."

"Not really. Actually I'm very easygoing." But her crisp tones belied her assertion.

"Interesting. Ol' Dad warned me about situations like this."

"What do you mean?" she asked curiously.

"He said women, like apples, tended to be tart and crisp when you expected them to be sweet and juicy."

"Interesting." She echoed his earlier comment, indicating the opposite.

"Ol' Granddad added his two cents to that pearl of wisdom," he offered with calculated offhandedness.

"And made you a very apple-wise guy," she inserted tartly, but she was curious for all that.

"Yep!" Matt sounded almost strangled, and she realized he was trying not to laugh. "Ol' Granddad agreed

135

that some apples taste sour at first bite." The pause was deliberate. "But if you sweeten them a little, they make the best pies."

"Good grief!" she said with a touch of disgust. "You've managed to incorporate three generations of apple philosophy into one good set of theory and application. Which one of you decided apples are cheaper by the bushel?" she asked too sweetly.

"I haven't, you know." His voice was quiet, serious.

"Haven't what?"

"Been in the market for a bushel. Not for months."

"Did Ol' Dad and Ol' Granddad teach you to lie through your teeth?" A vivid picture of Bibbi and Stacy was in her mind.

"You know, Katherine Meadows, if I were there with you, I'd shake you till your skinny little bones rattled," he bit out in sudden annoyance. Then, incredibly: "Have you thought about what I asked you last Saturday?"

Only with every waking breath, but her answer was evasive. "What do you mean?"

"I mean I want to be with you, dammit!" he barked in exasperation. Her silence seemed to get through to him, and he added more coaxingly, "We could arrange something that would work, Katherine."

"For how long, Matt?"

"Why put time limits on it, Kat?" he countered unwisely.

Because of wanted commitments, like forever, from this day forward, till death do us part, her mind screamed, and she was more than appalled at the direction of her thoughts. When had visions of marriage crept into her head? But her answer was quiet and unequivocal. "No, Matt."

It was Matt's turn to fall silent, and she could almost feel his anger over the wire. The self-assured Mr. Clinton didn't like being told no. When he finally did speak, it was in terse, clipped sentences.

"I'll be home in a few days. You be there!"

The phone was slammed in her ear, and she held the receiver away from her, wincing.

Rat! Who did he think he was? Ordering her to be here like some well-trained dog being told to heel by a terse master! Katherine's groan was full of self-disgust. How could she love a man like that? And then she groaned for an entirely different reason, knowing she was lost. Love and marriage? *Why not wish next for the moon, Katherine?*

The hammock received Katherine's slender weight with a small creak. She lay back in its bowed length with a disquieted sigh, letting the warm May night surround her with soothing touches. The light breeze teasing the skirt of her sundress felt like a tranquil caress against her bare shoulders and legs. The soft sounds of chirruping crickets were almost musical to her ears, and the winking lights of fireflies prompted her memory of two small cherubs' delight in catching them and putting them inside glass jars to watch their winking brilliance at close range. So many years ago that had been, yet she could still hear Barry's voice gently explaining to Laurel and Tim that fireflies— lightning bugs he called them—were magical beings. She remembered their exclamations of awe and Barry's laughter as he hugged a child on each knee, her own answering laugh as she delighted in the simple pleasure of fireflies and small children and a straight, slim husband full of warm, gentle humor.

Shifting on the hammock, she turned to look across the sweep of back lawn to the line of oaks that had grown as tall and straight as her children over the years.

"Oh, Barry," she whispered into the night's stillness.

137

"You were so good, and I've missed you." But there were no tears in her voice, only a kind of quiet acceptance.

Barry had been good—a sweet, gentle young man with love and tenderness the most endearing of his qualities. He had possessed strength, too, of course—a kind of quiet ability to plan and work and strive for his family, a dedication of himself given without reserve.

Strength was an admirable quality, taking many forms. *Matt.*

The name rang through her mind like a discordant note of an amplified guitar. Another strong man, but this one mostly in the physical sense—big, muscular, powerful of body. Powerful of will, too, she acknowledged grimly.

For almost two weeks the house next door had been empty. Yet the force of Matt's personality was with her at that moment—the remembered resonance of his voice, the vision of his green eyes stripping away her cool reserve, the taunting jeers and self-confidence that practically oozed from his pores. Even over thousands of miles separating Texas from Paraguay he had managed to affect her thinking, her composure, her very heartbeat. How would she handle the next encounter with Matt? That there would be one, she had no doubt, probably tomorrow. His last words the other night had indicated his return in a few days. That, and his overbearing order for her to be here waiting for him, had her wishing tomorrow's encounter would be more pleasant. Maybe tomorrow . . .

Tomorrow, nothing! You're a fool, Katherine Meadows. There will be no tomorrow with Matt. Matt's a hard-core realist, thinking only in terms of expediency and today. And today he wants you. Tomorrow? Tomorrow he might want another woman, a new challenge, freedom to walk out of your life. . . .

"Comfortable?" asked a deep, familiar voice near her ear.

138

Twisting abruptly, she turned to see the man of her thoughts hunkered down beside the hammock, his face inches from hers, his features shadowed in the moonlit night. Her heart picked up speed against her breast as she surveyed him in silence. The usual jeans, boots, and western shirt clung to his broad, muscular frame and teased her with their casual emphasis over the ruggedness of his body. There was a possessive quality in the gaze fixed so intently on her face, and the strongly jutting chin announced his determination and aggression, boding ill for her peace of mind. Katherine felt robbed of voice and thought, gazing at him with a curious mixture of wariness and need. His own gaze shifted to her slightly parted mouth, his face moving slowly, inexorably forward.

Before that hard, seductive mouth could find its target, Katherine reacted, coming out of her frozen silence to emit a funny little moan and to scramble away. She knew reason and cool thinking would be lost once he started kissing her.

The hammock did a violent swing at her abrupt move, and her arms fought air until one hand found a steadying hold in thick, dark hair, another near a muscled throat. She heard Matt's strangled laugh and her own high-pitched wail as the hammock rocked crazily and then his brusque yelp as her fingers locked into his tobacco brown strands to gain more security out of the insecurity of her position. His two big, sure hands clasped her waist, pulling her completely free of immediate disaster, the swirling flare of her dress flying precariously about her thighs as they drifted back to the lawn. Matt was flat on his back with Katherine cushioned on his obliging chest. Her hands and fingers were desperately entwined in his scalp and the collar of his shirt, her cheek pressed into the metal buttons on a pocket tab, her heart beating as erratically as the one beneath her ear.

"That was quite a welcome" was said huskily and with a chuckle into the top of her head, effectively bringing her eyes up in mute denial. "I would have settled for a kiss, but this isn't bad, Kat," he told her complacently, his hands splaying over her back to hold her more securely and finding a smooth expanse of her bare shoulder and naked back to caress.

"You big jerk, that wasn't a welcome!" she retorted, gasping for breath.

"No?" was accompanied by a lifted brow, his hard mouth quirking crookedly. "Felt kinda like one. Except for that tenacious hold on my scalp. That stings a bit."

"Oh!" she whispered, flushing guiltily, loosing her fingers quickly and laying them on his shoulders to push away. The hands at her back firmed, one moving to the curving of her hip to settle her more comfortably along his length.

"Where are you going?" he whispered huskily, ignoring her efforts to strain away from him.

"Let me up, Matt."

"Why?"

"Because I said to," she retorted promptly, but not as vehemently or as convincingly as she should have or as she intended to. The warm touch of his hands on her bare flesh and the heady whisper of his breath fanning her face created sensations which threatened to undermine her resolve.

"Is that right? But it's nice and comfortable like this. Kinda romantic, too. Moonlight, warm breeze, warm woman." His hand cupped her shoulder as if to testify to her warmth, stroking softly over her smooth flesh.

"Warm man?" she queried with a soft bite.

"Absolutely" came back with unabashed roguishness.

"But the wrong combination," she insisted, although she still made no effort to gain her release.

"Oh, no, Katherine, very, very right."

"Because you say so?" she questioned with soft irritation but with a reluctant smile for his complacency teasing the corners of her mouth.

"Because I know so," he said quietly, with conviction.

"Hogwash!"

"Hogwash?" He laughed at her inelegant term. "How's that?"

"Because any woman, warm or otherwise, would suit your purposes, Mr. Clinton."

"And you don't want the opportunity to suit my purposes. Seems I've heard the same sentiment before," he told her with a flashing grin, but his eyes weren't smiling.

"No, thank you, I believe I'll pass on the dubious honor." And this time her hands pushing against his shoulders had a strength-filled purpose, the sudden hard glitter in his eyes telling her the game was over.

He let her up, loosening his embrace so that she could move away from him. The realization that he had allowed her up, the power in his hands capable of keeping her anywhere he wanted her, had her kneeling beside him instead of moving farther away. Sitting back on her heels, she watched Matt turn and raise himself on one elbow to look at her. For a moment there was silence while Katherine endured the intense assessment of his gaze, which seemed to strip away the light covering of her halter-topped dress. He finally dropped his eyes to the lawn, idly uprooting a long runner of grass and winding it through his fingers.

"Where did you run off to two weeks ago?" he asked suddenly, sending her an ironic glance.

"Are you asking where we went that evening?" she asked carefully, not liking the implication that she'd run away from him.

"Yeah," he said flatly.

"For a much deserved outing with my children. A movie, pizza, and the Water Garden," she told him slowly, sitting back on the grass and drawing her knees to her chin, carefully arranging her skirts to cover her legs. "Laurel and Timmy had a great time that evening, and we were back before ten o'clock."

"I had to leave for Paraguay at eight that night. I tried to call you several times before I left." The narrowed slits of his eyes reminded her of Marigold in sight of some unsuspecting prey in the flower beds.

"How's your road progressing?" she asked brightly, wanting to change the subject.

"Like any road. Slowly, one section at a time, but I plan to speed the construction up a bit." His grin was slow and wicked, and she knew he wasn't referring to a Paraguayan road.

"Do you enjoy working in Paraguay?"

"It's a job," he replied laconically.

"How . . . interesting," she commented lamely, his attitude not very encouraging.

"Oh, very," he acknowledged with a short laugh. "If you like mud and sun and flies and damned mosquitoes."

"And you don't?" She giggled suddenly, relaxing again. "Sounds heavenly."

"Not so bad for short stretches," he admitted. "But when the rains start, I begin hankering after the Texas sun. You have any family, Katherine, besides Laurie and Tim?"

The sudden change of subject startled her, but she answered easily enough. "No, all my family are gone. Although Peter and Martha have been like parents over the years. They're very special people."

"Do they help you financially?"

"No! I wouldn't want them to. Besides, I haven't needed

142

any help," she asserted with a proud, determined lift of her chin.

"Never?" He looked skeptical.

"No more than other working parents. I'm not complaining, although"—she smiled wryly—"I don't object to an occasional night away from cooking and housekeeping. Typical complaint, huh?" she ended with faint irony, and then curiously; "What about you, Matt? Where are Ol' Dad and Ol' Granddad?"

"Died twelve years ago. Granddad died from oldness and orneriness. Pure meanness got him," he said without a trace of rancor. "Dad drove himself too hard and keeled over from a heart attack at the age of fifty. He was a contrary old devil, too," he said, grinning up at her.

"That's a shame," she remarked quietly, meaning it. "Death's a hard reality to accept, especially of a loved one."

"Did I say I loved them?" he asked with careless irreverence.

"You did, didn't you?" She gave him a direct look.

"Yeah, I guess I did," he admitted slowly, his fingers idly twisting the runner of grass. His gaze, anything but idle, swept from her mouth to the cleavage her sundress exposed and then across her slim, bare shoulders.

Silence fell over them, and Katherine pondered the serious yet relaxed turn of their conversation. She covertly studied the big man on the ground beside her, thinking how strangely peaceful it was without the abrasive conflict that directed most of their encounters. She was acutely aware that Matt had found it difficult to admit loving his father and grandfather, and she wondered why. All his reflections of the two men spoke of respect and caring, yet the admission of love had come reluctantly. Would he admit love for a woman with equal reluctance?

Caught up in that last unsettling thought and half ex-

143

pecting Matt to bring up the subject of their relationship, Katherine met the gaze he directed her way with a solemn expression.

"You ever gone camping, Katherine?" he asked unexpectedly.

"What? . . . Camping?" she questioned blankly, then with a faint smile: "No, I haven't. Timmy's always . . . Why?" she asked warily.

"Tim," he answered laconically, outlining the length of her thigh through the dress with the tickling touch of the grass.

"What about Tim?"

"I invited him camping a few minutes ago. Laurie, too, but she wasn't quite so keen as your son. What about you?"

"What about me?" she asked evasively, suddenly nervous of his motives.

"We could drive down to Lake Whitney tomorrow, spend the night, get in some fishing, and be back Sunday afternoon. Tim is anxious to give it a try. Says he'll be away for the summer and might not get another chance for several months. Most boys his age need a little experience in that sort of thing. You and Laurie don't melt in the sun, do you?" he jeered softly.

"Of course not." She came back with a small show of indignation. "But I don't understand why you would want Laurel and me along. Neither of us is an all-American sportswoman."

"Is that right?" followed a great guffaw of laughter. Obviously he agreed with her. "Come on, Kat, you might enjoy it. Tim needs a chance to be a boy. And the three of you would have an opportunity to be together as a family."

"Well . . . all right," she agreed slowly, thinking it sounded like harmless fun, and Matt couldn't possibly

144

pressure her about their relationship with both her children around. "But we don't own any camping gear and—"

"No sweat," he interrupted lazily, feathering the delicate line of her jaw with the runner. "I can put together everything we'll need. Just bring some warm shirts and jeans to sleep in. Nights are cool on the lake."

"What about food?"

"Don't worry. This is my idea, my treat."

"Okay," she responded with a quick gamine grin. "But I hope you know what you're asking for."

Matt's answering smile was slow, wide, full of hidden depths.

CHAPTER SEVEN

It was one of those glorious spring days that foretold of the heated summer to come. A soft, warm breeze stirred the surrounding trees and vegetation and rippled gently over the surface of the lake. High in an unbelievably blue, blue sky, the sun shone brilliantly, inviting well-being to all under its heated rays. Glinting blindingly off the blue-green waters of Lake Whitney, its warm blaze deliciously beneficial to the flesh, that fiery orb brightly defined the peaceful setting Matt had chosen as their fishing locale. Almost two hundred yards from their campsite, the secluded inlet offered privacy from other campers and fishermen, enclosing their party of four in a cozy world of nature's serenity.

Katherine's gaze delighted in the beauty of the day, studying the scene with keen enjoyment, until it settled, perhaps for the hundredth time, on the object at her feet. That small white container and its contents rang a discordant note in her otherwise pleasurable contentment. Her brow furrowed uncertainly. Could she do it? More precisely, could she do it without getting caught? She lifted her eyes, bright with resolve.

No one would know. They were each too involved in their own pursuits to be concerned with anything she did or too far away to discern any move she made. Nobody would see or suspect her furtive, desperate measure . . . if she were very, very careful.

Tim was at least a hundred yards down the shoreline, his thin figure outlined against a backdrop of cedar and oak and mesquite. His attention was totally absorbed by the rod and reel in his hands and the yield he was enthusiastically exacting from the lake. About half that distance away Laurel was dozing in the sun, stretched out on a blanket atop a flat limestone rock. A transistor radio near her silvered head, she was more interested in soaking up sun than in anything the other three were doing. In the opposite direction Matt stood close to the water's edge, lazily fishing, occasionally unhooking a catch or rebaiting his line, seemingly at peace with nature and pursuing his own pleasure.

A saucy little grin twitched the corners of Katherine's mouth. The peaceful, almost soporific, setting of Lake Whitney's tree-lined banks had worked its magic in varying degrees on each of them. The kids and Matt were relaxed and content. Her gaze straying to the small receptacle at her feet, she knew her own contentment was just moments away.

The bait cup at her feet held eleven tiny minnows—silver, pathetic, and with glassy, accusing eyes. Her own eyes troubled, Katherine counted them once again. Yes, exactly eleven. Originally there had been an even dozen inside the foam cup, but Matt had threaded one onto her fishhook. He had ignored her diffident expression as he instructed her to watch the procedure so she'd be able to do it without help the next time. And she had watched, patiently, albeit with hidden dismay and the growing certainty that there would be no next time, as he pierced the hook between the minnow's eye sockets, thus securing it firmly on the end of her line. If her face had gone a trifle green, her mouth a little dry, she had nevertheless pre-

147

tended absorption and a casualness she was far from feeling, offering a bright, smiling thank-you for his help. Her thank-you had prompted one of Matt's provoking grins before he sauntered less than ten yards down the bank to set up his own fishing gear. That had been two hours ago. And during those two hours eleven tiny minnows had wriggled for space in her bait cup.

In a stance calculated to show nonchalance Katherine lifted the bait cup and edged slowly, negligently, toward the lake. She hunched down, her canvas-clad toes just touching the gently lapping waves, and her wrist moved, tipping the bait cup slowly over the water, while she avidly watched the spill of its contents. Ten little minnows swam eagerly away, wriggling toward a better life than the one they had been destined for just minutes before. Ten little fish lives saved . . . and Katherine Meadows was figuratively off the hook. Her soft sigh was triumphant, exhilarated . . . dismayed! *Ten* little minnows? A quick, furtive look inside the cup showed one tiny silver oblong, floundering helplessly, beached on the smooth white shores of the bait cup. Quickly, apologetically, she dipped the cup into the lake to wash the last poor creature into its natural habitat —the blue-green waters of Lake Whitney.

The smile hovering over her mouth and teasing a dimple into mischievous display was an acknowledgment of how very, very cleverly she had accomplished her subterfuge. Backing slowly toward her original spot on the bank, her fishing rod held rifle-ready and baitless in the crook of one arm, Katherine glanced surreptitiously to the right. Her smile deepened when she saw her children in the exact positions they had held just moments earlier.

"What was that? A Mercy for the Minnows campaign?" The deep, snide voice came from directly behind her.

The startled "Oh, no!" was torn from Katherine's throat when she jerked to attention and the foot poised to

148

take a backward step slid on a loose stone. She felt herself unbalancing, and a second later her high yelp of pain announced her less than graceful fall onto the seat of her jeans. With her cry echoing harshly behind her, she braced her palms on the bank to push up, standing to turn and face the overbearing witness to her deception.

Matt's dark head was bent toward his right shoulder. Katherine noted first the darkening stain on his shirt sleeve, then the hook and line trailing from the faded denim fabric and finally her own fishing rod lying guiltily at her feet.

"Oh!" was inadequate but all she could say as her dismayed eyes watched Matt calmly unhook himself, his expression grim. She rushed up the sloping bank, nervously twisting her fingers, her eyes huge.

"I'm sorry, Matt. Is it bad?" It looked terrible, blood rapidly soaking what seemed to Katherine a large area of his torn shirt sleeve. Swallowing convulsively, she quickly averted her gaze from the distasteful sight and stared anxiously at his face.

His eyes swept to her distressed figure, seeing the concern and worry in her expression before the lids dropped to veil a sudden glint. Positive Matt was hiding excruciating pain from her discernment, Katherine looked fleetingly, guiltily, back at the blood, her complexion paling to a sick shade of grayish white.

"Hurts like hell," he gritted, his voice muffled with emotion, his face etched into hard lines of tension.

"Oh, Matt, please forgive me. I'm so sorry. Do you have a first-aid kit? Let me go get it," she rushed on worriedly, her voice thready and her expression as pained as his should have been.

"I'll do it," he offered gruffly, hesitantly.

"Please let me. It's the least I can do. Is it in the pickup?" she asked anxiously, trying to concentrate on his face in an effort to avoid the sight of the blood.

"Under the driver's seat. I'll come with you," he murmured.

Katherine practically ran the two hundred yards back to the truck and reached it out of breath and sticky from nervous panic and the white-hot blaze of the sun. After scrambling into the cab of the pickup, she stretched across the passenger seat on her stomach, groping frantically under the driver's side for the first-aid box. Sensing Matt's presence behind her, she glanced over her shoulder and found his narrowed gaze on her tightly jeaned hips. Momentarily she stopped, her attention caught by the bright glitter in his eyes. But when he gingerly touched his injured shoulder and his eyes filled with what looked like torment, she quickly crawled out of the truck, the first-aid box clutched desperately in her hands.

"Sit down inside the truck, and let me tend it," she urged thickly, fighting back a wave of nausea.

With long legs braced outside the pickup, Matt obediently took the position she indicated. Katherine knelt between the spread of his legs, gauze and disinfectant ready.

"My shirt," he murmured huskily, reminding her it needed to be removed in order to cleanse the wound.

"I'll do it," she said immediately, gulping.

Her trembling fingers dropped the nursing aids into his larger, steadier hands before going to the snap openings of his shirt, which she quickly released to tug the tail of his shirt free of his jeans. Katherine was so concerned and half giddy that Matt's hiss of indrawn breath when her fingers brushed his tautly fleshed stomach sounded like an extension of her own shallow gasps of spiraling queasiness. First one and then the other sleeve was urged off his broad shoulders and muscular arms. The sight of his injury caused her to draw back quickly shutting her eyes on a

150

surge of dizziness. Then she blindly gathered the gauze and disinfectant from Matt's grasp and saturated the sterile pad. In her clumsy haste she spilled most of the liquid over her shaking fingers and onto the ground at her feet.

His hands spanned her waist. Katherine thought they squeezed because of the sting of the disinfectant when she hesitantly touched the gauze to his shoulder. She swallowed deeply to smother a moan, grateful for the solid feel of Matt's hands and arms that offered support to her trembling frame.

But despite all her determination to hold on to her equilibrium, her legs finally buckled, and she drifted helplessly toward a hard waiting chest, her pale face lifted to Matt's. Under Katherine's ear his heart seemed to be setting an all-time speed record, and when his hands lifted to her neck, she felt his warm breath moving closer to her mouth. The dark head closed in on her whirling vision and then paused just above hers. There was a suspended moment when his eyes trapped hers, and then Matt jerked back in surprise, abruptly aware that his nurse was about to pass out on his shoulder.

On a deeply growled curse Katherine's limp body was swung across Matt's lap and onto the seat beside him. Her head was pushed roughly between her knees, his firm hand at her nape keeping it in that position until the blood clambered back to her brain.

"Let go." Her voice was muffled but strong enough to be heard, and the pressure at her nape eased. "I'm okay now."

"What's the matter with you? Too much sun?" Matt asked gruffly, drawing her inside the circle of his arm, her head cradled onto his uninjured shoulder.

"Too much blood," Katherine explained, chancing a faint smile at his worried face.

"Blood? You mean . . . ?" His brows drew together in a fierce frown.

She nodded. "I'm sorry. Give me a second, and I'll bandage your arm."

"Like hell you will!" he grated disgustedly, lifting his arm away and pushing her back against the seat. "I'll take care of myself."

And he moved away to do just that, quickly and efficiently, roughly cursing under his breath while neatly taping a bandage over the torn skin. Without another word or even a glance in her direction, Matt stalked angrily away from the truck.

Lying back against the seat, Katherine felt weak and ridiculous and more than a little hurt by Matt's abrupt anger. Of course, she didn't blame him for being disgusted with her. It couldn't be a very pleasant experience to be injured and in pain yet still have to deal with a half-fainting woman. But neither did she understand such a volatile reaction to her display of squeamishness. While it wasn't something she was proud of, her aversion to blood wasn't a sufficient cause for such blatant anger either. Perhaps Matt was one of those men who had no tolerance for any show of weakness, regardless of who or why.

"Here, drink this." A mug of hot coffee was thrust curtly into her hands.

Katherine took it and sipped the sweet, steamy liquid until half was gone and she felt stronger. Then she glanced toward Matt. He was braced against the top of the pickup, and she was unable to see more of him than the lower half of his broad chest, his flat stomach, and a portion of denim-covered thighs. She wondered if he was still angry.

"Matt?" she called quietly.

"Yes?" He ducked down to peer inside the truck.

"I'm sorry about your arm. I should have called Timmy

152

or Laurel to help, but I was too rattled to think coherently."

"Shut up, Kat," he muttered, scowling ferociously.

"What?"

"Shut up and drink your coffee."

"But I—"

"I said shut up!" he bit out, each word said with hard
inflection, his voice as cold and sharp as the green eyes
surveying her pale, strained features.

Katherine's lips parted in astonishment, and she quickly turned to face the opposite direction, blinking back a
sudden sting of tears. *Well, that certainly answers the question about his anger. He's seething and seems ready to erupt
at any moment.* As she gulped down the last of her coffee,
she was silently cursing the unfortunate end to their peaceful day. Up until the small disaster with the fishhook, Matt
had been an exceedingly congenial host, organizing their
little camping expedition with a confidence and humor
that put everyone in good spirits. She felt guilty about
being the cause of his bad humor and at the same time a
little indignant that he hadn't had more patience with her.
Quietly she let herself out the far side of the truck and
walked to a nearby picnic table to deposit the empty mug
beside a cache of supplies. Calmly, straight-backed, and
outwardly composed, she turned to walk back to the lake.

"Where are you going?" His hard voice seemed to hold
more annoyance than anger, and Katherine glanced back
to see Matt shrugging into a clean shirt.

"Back to the lake."

"Two minutes ago you couldn't stand."

No doubt about it, Matt was exasperated, purely and
simply, and Katherine's voice was a little strained when
she replied, "I'm feeling better now."

"You don't look it," he told her with brutal honesty.
"You're as pale as a ghost, hollow-eyed, and your legs are

153

about as steady as willow limbs. Come back here and sit in the shade."

"I don't need to," she insisted, and she didn't really. The storm of nausea and dizziness had passed with the disappearance of the blood and the realization that Matt was as strong as an ox and not the least incapacitated, despite his injury.

"Get back here, you silly female!" was barked out in a booming roar when she started once again for the lake.

Her abrupt gasp was mild compared to the billowing eruption of anger that stopped her in her tracks. *Silly female! Why, that condescending, dictatorial . . . male!* She whirled to vent some of her indignant steam at his head, her head snapping almost viciously back on her neck when she found Matt directly in front of her. Bracing her hands on her hips, she glared up at him angrily.

"Female I might be, but silly I am not!" she snarled. "Neither am I some frail little creature in need of pampering or some cowering dog to receive curt orders with an apologetic whine!"

Her luminous eyes defied him to contradict her, and Matt appeared truly impressed, his eyes glinting approvingly over her flushed countenance, almost as if he enjoyed her anger.

"You're right about that," he agreed levelly, and the laughter coloring his eyes a vivid shade of jade had her clenching her fists. "You definitely don't cower or apologize. You plow head-on into every challenge, be it real or imaginary."

"And you take great pleasure in issuing those challenges!" she gritted, barely moving her lips.

"Okay, Kat, simmer down and let me apologize for my erring ways." The pause was to see if she was listening or just silently steaming. Apparently satisfied that her widening gaze meant she was listening, he took her by the shoulders and dipped his head to look directly into her eyes, his almost solemn. "First of all, my arm received a scratch, a skin wound that bled a little. Nothing serious, nothing painful. Secondly, if I'd known your aversion to blood, I never would have accepted your help."

"You mean you weren't in pain?" she asked in confusion. "But you acted so—"

"I acted, period. I apologize. But at the time it seemed a good way to receive some tender consideration," he explained soberly, his eyes searching hers for understanding and receiving a censuring glare instead. Undaunted, he gathered her stiff body close to his chest, placing her arms around his waist to link at his back under the opened shirt. His persuasive murmur was breathed penitently into her forehead. "I've apologized."

The unexpected pleasure she received from the feel of his hard muscle under her fingertips and the scent of his sun-warmed flesh in her nostrils aided in her capitulation. With a small sigh she relaxed against him, querying softly, "All right, but why were you so angry?"

"Because I played a ridiculous game for sympathy and caused you unnecessary discomfort."

"So you punished yourself by biting my head off. Makes perfect sense," Katherine commented sweetly.

"Yeah, something like that," Matt admitted with a soft laugh, not terribly ashamed of his tactics. Then he confessed bluntly, the laughter directed at himself, "Besides, I was getting as aroused as hell back there, and the discovery that your weak trembles were a product of nausea instead of desire was a low blow to my ego."

Briefly she stiffened in his arms, a little disarmed by his outspoken acknowledgment. Then she shrugged away her sense of amazement. After all, Matt was a very sensual man, and his confession shouldn't have surprised her. Perhaps if she hadn't been so swamped by a mixture of guilt and panic earlier, she would have sensed his aroused state. Suddenly she remembered the erratic beat of his heart when she'd drifted in a half faint against him.

A slight tug at the back of her head brought her face up to his. "Want to kiss and make up?"

A slow, enticing smile curved her lips as she gazed up into twin green flames, and it urged the unerring descent of his mouth. Matt's lips were warm and gentle on hers, subtly demanding the response Katherine couldn't or didn't hide. She welcomed the delicate exploration of his tongue, enjoying the texture and taste of him, her lips clinging to his with sweet adhesion.

It was unlike any of the kisses Matt had subjected her to in the past. With a warm rush of pleasure Katherine realized it was because the kiss was a total giving on Matt's part, an extension of the apology he had voiced and the remorse he felt for causing her upset. Despite the male need and impatience she could sense smoldering under the surface of his control, he was making no demands, no taunting claims on her emotions. The restraint and sensitivity of his kiss had Katherine arching closer, her fingers at the back of his waist pressing into his warm flesh to claim a tighter contact.

His "Katherine, the last two weeks dragged by like an eternity" was breathed raggedly into the smooth hollow of her throat a second before his hands spanned her slender waist. With an easy strength he lifted her free of the ground, his mouth tasting a delicious path along her smooth jawline to her temple. Her pleasure increased tenfold at the sensation his moist, compelling mouth induced along the receptive flesh of her face. Her hands cupped his strong jaw, gently forcing his head up to meet her gaze, her fingertips as soft and questioning as the gray eyes meeting his.

"Are you saying you missed me?" Her voice was low

156

and throaty, and the soft appeal of her words lit a lambent fire in his eyes.

His answer was a direct and unequivocal "Yes!" and Katherine's heart soared into her throat. His next words filled her with a wonderful excitement. "I rushed through my work in Paraguay. I had to come home—to you."

"Oh, Matt," she whispered, her whole expression softening with an answering need.

"Is that it? Just 'Oh, Matt'?" he asked with a tense expectation, and for a moment she thought he was angry again until he abruptly chuckled. The sound was rawly sensual, low and deep, almost a groan. "That's what you said over the phone the first time I called from Paraguay, and just those two words, said like that, completely undid me."

His words were wry, but his eyes held total sincerity, and hers widened in amazed comprehension. Her hands dropped to his shoulders as she remembered how quickly he'd hung up that night and also how affected she had been by the sound of his voice, the content of his words.

"Don't look so startled, Kat. Surely you know by now how much I want you."

His eyes reaffirmed his words, stroking over her features possessively. Then his hands deliberately guided her body down the hard length of his until her toes again touched ground. The very intimacy of her breasts raking softly down his strong chest and her slender thighs gliding along his muscular ones had her gasping at the realization that Matt wanted her at that moment. Her blood clamored through her body, and she wanted to wind her arms around his neck and give in to both their needs. But instead, all she managed to do was stare up at him mutely, uncertainly, watching his expression grow a little grim, a little frustrated.

"This isn't easy on me, Kat. I can't come near you

without wanting to make love to you, but I'm trying to play things your way." Once again his abrupt humor dispelled the tense moment, and she eyed him quizzically when he grinned. "Your way. The widow's way," he explained softly, his eyes reflecting a grudging amusement. "Rob and John predicted weeks ago that before long I'd meekly do things the widow's way."

"I can't see you doing anything meekly," she retorted on a self-conscious laugh, wondering what Matt and his friends had been saying about her, and then curiosity had her questioning, "What exactly is the widow's way?"

"John claims that a woman with your cool courage can't be bullied into submission. Rob insists that a woman as intelligent and capable as yourself won't be coerced into surrender."

A little disconcerted that her relationship with Matt was open to his friends' speculation, she nevertheless couldn't help being pleased by the admiring tenor of their comments. "Did you offer an opinion of the widow's way?"

She was warned in advance by the wicked light entering his eyes. "Yeah," he admitted, straight-faced. "I've made a careful study of widows over the last few months and found them to be a special breed—stubborn, aloof, a little wary. They have to be approached with delicacy."

"Delicacy? When have you ever—"

"You don't think I've used a delicate touch in my dealings with you?" He sounded hurt.

"Matthew Clinton, I have enough battle scars from your *delicacy* to make me a cripple for life!" But she was smiling, his hurt expression so false that she couldn't help being amused.

"I guess I'll just have to try again," he murmured huskily, his head bending to hers.

And with a masterstroke of delicacy his lips gently

prized hers apart. His hands as light as feathers skimmed her back and waist, one brushing almost insubstantially over her breast, lingering there to evoke a response from the nipple delicately—a response that had him emitting a low, disturbed groan into her mouth.

It was a loud wolf whistle that broke them apart, Tim and Laurel gamboling into view, loaded down with all the fishing equipment and a heavy string of fish.

Katherine's attempts to back out of Matt's embrace were foiled by his determined arms that let her turn but kept her firmly against him, her shoulder blades digging rigidly into his chest when his arms locked at her waist. She faced her children with steady eyes but a very pink face, wondering at the approval she saw in their eyes. Laurel and Tim looked as pleased as punch, exchanging sly grins before laughing their way into camp.

CHAPTER EIGHT

Near the water's edge Katherine sat breathing in the cool night air with deep welcoming breaths, marveling at the peaceful beauty of the lake. Scooping up a handful of pebbles near her outstretched legs, she idly tossed them one by one into the almost black waters, glad she'd come down to the water to ward off her sleeplessness. The night air penetrating her flannel shirt and corded jeans was cathartic, relaxing her tensed muscles, and the moon's reflection shimmering over the surface of rippling, dancing waves was hypnotic in effect. The night sounds enveloped her in a soothing cocoon. The lapping water, the breeze playing through the trees, the quiet sound of insects played along her body like a soft stroke of velvet.

Relaxed as she was now, it was difficult to recall the disquiet that a whole day of Matt's company had produced. Often abrasive, sometimes endearing, he always managed to leave her slightly shaken, but tonight sleep had been impossible. With memories of their day fixed indelibly in her mind, she had found the peaceful blessing of sleep an elusive retreat, tossing and turning until fear of wakening Laurel had sent her scurrying out of their tent and down to the lake.

Tossing another pebble at the moon's wavering reflection, she hardly heard the quiet approach of footsteps, until another sound, this one the crunching of a booted

160

heel on the graveled embankment, had her turning to find the source of her earlier insomnia taking the last two steps to her side. Matt lowered himself beside her, stretched one long jeaned leg out in front of him and leaned an arm on the bent knee of the other.

"Couldn't sleep?" he asked quietly.

Katherine slowly shook her head, wishing she'd stayed in the tent. Coming down to the lake had been an attempt to gain a measure of relaxation, and somehow she knew that another dose of Matt's company was the last thing she needed to prepare herself for a restful night.

"Me either. Your young man snores," he told her, smiling.

"I'm sorry," she murmured quietly.

"No sweat. I've slept with worse distractions."

"I can imagine," she retorted with soft acidity, doing just that, the images of Stacy and Bibbi all too ready to surface.

"I was referring to my stint in a marine barracks and to camping trips with Dad and Granddad," Matt informed her with a grim smile. Although she didn't comment, Katherine did raise a skeptical eyebrow. Bending closer to her face, he asked curiously, "Do you snore, Katherine?"

"Not that I'm aware of."

"Those three creeps you were involved with—they had no complaints then?" His grin was taunting, but his eyes in the moonlight held not a grain of teasing.

"About me snoring? Hardly," she answered with a lame little laugh. The conversation was taking an unexpected turn, and she felt decidedly uncomfortable, wondering at how completely Matt could change from one moment to the next. Earlier that afternoon his anger had been swept away by her indignation, and he'd become a gentle lover. Now his smiling approach in the darkness was giving way

161

to the hard mockery she generally associated with Matt and didn't particularly like.

"That good, huh?" he jeered softly.

"What are you getting at?" she asked warily.

"Just plain speaking. You're telling me you're so good that your men ignore any little idiosyncrasies on your part, like snoring or cold feet or crackers in bed, right?"

"That's not plain speaking," she hissed, her annoyance rising to meet his mockery. "That's vulgar curiosity. Why did you bring up this subject?"

"I brought up the subject of snoring and sleeping. You put the curiously vulgar slant on it," he informed her with rude accuracy.

Katherine clamped her lips tightly shut. Infuriating devil! How had he managed to put her in the wrong?

"No comeback? No denial?" he continued to gibe. "I'm as interested in your sex life as you are in mine. Go ahead, ask away. Whatever you want to know, I'll tell you, but I'll expect reciprocal answers to my questions."

"I'm not interested in your sex life, thank you," she informed him coolly and was chagrined by his snort of skepticism. Damn him! Of course, she was interested! It tortured her to think of him with other women. In an effort to change the subject, she asked the first thing that popped into her head. "When do you go back to Paraguay?"

"Now how should I answer that, I wonder?" he retorted dryly. "Are you telling me you'll be glad to see the back of me, or are you interested in my . . . activities . . . in Paraguay?"

"Your activities be damned!" Her reply was crisp and succinct.

There was a pause while Matt seemingly digested her statement, and Katherine almost breathed more easily, thinking he had decided to let the subject drop. Then his voice came, riddled with impertinence. "You want to go to Paraguay with me next time? Check out all the action? You could bunk with me."

"I wouldn't take a ride down the street with you!" She flared, fed up with his deliberate innuendos. Why was it that conversation with Matt couldn't stay on safe, ordinary topics? Why, always, these strong emotional undercurrents?

"Yet you came to Lake Whitney with me for an overnight camping trip."

"That was different," she mumbled, averting her head so he wouldn't see the glimmer of guilty recognition in her eyes.

"How?"

"My kids enjoy this, and you were nice when you invited us!" she supplied tartly, raising her chin as she glared at him.

And he supplied her unspoken accusation, his own chin thrust aggressively forward. "But I'm not now?"

"Not particularly."

"In what way? Because I bring out into the open subjects you only hint at?"

"Oh, forget it. I don't want to talk to you anymore. I'm going to bed."

"Oh, no, you don't!" He stayed her with a quick grab on her wrist that jerked her alarmingly close to the warm strength of his flannel-shirted chest. "I enjoy talking to you. I like other things more, but talking will do for the moment. You scared of something, Kat? Afraid I'll discover you're as interested in my life as I am in yours? Frightened I might guess you want me as badly as I want you? Alarmed I could make you admit it?"

No, I'm terrified you'll discover I love you and fearful of what you could do to my life with that knowledge in your power, her mind screamed, but her lips were stoically

163

silent, stubbornly refusing to answer. She wouldn't give him the satisfaction of admitting he was right . . . and more.

"Perverse tonight, aren't you?" he said, taunting her moodily.

But she didn't rise to the bait, silently gazing out over the lake while trying to ignore his long fingers stroking caressingly over her wrist and under the edge of her flannel cuff.

"You know, Widow Meadows, I'll lay odds you speak before the next ten minutes are up," he murmured silkily, sounding disgustingly sure of himself.

Her eyes shot him a glacial denial that clearly damned his assumption to a freezing death. And that made him smile—a slow, lazy, calculating smile that alarmed her by its very aura of supreme self-confidence. She watched cunning green eyes dip to the gold watch on his wrist and then come speculatively back to her face.

She was on her back with him on top of her before she could possibly have guessed his intention, her slender body pinned to the embankment by his superior strength. She opened her mouth to order him off, but the expectancy in his eyes just inches away reminded her of his assertion that she would speak before ten minutes passed. Her mouth snapped shut defiantly, her arms coming up between them, her hands pushing ineffectively against his wide shoulders.

"Nothing to say?" he jeered softly, managing to convey the impression that he would be disappointed if she did speak. "My old man always vowed that a silent woman was a blessing, and his old man never failed to add that a silent woman was a compliant woman." His eyes sparkled with devilish lights. "Now me, I never figured Katherine Meadows as a compliant woman—defiant maybe, but not compliant. But who am I to argue with the time-worn truisms of my elders and betters? Are you compliant, Kat?"

She shot him a murderous look, but predictably enough he didn't expect a verbal reply. He was smiling, nearly laughing, as if the way the game was played were more important than the win.

"You know, darlin', your docility could make this short and sweet." His voice was husky, caressing, the tone and words offering seduction as surely as the warm breath teasing over her face and the gentle touch toying with the buttons at her shirtfront.

Oh, the devious rat! She felt sure that his sensually drawled "darlin' " was a deliberate ploy to melt her resistence. Subduing a sudden urge to laugh, she cast her eyes to the top buttons of his flannel shirt, concentrating on the curling tuft of dark hair just visible in the moonlight at the opened collar of his shirt, determined not to let him outmaneuver her.

"Ah, you're shy, darlin'," he observed sardonically, adding dryly as his fingers slipped a button or two, "Isn't it a good thing I'm not? Otherwise so much *time* could be wasted."

Time again! She wondered how much of that precious commodity had elapsed and then tried to prize his hand away from the buttons of her shirt. Beneath her shirt was bare, tender flesh, the restricting bra having been removed when she had made ready for bed earlier. In seeming capitulation Matt left the buttons and grasped her hand, bringing it to his mouth, his tongue delicately flicking her palm before she snatched it away. Her eyes scolded his audacity, sparkling with defiant reproach and a touch of reluctant humor.

"Give in, Kat," he urged softly, a surge of warm laughter teasing into her hair with his words. His mouth at her temple edged downward, gliding, warm and moist, across the delicate line of her cheek and jaw. His hand tangled in her loosened hair, caressing her neck, while the other one went determinedly back to her shirt. Katherine sucked in a shallow breath as she steeled herself not to respond, fighting against an urgent desire to turn her head and stop that tormenting mouth with hers.

Strong teeth gently nibbled along the sensitive side of her neck; strong fingers stroked carefully inside the completely unbuttoned front of her shirt to claim a possessive hold on her bared midriff; strong heartbeats pounded like rumbling thunder under her hand. Weak shivers of excitement underlined her reaction to his touch; weak senses clamored out a yielding message that wildly contradicted her continued resistance; weak defenses rapidly crumbled as she arched her throat to oblige the compelling seduction of his mouth.

"Stubborn woman, you're destroying the heroic images of two strong men" was whispered in husky rebuke, his mouth at her ear.

The disturbed tenor of his voice affected her so forcefully she scarcely heard the content of his words. The teasing play of his mouth moving to the hollow of her throat drove her hands to his chest, unsteady fingers dealing with the buttons of his shirt to bare the hair-roughened flesh to her touch. The tip of his tongue flicking over her breast teased a soft moan from her throat, and immediately his mouth moved back to hover over hers.

"Ol' Dad claimed a stubborn female was trouble," he groaned softly against her lips, his weight shifting so that her breasts were flattened by the muscled wall of his chest. "But Ol' Granddad was closer to the truth when he insisted it was desirable trouble."

His mouth bruised hers, causing a shudder to course down the whole of her slender length, in turn illiciting an

166

uninhibited response in the devouring pressure of his mouth, the expert teasing of his tongue.

"Oh, Matt," she moaned against his lips, then shallowly, desperately: "Please . . ."

He went curiously still, raising his head so that the direction of his gaze was on the hand in her hair. "Eight and a half," he murmured thickly.

"What?" Her hands at his neck were urging his head back down to hers.

His smile was strained. "You spoke before the ten minutes were up."

It was Katherine's turn to go very still, her weakened senses at war with her confused thoughts. He was telling her he'd made her speak before the allotted time had passed. Was that all this had meant to him? Another little challenge met and won? Her eyes clouded as her whole body tautened beneath his.

"Don't withdraw from me, Kat." He didn't sound either teasing or triumphant. He sounded frustrated, urging her roughly, "Stay alive for me."

"I don't like your games," she managed to whisper, but bewilderment and hurt were equal parts of her declaration.

His denial came swiftly, hoarsely. "No games, Kat. This is real. Can't you feel how real? My God, woman, can't you tell how much I want you?"

His hips surged against her, and even through the layers of cloth that separated them his physical state couldn't be denied. Just as she couldn't deny her own. She wanted him, too. Her body felt on fire with the heated urgency she could feel in his, the conflagration in her lower belly proof of the plaguing ache to belong to him.

His hand moved to her breast, circling it, surrounding it, kneading the pliant flesh. When she felt his fingers gently tugging a response from her nipple, her hands went to his wrist to halt the torment.

"Stop!" There was a ragged edge to her voice, desire intermingling with the protest.

"Stop what? Stop touching you? Stop desiring you? I can't. As surely as I draw breath, I'm driven to hold you, touch you, make love to you," he told her with harsh urgency. "You ask the impossible. You deny not only my needs but your own."

The mute shake of her head was more confusion than denial; but Matt didn't realize that, and his mouth crushed down on hers, driving her lips apart. Then his lips moved down to her breasts, fully exploring the taste of each creamy mound.

"Matt, no!"

Her hands tangled in his dark hair, trying to move his head away; but he was determined, almost desperately so, and the fingers in his hair turned traitor and urged his mouth to continue the sensual assault, a low, hungry sound rolling from her throat as she arched into him.

"Admit it" was the hoarse command hovering above her lips. "Admit you want me as much as I want you. You've never said it, and I need to hear you say it."

Oh, Matt, and what of my needs? What of love and trust and mutual affection and emotional security? She stared helplessly at his features, seeing the frustration and desire warring in his eyes and realized Matt might never understand her needs. He was too self-sufficient to want a total commitment to another person or perhaps even to acknowledge the emotions that guided her thinking. His needs were more basic, his understanding limited to the desires of his body and the response he could draw at will from hers.

"God, Kat, say it," he groaned from somewhere deep in his chest.

And knowing she didn't lie, knowing her concession was only a fraction of what she really felt, she heard herself voicing the response he demanded. "I want you, too, Matt."

Some of the tension left his body, and his hands gliding up her neck to secure a hold on her jaw were almost gentle. The light in his eyes was victorious but also unbelievably tender.

"Then, darlin', we're finally in accord," he rasped out on a soft explosion of breath.

And this time, when his mouth covered hers, there was no denying either his need or hers. Their tongues met and teased, skillfully playing out a little dance for supremacy that ended with the force of Matt's hunger, Katherine compliantly entwining her arms across his broad shoulders as she gave herself up to the inevitable possession. At her waist his hand was warm, and it dealt easily with the snap of her cords, executing the zipper, the feathery touch across her bare stomach rippling through her insides like a scorching tongue of flame.

"You're so damned *soft*, Katherine," he whispered with thick resonance below her ear, his hand enclosing her breast with almost fragile care.

"You're not," she told him breathily, her mouth against his hard shoulder, her hands gliding over his tautly fleshed ribs, tactilely testifying to the hardness of his body.

His laugh was low, sexy, muffled in her hair. "No, I'm definitely not."

Her soft gasp acknowledged his blunt assertion, the evidence of his arousal hard against her thigh. And when he claimed her lips again, she met his mouth with mindless need.

His "Let me make love to you, Katherine" was burned into the erratic pulse at the base of her throat.

Her "Matt!" wasn't an answer at all, but a throaty reaction to the sensual bite on her earlobe.

Matt's mouth merged with hers, thrilling her, destroying rational thought. His tongue explored while his hands moved over her, growing bold and more urgent with each ensuing caress. Excitement mounting, her head went back, allowing the scorching search of his lips to heat the hollow of her throat, then downward to burn the ache of her breasts, spreading fire into her veins. Her need for him became a raw necessity, and Matt built it into unrelenting proportions.

The sinewed sculpture of his chest was hot under her palms, then salty to her tongue, and with tantalizing delicacy she moistly traced a path over to his shoulder, circling the bandage on his right arm. He groaned, crushing her to him as he rolled onto his side. His lean fingers worked at her clothing, gliding it away; her silken curves were studied first by his hungry emerald eyes, then learned intimately by his knowledgeable hands. Her lithe form shook with the fervor building inside her, and her mouth grew demanding under his.

She felt his hands slip between them to loosen his clothing, and her exploring fingers moved over the taut flesh of his belly, then lower, finding and gently claiming him. The shudder that coursed through his long frame was explicit with pleasure, and his hand covered hers, ensuring the contact.

The spill of her hair obscured her face as Katherine bent over him, and when her lips moved over his warm skin, strands of honeyed silk tangled with the brown crinkly hair of his chest. To the sound of a hoarse, inarticulate murmur, his hand found her neck, drawing her mouth up to his, their kiss deep and fierce as their tongues met and their mouths slanted across each other's in escalating hunger.

170

For a moment Katherine lost the security of his warm embrace, and her eyelids fluttered down, her heartbeats arrested. The soft rustle as Matt removed his clothing blended with the whisper of night breeze and her shallow intake of air. Cool shadow clothed her; nature's breath moved over her; suspended desire held her in its thrall.

Vaguely Katherine was aware of the tremors in the arms reaching for her, enfolding her; then she felt the sensual tautness of his hard body molding to hers, reestablishing a physical demand. His hard chest crushed the softness of her breasts. His leg moved heavily across hers, holding her willing prisoner. His palm, sensually rough, stroked lightly along the satin curve of her hip, then boldly to her inner thighs.

His rasping breath, the low whisper of her name huskily called out to her, and her eyes flickered open. The gaze beating down on her was heated, and she saw his mouth forming words that were low and lost over the thundering beat of her heart. Under the persistent search of his hand, her thighs quivered, and his intimate caress spread a passionate yearning throughout her body, waves of delight tingling her every nerve.

Hot and moist, his open mouth seared her breasts, his teeth and tongue enticing the malleable nipples, bringing them to swift, aching excitement. The wild flood of pleasure had her holding him to her, arching into his caresses, her fingers digging imperatively into his back as she softly cried his name.

His head came up, his gaze searched through the shadows to read her expression and blazed at what he saw. His eyes never left hers as his knee gently nudged her thighs apart, and he came over her. Poised at the edge of endurance, he claimed her with a piercing sweetness, softly groaning her name. She welcomed him with the pliant surging of her body, knowing nothing, feeling everything,

171

experiencing a longed-for ecstasy. Bodies entwined, movements blending, their passion played itself out under the soft illumination of the moon, and when Matt felt her quaking response, he kissed her deeply, shuddering, finding his own completion with the taste of her name on his lips.

Disquiet came within moments after the last tremoring shake left her body. Disquiet and reality and an emptiness when, after murmuring a low, satiated incoherence against her neck, he moved away from her. Standing, he stepped into his jeans, his tall body relaxed and coordinated. She watched his movements. Her troubled eyes followed the rippling fluidity of moon-gilded muscles, locking onto the strong profile etched against the night's skyline, and then flickered down to veil their distraught reflections from his shadowed green gaze swinging her way.

His voice came to her, suggesting quietly, "You'd better get dressed, Kat. The night air is cool."

Katherine's mind and heart screamed a violent protest, and her body shivered with a chill that was only partly due to the night breeze. No sweet words, no tender caresses, just "You'd better get dressed, Kat." Her uneasiness swiftly propelled into heartache and self-disgust, and she fought back a sickened groan.

Her shaky fingers groped for and found soft flannel, and she sat up, jerkily shoving her arms into the shirt sleeves. *How could you, Katherine? How could you mindlessly give in to him, knowing full well how little he cares for you?* Frustrated both by her thoughts and by sleeves suddenly too long and buttons maddeningly where there should be buttonholes, she gave up her attempt to fasten the shirt and grabbed up her cords and panties. Frantically tugging them on, she was on the verge of hysterical tears.

Love? Respect? Commitment? You didn't receive any of

those things. You just freely, idiotically, let yourself become one more of Matt Clinton's women. She was down on her knees, her brimming gray eyes trying to spot her misplaced shoes. Irritably she shoved the bothersome flannel sleeves back from her fingertips, turning on all fours in her blind search, bumping into something warm and solid. Glancing up sharply, she found Matt kneeling in front of her, his chest bare, his eyes quizzically examining her confused distress.

He raised her to kneel in front of him. "Why are you scrambling around in such a dither? There's no rush."

Her mouth went dry, and she blinked furiously, whispering, "Laurel . . . Timmy . . . they might wonder where we are."

"They're asleep, Kat," he whispered back, softly mocking her hushed tone. "You worry too much, and about the wrong things."

Katherine stared into his relaxed features, helplessly and unwillingly aware that she was responsible for the warm contentment in his eyes, the relaxed curve of his mouth, the total lack of tension in his body.

"Let me go, Matt." It was a weakly whispered plea, and he brought her closer, his chin nuzzling the top of her head. His chest rose and fell on a deep, gusty sigh, his hands splaying possessively over her rib cage.

"Darlin', the way I feel right now, that's asking a lot. I enjoy holding this sexy little body of yours." His low, rumbling laugh punctuated both his feeling of well-being and Katherine's growing disturbance.

With a soft moan she wrenched away, quickly rising. Aware that Matt rose more slowly, she was more aware of his soft snort of exasperated amusement. She found her shoes and hopped clumsily into them, then once again tackled the buttons of her shirt. Only to groan in dismay. Because it wasn't her shirt at all. It was Matt's.

A low, subdued chuckle had her eyes flying to Matt. Clutching the shirt over her nakedness, her expression distraught, she watched him move nearer. For a moment he stared down at her, studying her; then she was grabbed about the waist and lifted high against his chest, her feet dangling, her protesting mouth soundly kissed into silence.

"Don't fret, Kat. The shirt looks great on you," he growled playfully, enclosing her in a bear hug that had her gasping for breath. Then he was covering her face in fierce little kisses. "You confounding bundle of contradictions, don't tighten up on me now." His tone was softly chiding, his features displaying confidence and depicting total ignorance of the reason for her stiff distress. "Come on, darlin', relax. I told you two weeks ago we could be together without involving your children. And now I'm promising not to do anything to hurt your relationship with those two. It's only another month before they leave to visit their grandparents for the summer. Weighed against the prospect of a whole summer with you, a month of abstinence won't kill me." A crooked smile mocked his self-control. "Of course, you could take pity on me and let them spend the night with their friends."

The confounding bundle of contradictions in his arms proved worthy of her title and became a squirming bundle of resistance, choking a strangled "Noooo!" before pounding one tight fist into an unflinching chest and gazing at him in horror. "There won't be a repeat of tonight!"

His relaxed humor was slow to disappear; his understanding, reluctant to come. But her hands pushing desperately against his shoulders finally got through to him, and his head reared back, his eyes narrowing warningly. "What is it now, Kat? What contrary objection is rolling around in that frustrating little head of yours this time?"

"The seduction's over, Matt," she asserted grimly.

"You got what you wanted, but don't expect it to happen again." Her voice was tight, but the seduction itself was just a moot point. It was the knowledge that to Matt, she was just one more woman. One more willing woman. Who happened to live next door. Who happened to be handy for a summer affair. The desire to be free of his touch, the need to deny his easy command over her emotions, fierce.

His hands bit into her waist as he set her on her feet. "If I hadn't promised myself to be gentle with you, I'd snap every bone in your skinny little body."

"How romantic!" she whispered acidly, hating his single-minded determination to have her on his terms—his hatefully unacceptable, *temporary* terms. *Why didn't you just make love to me, Matt? Why didn't you just take what I foolishly handed you and not ask for more? Why did you have to remind me that I am not, nor probably ever will be, more to you than a brief affair, a temporary lover, a convenient playmate?*

Disgust entered his eyes, and she knew it was put there by her reference to romance. But when he spoke, his words were patient. "You're thirty-three, Kat, and I'm thirty-seven, and neither of us is a starry-eyed teen-ager. What we shared tonight, what we could share again, is good. And if you're honest, you'll admit it."

Stung that he could overlook so callously the need for words of sweet desire and love and assurance, she cried, "We didn't share anything tonight that you haven't shared with two other women in the last month! You be honest, blast you! You don't want me! I'm just conveniently close at hand!"

"Kat, there's not one damned convenient thing about you. You're muleheaded and obstinate, and you jump to conclusions," he gritted tersely, shaking her a little. Then, with hard amusement: "But I want you. Only you. There are no other women."

175

"Have you already forgotten Bibbi and Stacy?" she questioned grimly, hating him.

"No, I haven't forgotten them, but I think maybe I'd better explain them." There was a suspicion of a grin on his face, but it evened out under the cold surveillance of her silver gray eyes. "Stacy's my secretary. She's also married, loyal to her husband, and I've never been tempted to want anything from her but a business relationship. Bibbi . . ." He issued a self-disgusted sigh. "Bibbi was an attempt to get a cool little widow out of my brain. She didn't work." His hands framed her face, his thumbs rubbing gently at the corners of her mouth. "Nothing works. Not even having you tonight. You're still there, Katherine. Only now you're a potent reality, not just an idle fantasy."

"And you want to exorcise me by having a summer fling!"

His jaw tightened, and his chin angled aggressively forward; but he made no response, abruptly releasing her to move away. Grabbing her shirt from the ground, but not offering it to her, he let his eyes flicker over her partial nudity, glittering with anger and frustration and the lingering heat of his desire.

She held out a hand for her blouse, and when he calmly looped the sleeves about his neck and shot her a look that dared her to take it, she fumbled once again with the buttons of his shirt, knowing to play his game would be to court disaster. She was out of his arms, and out of his arms she wanted to stay. It was safer. With a last glare she would have left him, but he stayed her with a firm hand on her arm, his gaze beating relentlessly into hers.

"What will it take to convince you we could make a relationship work? Are you waiting for more assurances that there will be no other women? You've got them. I'll be faithful. Do you doubt my ability or my desire to be there for you? I like you, Katherine. I'll be your friend as well as your lover. Do you want a declaration that I enjoy being with you? I'll give it freely. But you give it a chance, Kat! Don't throw away the possibility of sharing something good!"

His rough, vehement words swept away all her doubts but the most important one. Not one word of love had been spoken. And how does a woman go about asking a man to love her? So, a little subdued, she answered his charges, her voice quiet. "I'm not asking for evidence of your friendship and fidelity, Matt. But there's more to a good relationship than that."

"Then I don't get it!" He raged with barely tempered violence, his fingers biting into her flesh. "More than once you've shown you want me. Just minutes ago you demonstrated it. And you must know by now how much I want you!"

"Desire and physical attraction aren't enough for a relationship. How many women have you desired? Did you offer them all a summer affair? I want more than to be someone's temporary lover!"

"Sex is the primary basis for any man-woman relationship, whether it's an affair or a quick toss on the sheets," he retorted bluntly.

"And when I balk at more than one quick toss on the sheets, you resort to proposing a temporary arrangement. You see me as some kind of challenge!" she countered with equal bluntness. In her belief that summed up Matt's feelings for her.

"Oh, you're a challenge all right, Kat. To my sanity. But don't kid yourself into believing you're not subject to physical desire like the rest of us mortals. Your cool control is superficial." She didn't like his smile. It was derisive and knowing. "You've got some tight little picture in your head about relationships meaning perfection, but your body responds to me. Don't lie to yourself. Don't tell yourself that high-minded dreams are enough to keep you warm at night, because there's a hunger in you that's clamoring for satisfaction. I've felt it almost every time I've touched you. And I damned well experienced it tonight." He muttered an expletive that made her flinch, turning for the embankment, pulling her stiffly behind him. "Let's get back to camp before your children become orphans."

Katherine twisted out of the tight hold on her elbow and walked stiffly beside him. And then abruptly stopped, remembering her shirt. Embarrassment made her voice clipped and tight. "I need my shirt, Matt."

He turned, frowning ferociously, and then jerked her shirt from his neck, tossing it to her. Crossing his arms over his chest, he smiled nastily, waiting for her to make the change from his shirt to hers. The cold contempt in his eyes as she turned her back on him made her movements stiff and her fingers clumsy. But she managed the transfer without undo fumbling and turned back to face him, her composed expression belying the tight ball of misery in her chest.

The walk to the tents was accomplished in a strained silence, and when Matt left her outside the tent she shared with Laurel to stalk rigidly, angrily, to the one he shared with Tim, Katherine watched his departure, a maelstrom of chaotic emotions coloring her thoughts.

CHAPTER NINE

The tantalizing aroma of freshly brewed coffee drifted inside the tent with the first hint of daylight, and Katherine was immediately awake. In fact, she wondered if she had slept at all. Long into the night she had lain awake, trying to sort out her upheaval of emotions. As she carefully stretched inside the downy sleeping bag to relieve a cramped muscle, two undeniable facts hammered relentlessly through her mind, filling her with a sense of urgency.

It was very simple really. She loved Matt Clinton, and he wanted her. Not necessarily the best of odds, but not a complete losing situation either.

She almost groaned aloud and then covered her mouth to smother the low, betraying sound, her gaze sweeping to the sleeping Laurel. *She loved Matt. Matt wanted her.* It burned like a refrain in her mind, just as it had during the long night. It instilled her with hope.

No man wanted a woman as badly as Matt claimed to want her unless he felt something strong, did he? Something stronger than physical desire? Perhaps not love, but surely more than lust?

Behind Matt's taunting façade was a complicated man. Strong, hard, supremely masculine, and self-sufficient, Matthew Clinton also displayed odd touches of tenderness. Aggressive and determined to the point of bullhead-

179

edness, he could show gentler emotions even while refusing to label and recognize them. Last night he had shown caring along with the desire, humor with the seduction, tenderness with the passion. Last night he had vowed friendship, fidelity, a certain measure of affection, a promise of passionate ecstasy. In fact, he had offered everything but an outright avowal of romantic love. And with a cowardice she now regretted, Katherine had wanted words—commitment . . . love . . . romance—rejecting out of hand Matt's more basic approach.

If a self-contained man could offer friendship, mightn't he be capable of love? If a self-sufficient man could hint at a desire for companionship, couldn't he eventually feel a need for a more permanent relationship? If an aggressive man could make love with tender passion, wasn't it possible that tender sentiment guided his actions, if not his words?

Words. What was the old axiom? "Actions speak louder than words." Matt wasn't skimpy with actions, even if he was cautious with words. He boldly said he desired her, she interested him, in everything he did. Teasing, tormenting, he kept her on a knife's edge of awareness. And had since that first day back in January when bold green eyes captured hers in insolent assessment. He sparked in Katherine an intense response she had exhibited to no other man, not even Barry, whom she'd loved with all her heart. Matt ignited a conflagration of passion, turning her world upside down with a hard kiss, a challenging taunt, a scoffing reminder that perfect relationships were an unrealistic goal.

A perfect relationship? No, she wouldn't have that with Matt, but she might find an association that would fulfill a lonely gap in her life. For ten years she had lived her life on a level that excluded the chance for companionship between a man and a woman. For an entire decade she had denied herself the pleasure of being a woman. Now she was burning with a need to grasp that pleasure in her hands and cling to it for dear life, to take what Matt had to offer and return it with all the love and passion inside her.

What was it Matt had said yesterday? That he was doing things her way, the widow's way? *The widow's way.* The memory of that phrase instilled Katherine with a new resolve, and the small upward curve of her lips showed a resurgence of confidence.

The widow wants you, Matt Clinton—all of you—and she accepts the challenge to gain that totality. She'll have an affair with you. She'll accept your terms. And although you may not realize it, the widow's way is love.

Almost buoyantly Katherine pushed out of the sleeping bag, a quick scan of Laurel's huddled figure confirming that her daughter was dead to the world and hadn't been troubled by her mother's restless night and early-morning fidgeting. After slipping into her shoes, she brushed through the tent flap to greet a day that was just breaking, the landscape shaded in glorious pink and golden hues. Her eyes sparkled, spiriting across the campsite in search of Matt, but she found the immediate area void of his presence, the simmering pot of coffee atop the campfire the only sign that he was up and about.

A frivolous feminine instinct to be seen in an attractive light had Katherine pausing for a quick spruce-up before setting out to find Matt. She washed her face, brushed her hair and her teeth, and gave her clothes a cursory straightening. Then, her strides springy and positive, she made a direct march down to the lake, knowing her man would be there, determined in any event to search until she found him.

He was there. Near the water's edge Matt was hunkered down on the balls of his booted feet, his forearms resting atop his jeaned thighs, his hands wrapped loosely around a steaming mug of coffee. Katherine's heart skipped a beat when she spotted him, recognizing the location from the night before and wondering if Matt's thoughts had returned to what had happened there just a few short hours ago. He looked pensive—grimly so.

With his casual clothes and posture, his hair darkened to mahogany from a recent wash, his muscles seemingly fluid and relaxed, Matt's frowning countenance was a sharp contrast. In profile he was an impressive sight: his strong jaw clean-shaven, the bold cut of his nose and chin suggesting tough strength and grim implacability in equal measures. Smiling, undaunted, Katherine made her way to him on silent feet, halting within yards of his hunched form.

"Matt?" she called softly.

He turned on the balls of his feet but didn't rise, squinting up into the sun at her back, his face stony and a hint of combativeness in the angle of his chin.

A "Yes" was clipped back clearly but not encouragingly.

"About last night, I—"

"Forget it." The gruff timbre of his voice was hard and unyielding.

"I can't," Katherine answered, feeling a lessening of confidence at Matt's brusque manner but determined to take the plunge. "I've changed my mind."

One dark eyebrow rose a fraction of an inch, but otherwise Matt gave no indication that he understood what Katherine was trying to say, his expression seemingly carved out of granite, not inviting her to enlarge on her statement. Even his squinting eyes gave no clue to his thoughts, their narrowed slits unreadable.

"If you still want to"—she gulped back a returning surge of cowardice and rushed on—"to have an affair, I agree. I've thought about it and decided you're right. There's no sense in waiting for the perfect romance. It's not that important. But you were wrong about my expecting it. At least, I don't expect you to be romantic," she finished lamely, knowing she was expressing herself feebly but unable to find the right phrases in his continued silence.

Grimly, bleakly, Matt stared up at her, his mouth a firm, obdurate line. Shakenly, horribly, Katherine came to the belated realization that his first denial, that terse "Forget it," had meant exactly that. Her eyes widened in dismay, realizing her lamely phrased acceptance was being harshly rejected. One shaky hand came up to her breast, and the other to her mouth. For a long moment she was frozen in that posture, her eyes huge and shot through with horror and then with a hint of sickness under the persistence of his grim surveyal.

Had it all been a joke? A taunting little exercise to keep her whirling, his huge hands figuratively batting her back and forth like a big confident cat playing with a desperate little mouse? A thick, nauseated moan escaped her throat and was a prelude for action on both their parts. Matt jackknifed to his feet, tossing the coffee mug to the ground, at the same time that Katherine spun on her heel, determined to get as far away from him as possible.

Two steps up the embankment she was grabbed from behind. His hands on her shoulders whirled her about, and although she twisted both her body and her head, his mouth nevertheless found hers accurately and quickly, burning hers like a brand. His strong arm clamped around her waist, effectively pinning her straining hands between them, while his fingers went to her neck, tunneling through her hair to still the frenzied struggles of her head.

Katherine quieted slowly under the fierce kiss, desperately fighting Matt's dominance until the hunger of his

183

punishing mouth transmitted itself to her and she sagged weakly against him, her lips moving helplessly under his. Only then did his mouth gentle, still burning her into submission but not so bruisingly. Lost to anything but feeling, Katherine sighed tremulously, and immediately his kiss deepened. Not forcefully but erotically, his tongue probed her teeth and beyond, its velvet roughness evoking bright darts of sensual pleasure that stabbed through all her defenses.

The crushing embrace gradually loosened to allow her hands to scrabble up his chest. Behind his head her nails flexed into his hair and scored lightly across his neck and shoulders. A series of rough, stinging kisses went hotly over her face. The possessive trail of his hands had no pattern, only purpose, kneading imperatively over her back, brushing lightly down her thighs, gently cupping her breasts, carefully shifting her length to allow his thigh to glide between hers in more intimate contact.

"I just spent one hell of a night, Katherine," he told her almost accusingly, rasping out the words against her neck so that her nod of agreement became a trembling shudder. Loosening his hold, Matt pushed some space between them, allowing their gazes to meet and lock.

"You'll move in with me," he informed her roughly, and when her eyes clouded with uncertainty, he added adamantly, "In my house, Kat. There won't be any separate roofs and occasional nights together."

"All right, Matt, if that's what you want," she answered cautiously.

"What's your objection, Kat? You've fought me every inch of the way, and I can see you're struggling with some reservations even now." Somewhere, underneath the flat statement, was a shading of grim humor.

"No, I'm not," she denied swiftly. "I was only thinking that between your traveling and my erratic work schedule, it might be easier to live in our own houses. And Timmy and Laurel won't be gone forever, Matt. I can't live with you after they get back from Big Spring."

"We'll see about that," Matt murmured, casually looping his hands around her neck, his eyes sparkling with determination.

Twisting away to stare warily up at him, Katherine hoped he wasn't going to try bulldozing his way around her reservations. Her troubled eyes reflected her suspicions.

"Kat, trust me," he advised warningly, folding his arms across his chest in an attitude of heavy patience. "You just told me you'd thought everything through and decided I was right."

"Are you expecting me to jump every time you yell frog?" she asked, frowning, ready to combat him on the subject of her children.

Matt surprised her by laughing heartily, his long fingers snagging her neck and bringing them forehead to forehead. His words broke over her face with warm amusement. "The day Katherine Meadows docilely falls in with all my plans will probably be a snowy day in July. What are *you* expecting, Katherine?"

"An honest relationship," she answered simply.

And he smiled—a slow, wide smile that reached his eyes until they shone with brilliant dancing lights.

"You'll get it." He laughed, framing her face in his warm palms. "I promise you that. I'll impatiently sweat out the next month, and then you'll get your way, complete with pledges of fidelity and trust and respect. I'll search for the damned cat when she escapes into the night, and I'll even take over the first-aid duties when one of us has an accident."

"Sounds very domestic," she ventured with a strained

smile, wishing she hadn't noticed the absence of love among his pledges. "Are you certain you're up to it?"

"Yes, my doubtful darlin', I'm up to it. I'll see to my side of it. What about you?"

"Me? Oh, well, I'll try my best to fulfill your expectations, if I can manage it from under the weight of your controlling thumb," she said teasingly, but there was a shadow of uncertainty in her eyes that prompted the narrowing of his.

"My thumb promises to be as light as a feather on you," he promised solemnly. He drew her firmly back into his arms, kissing her forehead. "You're not going to regret this, Katherine."

Dropping her face to his chest, she managed to hide more doubts from his discernment. Matt's primary expectation was a satisfying sexual union. Could a widow of ten years possibly match the experience he was accustomed to?

Matt was slowly gliding his fingers over her rib cage, outlining the almost fragile slenderness, shaping the bones under his touch. He sounded concerned, murmuring, "Why don't you eat more, Kat? A big puff of wind would blow you away."

Katherine automatically tensed, then forced herself to relax. Romance? Flowery speech? Adoration? Expecting those things from Matt would be like going to a goat's house after wool. If she intended making their time together as problem-free as possible, she would have to learn to accept what he offered and not expect more. Her smile against his chest was determined, even as an insistent voice whispered mockingly, *Not even love?*

"Let's get back to camp, Kat, and rouse Tim and Laurie. I made some promises to those two last night that need to be set into action. How does a trek through the woods and then a lesson on driving a pickup sound to you?"

186

She smiled up at him. "Like Timmy wants to explore and Laurel has implored."

"Smart lady. You know your teen-agers."

With his arm possessively about her waist they walked leisurely back to the campsite. Tim and Laurel were up, barely awake but eager to start the day, chattering volubly about who got to do what first. Matt laughed at their eagerness, standing behind Katherine as he outlined the plans for the day, his fingers kneading caressingly into her shoulder blades.

For the second time in as many days Katherine was made aware of her children's keen powers of observation. Two brown glances covertly noticed Matt's possessive stance behind their mother, two suppressed grins said questions would come—but not at that moment.

"When's Matt coming back from Paraguay, Mom?"

Katherine faced her son across the breakfast table, noting the bright curiosity in his brown eyes. "Probably next week, maybe the second week in June."

"He calls a lot, almost every night," Tim commented idly, his lean cheeks sunken with a held-in smile.

"Not every night, Timmy," Katherine corrected. Almost every night, to Tim, was five calls in the past three weeks.

"What do you guys talk about?"

"Lots of subjects. You and Laurel. Matt's Paraguayan project. How busy we've both been." *How many days are in the month of May. How long those days are. Pensive doubts surfacing from a long separation. Gruff, exasperated warnings not to put up stumbling blocks to our relationship.* "Finish your cereal, Timmy. If you miss your school finals today, you'll have to make them up, and that will delay your trip to Big Spring next week."

With a quick grin at his mother's uncomfortable expression Tim obediently applied himself to his breakfast. And Laurel took up the questioning.

"You don't hate Matt anymore, do you, Mother?"

Gray eyes met probing brown ones. "I never hated Matt, Laurel."

"Well, you didn't exactly like him at first" was pointed out with a casualness that was belied by the next acute observation. "Matt's close to your age. You two probably have a lot in common."

Like mutual attraction and physical desire. But don't get your hopes up, children, because your wonderful pal doesn't want your mother on a permanent basis. "You'd better eat, too, Laurel. We have to leave here in fifteen minutes in order to get to school and work on time."

"Which means she's not going to admit knowing she turns Matt on," Tim informed his sister under his breath.

"Timmy!"

"Sorry, Mom." The thirteen-year-old apologized quickly, cramming the last of his cereal inside a grinning mouth.

Politely Laurel excused herself from the table and paused to rinse her breakfast dishes at the sink. Then, with all the wisdom of an experienced woman of the world, she added her two cents' worth. "Or that Matt is a total fox and turns *her* on. She's afraid we'll be shocked. She thinks we're c-h-i-l-d-r-e-n and don't understand l-o-v-e and s-e-x."

Katherine's "Laurel!" was lost over the quick "Better finish your coffee, Mom, or we'll be late," as Tim scraped back his chair and followed his sister to the sink. While Katherine stared, caught between laughter and reproach, both teen-agers gave in to their naughty humor and laughed uproariously, hurrying out of the kitchen. From the hallway came a hummed duet, sounding suspiciously like the wedding march but which their uncontrolled fits of laughter made difficult to identify positively.

188

The smile that finally touched Katherine's mouth was poignant, and she stared unseeingly into her coffee cup. Love and sex and marriage. How gloriously simply the three things had come together in her children's minds. And she knew the reason. Matt. None of the other men she'd dated had captured the hearts of her teen-agers —had captured her own, for that matter—as Matt Clinton had done without even trying. Three hearts in the palm of his hand. Three reasons to find out if a similar organ lay dormant, encased in that iron-hard chest.

Damn you, Ol' Dad and Ol' Granddad! Why didn't you teach him that loving is part of being a strong man?

The sunlight filtering through the drapes of the bedroom's east windows boldly announced the lateness of the morning. Much later than the usual time for awakening. Her thoughts as lethargic as her body, Katherine tried to summon up the alarm that would have her jumping out of bed and dressing for work. But the warm arm lying heavily across her stomach promoted memories of the past night, excusing oversleeping and prompting unruly urges to snuggle deeper into delicious inertia. Common sense and dreamy lethargy dueled. An unequal battle. One fought sensibly for leaving the bed, recounting the work waiting in the offices of Kendall Realty. The other whispered slyly, insidiously, *Just a few more minutes to relish the memories, just awhile longer to enjoy the warm feeling of pleasure those memories bring.*

Turning her head on the pillow, Katherine examined the sleeping man, sprawled on his stomach, at her side. The sinewed structure of his back rose and fell with the steady rhythm of his breathing; his fatigued body relaxed in slumber. His head was half buried under the pillow, his dark hair tousled and hiding his features. A small smile played with the corners of her mouth, and her fingers gently brushed the brown hair into order. With a soft, drowsy groan Matt shifted, bringing his face to her view. Her eyes brightened, lethargy receding, and she studied the sleeping face.

His features were deliciously haggard from a night that had extended into dawn, and with a ripple of renewed pleasure she heard again his words in the night; rasped urgently against her mouth: "The month was too long, Kat." His jaw was shadowed by an overnight growth of beard, the chin just as prominent in sleep as in wakefulness, she noted, and his eyes were wearily circled. Her heart thudded a quick rhythm, recalling the midnight vision of taut muscular strength above her, more words, low and breathed thickly over her face: "You, Katherine, are an addiction." His mouth was firm, even in sleep, but his forehead was smoothed of tension, and her smile tilted crazily, hearing his words at dawn, weary and satiated, whispered feelingly into her tangled hair: "Darlin', I'm bushed."

As she filled with delighted laughter, her eyes lifted to the ceiling. A small, satisfied sigh came whispering through smiling lips. Qualms or doubts about Matt's terms had been smothered at dawn, she thought whimsically.

His fingers played caressingly over her ribs, becoming a part of remembrance, and her flesh quivered. Her smile softening on another memory, her mind replayed other words, heady and sweet, issued with quickening need: "You feel right to my hands, Katherine. . . ."

"You're awake."

It sounded like an accusation, and she turned, her gaze colliding with his bleary green eyes, barely open, mildly censuring. A soft laugh bubbled helplessly from her throat.

"We both should be. We've overslept."

"Why don't you look like I feel?" he wanted to know, yawning hugely. Then his grin surfaced with crooked pleasure, his eyes becoming polished emeralds as they traced her soft, contented features.

"Must be because I have more stamina than you," she informed him smugly, knowing she was stretching the truth. She had been as exhausted as he, exquisitely so.

"Must be because I allowed you to nap on and off during the night," he corrected dryly, pulling her onto his shoulder. His mouth nuzzled the top of her head. "Any regrets, Katherine?"

She knew his reference was to their whole arrangement, not just the past night. Perhaps a little slow to come, her answer was a solemn "No regrets, Matt."

"And there won't be," he murmured, just as solemnly. *Not for the summer. But come fall and the end of our arrangement? What then, Matt? Will I still be able to say, "No regrets"? . . . Will you?* Aloud she said, "We're going to be late for work if we don't start moving."

He pushed her gently onto her back, his forearms jailing her shoulders, his fingers toying with her mussed honeyed tresses. "We could always play hooky."

Her fingers found an interesting swirl of dark hair on his chest, investigating it with teasing fascination. "We might get caught."

"You might," he corrected huskily, a muscled thigh moving between hers.

"Aren't you tired?" she breathed, liquefying beneath his weight.

"No."

His kiss was deep, his mouth twisting warmly over hers. His hands searched out her soft, aching breasts, his fingers creating exquisite new aches. Her hands sought the curve of his hips, her body making a sensual adjustment to accommodate his. Amazed at how quickly she could again

191

respond, she met him with an ease established during the night, answering his softly taunted "Show me your stamina, darlin'," with a confident smile.

Leisurely lovemaking whiled away another hour, and bathing and dressing were a hurried affair. Over a rushed breakfast of toast and coffee, consumed standing, Matt zipped the back of her dress and straightened the collar of its matching jacket. She thanked him with a soft glance over her shoulder, her mouth full of toast.

"Matt, would you mind if I had my calls forwarded to this number? Clients expect a number to call in the evenings, and Laurel and Timmy might need to get in touch with me."

After a moment he said slowly, "No problem."

His smile was a shade quizzical; the study of his gaze, a little unsettling. What was he thinking? Had she overstepped the bounds of their agreement by wanting to have personal and business calls forwarded to his house? She watched him swallow the last of his coffee, then place his plate and cup in the sink, his movements unhurried. With a last bite of toast she joined him at the sink, but before she could dispense with her dishes, he caught her by the shoulders, his eyes questioning.

"Why don't you move the cat over here? That would save your traipsing back and forth to see to her."

"All right." She smiled.

"And your clothing? Do you intend spending the rest of the summer living out of a suitcase?"

"I hadn't thought about it." *The rest of the summer.* Her smile wavered.

"Think about it."

Three evenings later Katherine entered Matt's house, her arms full of clothing, her gaze immediately spotting the suitcase by the door. Frowning, she walked to the den

192

and paused in the doorway. Matt was on the phone, making arrangements for a limousine service to the airport. Her stomach lurched with disappointment.

"Twenty minutes? Great!" His finger pressed the button to break the connection and immediately began stabbing out a new number. "Skip? Did you get the information we need?" As he listened to the answer from the other end of the line, he became aware of Katherine poised in the doorway, and his mouth curved into a wide smile. Smiling back, she moved into the room, laid her clothing over the back of a sofa, and correctly interpreted his gestures toward the bar across the room as a request for a drink.

Behind the bar Katherine fixed the whiskey and water she'd seen him drink the last few evenings, judging the proper mixture more by remembered color than actual know-how. Her nose wrinkled at the pungent aroma, and when she took it to him, her questioning gaze silently asked if its taste suited him. He swallowed deeply, nodding his head, then pulled her to his side, his mouth covering hers while a brisk male voice continued a spiel of words into the receiver at his ear. The warm flavor of whiskey was more pleasant than its aroma, she decided, savoring the taste, smiling when his mouth left hers.

"Yes, right. Our plane leaves in an hour. I'll meet you at DFW." He replaced the receiver, drinking deeply from his glass.

"Where are—"

"Paraguay. One last time. Skip Andrews, one of my engineers, is going with me and staying to see the thing completed."

"How long will—"

"Two days, three at the most." His fingers played lightly along her ribs. His eyes were watchful. "You received two calls about an hour ago. A harassed-sounding female

193

by the name of Gullidge and a guy named Hudson. Clients?"

Her eyes went a little wide on the latter name, but her response was composed. "Sara Gullidge is anxious to sell her house as soon as possible. Her husband was transferred out of state, and they've been living apart for several months."

"And Hudson?" His dark eyebrow lent a sardonic quality to his mild prompting.

"He's recently divorced and looking for a house that will satisfy the needs of his two young children and still allow him easy access to the downtown area." *And he's also bent on becoming reacquainted with me.* Despite her polite discouragement, Mike Hudson had contacted her several times since that first phone call back in May and had finally requested her help in finding a new house. He sounded lonely rather than aggressive, and although not interested in furthering a personal relationship with him, Katherine could relate to his loneliness. The loss of a mate, whether through death or divorce, was a difficult adjustment to make. But somehow, she couldn't explain the situation to Matt. She doubted he'd ever been lonely in his life. He would, no doubt, judge loneliness as a weakness.

Matt's quick grin didn't quite reach his eyes, making him seem tense. "Wanna tell them both to go to hell and come with me to Paraguay?"

Something in his voice told Katherine it wasn't just an idle suggestion, and although it was a heady temptation, she backed out of his embrace, smilingly shaking her head. "If you're leaving in twenty minutes, I'd better find Mari and move us out of here."

"Why?" he rapped quickly, a little tersely.

"Because if I left her untended for two or three days, you might not like your home when you returned." The

194

twitching of her nose said the tabby wasn't completely accustomed to Matt's house, despite the familiar litter box and cushioned basket that had moved with her from next door.

"I meant, why are you planning to leave at all? You live here now."

"Matt, that's foolish. While you're gone, I should—"

"Stay here," he finished for her concisely, his hand going to his dark suit pocket before grasping hers and folding her fingers gently around the brass house key he placed in her palm. Levelly he reminded her, "You agreed to live here, not to run back and forth to your house. I want you here, Katherine, when I get back."

A little puzzled, a little exasperated by his persistence, she nevertheless heard herself agreeing. "All right, Matt."

The first two evenings of Matt's absence Katherine spent in restless solitude, grateful for the company of a purringly attentive Marigold, watching reruns on television until late at night, listening for a phone that didn't ring. The third night she called Tim and Laurel, swallowing qualms about the size of her telephone bill during the summer months and smiling at her children's happy voices. It seemed Peter and Martha were spoiling them. Tim could talk of nothing but driving tractors, and Laurel was excited about attending a community dance. Martha's gentle voice was quick to say that they were enjoying the visit as much as or more than their grandchildren. Peter's smoke-rough voice extended the biannual invitation for Katherine to visit. The Fourth of July and Thanksgiving had been spent on the Meadowses' farm for more than fifteen years.

Hanging up with warm words and vague promises, Katherine broodingly wondered if Matt would object to her leaving for the Fourth. Would he miss her as much as

195

she was missing him? After only three nights together, there now had been as many apart, and he wasn't calling from Paraguay. Was he busy? Too busy to call? Did he think of her? Did he remember their nights and find it difficult to sleep?

Interrupting her musings was another call from Mike Hudson, confirming their appointment to view several residences Katherine thought might fit his needs. Once again he turned the conversation to a personal level. And once again she found excuses not to see him other than as a real estate agent. But she didn't come right out and tell him about Matt, and she despised the cowardice that kept her from being straightforward. *But how?* her mind shouted. *How do I announce I'm living with the man I love because he wants me . . . for the summer?*

It was past eleven o'clock the next night when Katherine inserted the new brass key on her key ring into the lock of Matt's front door. Under her arm was a slim leather briefcase, and inside it was a contract on the Gullidge residence. Sara Gullidge was thrilled to have sold her home and be able to join her husband, and the buyer was pleased with the spacious Gullidge house. Katherine was mildly elated at the success of another sale but very tired from the long hours she'd spent getting buyer and seller to agree. Deciding a warm bath would be providential to tense muscles, she headed toward the bedroom.

From the bedroom doorway her weary gaze immediately spotted the suitcase tossed onto the bed and just as immediately brightened. The sounds of running water from the open bathroom door greeted her ears with a welcome rush of pleasure. Her heart doing a funny little dance in her chest, she kicked out of her shoes and plopped down on the edge of the bed, expectantly waiting for the sounds of the shower to stop. She was no longer tired, only elated. Her sparkling eyes fastened on the bathroom doorway and were rewarded just minutes later by the sight of Matt striding into the bedroom, a towel draped around his lean hips, another being vigorously applied to his wet hair. His features were drawn by grim lines, but each was achingly, heart-wrenchingly dear.

When he spotted her, there was the briefest of moments when something curiously like relief crossed his features; but it passed quickly, and he rapped, "Where have you been?"

Used to his aggressive moods, Katherine smiled, asking, "How was your trip? When did you get home? Are you finished in Paraguay?"

He moved closer, the power in his half-naked body a bold intoxicant to her senses. Dropping the towel over his shoulders, he crouched down in front of her, his eyes shining. "The trip was long, and I hit DFW at six this evening. Do you know what time it is now?"

Leaning forward, she kissed his jaw, her fingertips outlining his eyes. "You look tired."

Firmly halting her caress was an ungentle hand. "Where the hell were you, Kat? I've waited for over five hours for you."

He was angry, she realized suddenly, not tired or mildly disgruntled. Very angry—his eyes accusing, his mouth tense. She tried to release her fingers from the punishing grip of his, but he tightened his grasp, gritting, "Where have you been at this time of night? Selling little houses?"

The condescension stung, more than the unwarranted anger or the obvious skepticism. Jerking her hand from his, she reached for the briefcase beside her, extracting the contract she'd worked so hard on, handing it to him as she stood.

"Selling *big* houses," she retorted crisply, turning for the bathroom.

Insensitive bully! Did he think she played around as a real estate agent for a hobby? Something to do instead of filing her nails or fluffing her hair? Anyway, who was he to question her? He didn't own her! He had no claim on her other than that of a temporary lover! He had been gone four days instead of the two or three he'd told her, and he hadn't bothered to allay her fears or nervousness with a phone call! What made him think she had to answer to him and report all her moves like a well-tutored mistress?

That last thought had her angrily stripping off her clothes. She practically vaulted into the shower, snapping the door shut with a little bang that threatened the stability of the glass panel. After jerkily lathering a washcloth, she rubbed it fiercely over her flesh. Under the heated spray of the showerhead, she cursed softly and explicitly, damning her vulnerability and his insensitivity, then gasped in surprise when the shower door opened to admit a large male body. Solemnly, his broad back taking the full force of the shower spray, Matt took the washcloth from her startled grasp, intent green eyes easily capturing her frosty gray gaze.

"You've already had a shower," she reminded him coolly, wishing the shower stall were larger, wishing Matt were smaller and less threatening to her peace of mind, wishing her anger sizable enough to combat her need of him.

"I know." A tiny movement at the corner of his mouth acknowledged her cold anger; smoky jade eyes probed its depth. "I was out of line, Katherine. I had no right to knock your job or your capabilities."

As an apology it was reasonably acceptable, but Katherine wasn't in a reasonable mood. Her eyes didn't melt, and her chin lifted with a hint of frigid haughtiness. "I agree."

Inexorably he crowded closer, backing her stiff body against the shower wall. The washcloth landed on the shower floor in a soggy heap, and his hands landed on her tense shoulders with firm purpose. His thumbs caressed droplets of water from her collarbones.

"I missed you, Kat. Don't close me out because of my lapse into stupidity."

Wide and defrosting against her will, her eyes watched the slow descent of his mouth. Her lips parted helplessly under the heated search of his, and she heard his low groan as he gathered her close against his length. With a tremble of awakening need her arms lifted to encircle his neck. His hand reached up to turn off the shower spray before he lifted her into his arms, his hungry mouth silencing any coherence as he carried her to the bed, neither of them caring that towels were left, unused, on the bathroom counter.

The next two weeks passed in a frenetic sunburst of shared passion, obscured only by Katherine's occasional doubts—doubts brought about only by Matt's odd moments of withdrawal. Despite that, Katherine fell more in love than ever and often found herself biting back the words, unwilling to subject herself to Matt's taunting ridicule of love. His feelings for her were still expressed by words of want and desire, and if she despaired of ever hearing a word of love or commitment pass his lips, she thrilled to his physical need of her that showed elements of the caring she craved.

One thing she had no complaints about. Matt was very attentive. Sometimes belligerently so—demanding to know her daily schedule and often unexpectedly showing up at Kendall Realty to take her to lunch or to bring her home. She accepted Charlie's knowing looks and comments without embarrassment.

"That man is crazy about you," Charlie commented one afternoon after Matt had deposited Katherine at her office following an extended lunch hour.

Katherine's answering smile was a little subdued. She was remembering the lunch hour. It had started at a near-by restaurant and ended at home. "I need to run by the house to collect something I forgot this morning," he'd told her, a funny catch in his voice, his eyes trained to the rearview mirror as he backed out of the restaurant parking lot. But once inside the house he'd stalked Katherine relentlessly into the den.

His wicked grin had been for the wary features watching him discard his jacket and strip off his tie. Startled but aware of his intent, she'd protested disjointedly, "Matt, you're not . . . we can't . . . I'll miss my one thirty appointment."

He'd taunted softly, "Not if you don't waste time fighting against this, darlin'," drawing her down onto the soft velvet sofa cushions. His hands quickly dispensed with buttons, his grin widening when her protesting hands, tired of counteracting his movements, had helped him with his task instead. He grinned tormentingly, watching her hands trace erotic lines on his chest, and whispered at her mouth, "This is what I forgot to collect this morning."

But moments later his grin had been an ardent smile as his mouth left hers on a fiery search for additional territory to conquer. His laughter had been a soft groan when she issued a surrendering sigh as his lips explored the satin of her stomach, his amusement lost in his need to taste and overwhelm the last summit of all her sensations.

And into the teasing, flurry-of-dressing aftermath a measure of discontent had unexpectedly surfaced. As Matt helped her back into her clothes, the phone had shrilled an unwelcome intrusion. While he fastened the

200

last of her buttons, she'd answered the phone, lamely offering her one thirty appointment, Mike Hudson, a faltering excuse for being late to pick him up at his office. As if the call of business were a crucially sobering one, Matt had become withdrawn, breaking the silence on the drive back to Katherine's office with one unsettling warning. "That call forwarding service is your own personal hot line, Kat. Watch it doesn't burn you," he'd told her. And before she left the pickup, he'd leaned across to bestow a devastating kiss on her mouth, somehow punishing in intensity.

Charlie's questioning voice brought Katherine back to the present. She blinked, and Charlie repeated the question: "Are you going to marry him?"

Her eyes clouded, and Katherine answered soberly, "He hasn't asked me."

"He will. Love has a way of leading to marriage."

"Matt doesn't love me, Charlie."

"He can't leave you alone!" Charlie laughed throatily. "In my book, that's love."

"You've forgotten the common garden variety of attention known as desire," Katherine mocked softly, but inside she was unwillingly remembering: *Your expectations are too high. . . . Affairs don't have to be labeled romance or prefaced with love in order to be fulfilling.* And recalling, too, that not once had Matt ever denied wanting anything but a temporary affair. And wishing she understood the contradiction between making love with gentle, hungering passion and almost immediately withdrawing into a shell of brooding discontent. *"Watch it doesn't burn you."* What had that unsettling comment meant? He had insisted she move in with him yet seemed to resent the permanent implications of her phone calls' being received at his house.

"But you love him," Charlie was saying.

"Yes."

"Then fight for what you want, Katherine. Nothing worthwhile was ever won without a struggle."

A brief, lopsided grin touched Katherine's mouth. "You, Charlotte Kendall, are a wise lady—optimistic, but wise. I'm fighting—sometimes a battle I don't understand —but I'm fighting."

CHAPTER TEN

The phone rang just as Katherine entered the bedroom from the bathroom doorway, a velvety peach towel wrapped precariously around her damp, glistening body. Securing the towel with a deft fold across her breasts, she hurried to the bedside telephone and grabbed up the receiver on the second ring. It was Charlie.

"Katherine, I hate to bother you at home, but I can't find the survey on the Warren Street property. You don't, by any chance, have it in your possession, do you?"

"I don't think so, Charlie, but if I do, it's in my briefcase along with the Lockwood estate survey. They both arrived in today's mail. Hold on a second, and let me check."

Having dropped the receiver onto the bed, she padded out of the bedroom. Her steps slowed to a stealthy tiptoe as she entered the den, her fingers pushing straying pins back into the loose upsweep of her hair. Matt was where he'd been two hours earlier, seated on the sofa, his shirt sleeves rolled up to mid-forearm, a scatter of blueprints and cost lists laid out in front of him on the coffee table. At the forefront of Katherine's mind was the brusque explanation that the plans for a bridge construction in an East Texas community had to be readied by the first of the week. Standing a few feet behind him, watching the hunching of one broad shoulder as he scribbled a notation, she bit her bottom lip, also remembering his gruff request not to be disturbed.

As quiet as a mouse, she neared the far end of the sofa, spying the soft tan leather of her briefcase reposing against the velvet cushions. She perched quietly beside it, careful not to break Matt's absorbed concentration. Wriggling only slightly, she adjusted the towel over the upper part of her thighs and folded long, gleaming legs at the ankles.

The soft snap of a pencil lead committing suicide on paper came right before the impatient click, click, click as more lead was advanced into the point of an automatic pencil. Calmly, her back to Matt, Katherine ignored the small warning and lifted the briefcase onto her lap, opening the zip with nothing more than the sibilant whisper of metal sliding against metal. With nothing less than loud exaggeration, paper rustled behind her. Nibbling her lip, she withdrew a sheaf of documents onto her lap and then blinked in surprise when a wadded paper missile flew over her head and crashed against the far wall. Whisper-soft and unobtrusive, her thumb searched through the papers and then abruptly stilled, an irritated drumming on the coffee table reminding her that any noise, however infinitesimal, was being duly registered and was unappreciated. When she found the Warren Street survey paper-clipped to the one on the Lockwood estate, her sigh was softly victorious and was echoed at her back in a long, drawn-out expulsion of barely controlled patience.

The back of her neck and bare shoulders prickled with the awareness of an exasperated gaze, and Katherine deftly—and wisely—slipped the papers back inside her briefcase and zipped it noiselessly shut. As she edged off the sofa, Charlie's survey dangling from her fingertips, she heard a loud, disgusted snort. Then her wrist was snagged, and she was hauled downward, unceremoniously dragged across Matt's lap.

"What are you doing, Kat? Trying my control?" The words were heavy with accusation, and his expression positively reeked of long-suffering patience.

She looked up into irritated eyes, her own a little annoyed. She'd made hardly any sound at all and had been attempting to leave when he grabbed her. "Trying to be stealthy—apparently without success."

"Next time you try stealthiness, do it when you're not gleaming with scented bath oil," he advised grimly. His narrowed perusal swept her length, and he added tautly, "That towel is a loud garment."

Her eyes glanced down at the garment in question, noting its velvety smooth texture, and then lifted defensively to meet his look of annoyance. "Actually this towel doesn't even whisper. Velour makes not the teeniest sound."

Something warm and brilliant flared to life behind his impatient gaze, but his deep voice remained terse, a little rough. "Maybe it was a visual loudness."

"Muted peach is almost invisible," she pointed out with a superior smirk, curtailing an urge to wrap her arms around his taut, unyielding waist and snuggle into his broad, inflexible chest.

"Not when barely covering light honey tan," he corrected, his tone clipped. His finger traced the line where honey tan left off and muted peach began. Steely watchfulness, then obscure withdrawal, entered his eyes. "Who was on the phone?"

"Charlie *is* on the phone, so if you'll let me up, I'll get back to her, thereby taking my offensive garment out of your annoyed presence."

His dark brow lifted sardonically. "Disruptive, Kat. Evocative, teasing, disturbing—all things to break my concentration and destroy my peace of mind, but not

205

offensive." Then, on a jeering note that said his annoyance hadn't lessened, he said tauntingly, "Feeling neglected?"

If her arms hadn't been caught between them, she probably would have smacked him. "Absolutely. I crave constant male attention, especially the irascible variety. Nothing turns me into a panting bundle of anticipation quicker than the exciting possibility of commanding the full attention of an irritable, cantankerous, ill-humored male." Her smile was sweetly supercilious, but when she saw retaliation coming in the form of his descending mouth, she quickly slithered off his lap, soft velour-toweled and gleaming honey tan legs moving with soundless dexterity. Standing above him, she announced blithely, "Get back to your work, oh, greatly impatient one. The loud towel and I are off."

"Something will be off if you stand there, daring me much longer," Matt told her evenly. His eyes said it wasn't an idle threat, by burning a path to the folded velour across her breasts and then gleaming a reluctant appreciation of her siren smile tossed over one honey tan shoulder as both "loud" towel and wearer disappeared through the doorway.

In the bedroom Katherine assured Charlie that the needed survey was in her possession. "Do you need it right away?"

"No, Monday morning will be fine. That's the closing date on that property. Though, before I hang up, I've got a message to relay."

"Oh? What's that?"

"Mike Hudson phoned after you left this evening. He wants you to call him tonight. Claimed it concerned the appointment you have tomorrow morning to view that house on Oaklawn Drive." Charlie's tone was definitely tongue in cheek.

"Did he leave a number to call?"

Charlie relayed the number, advising, "Do what you want to do about this, Katherine. Normally all clients are welcome at Kendall Realty, but I've got the feeling Mr. Hudson's more interested in you than he is in acquiring a new house."

"You could be right, Charlie, but I'll give him another chance. Maybe Mike is sincere in—"

"Wanting nothing but your professional services?" A soft laugh said Charlie doubted the possibility, and Katherine smiled ruefully, doubting it as well. "Does Matt know there's another male on the make?"

"There's nothing Matt need know, Charlie. This doesn't concern him."

"Okay, my naïve friend, play it your way."

"Thanks, Charlie," Katherine responded dryly, replacing the receiver in the cradle.

Frowning pensively, she sat on the edge of the bed, her back to the door, hesitant to call Mike. *Was* she being naïve? She wanted to believe he wasn't just on the make. She also wanted to believe she was intelligent enough to know the difference. Mixed with her mild dismay that he was trying to promote a personal relationship was the warm rush of sympathy for the loneliness she could sense in him. His divorce was a very recent thing, and he hadn't made the adjustment. Reluctantly she picked up the receiver.

Mike answered her call on the third ring, sounding warmly delighted to hear from her. "I would have called your home, but that guy who answers your phone sometimes sounds a little grim. Is he a friend of yours?"

Katherine's first reaction was surprise. Matt had never relayed messages from Mike after that first time. Her answer was vague. "Yes, Matt's a friend." Then, in a rush to get off a personal subject: "Is there some problem about tomorrow, Mike?"

"I'm afraid so. Something's come up at work, and I'll be in meetings all day tomorrow."

"Perhaps we can make it some night next week," she offered carefully, hoping the owners of the large residence on Oaklawn Drive would be agreeable to a new time.

"That would be great. Why don't we have dinner after seeing the house? I know an excellent restaurant not far from that neighborhood."

"Mike, I'm not sure," she said uncertainly, hesitant to repulse a dinner meeting rudely. It wasn't unusual to take prospective buyers out to eat, but with Mike, she feared a meal would insinuate more than a business interest on her part. "Look, why don't I call you sometime day after tomorrow? We'll see what we can arrange."

"All right, Katherine," he answered after a moment. Then, with bold probing: "Is Matt more than a friend?"

Unnerved by his persistance, she replied vaguely, "No, he's just my neighbor." Katherine felt uncomfortable at her less than truthful answer.

Mike's laugh was rueful. "You could tell me it's none of my business, Katherine, and you'd be right."

Her soft laugh agreed with him, but she responded diplomatically, "I wouldn't do that, Mike."

"Because I'm a valued client or because I'm a friend?" he said, flirting lazily.

"Well, you're both." There was a smile in her voice. It was difficult not to respond to harmless flirting. But deciding the conversation had digressed too far from business, she brought it quickly to a close, saying firmly, "Look, Mike, it's late. I'll give you a call Sunday."

As she hung up, she once again silently cursed her evasiveness. Why didn't she just come right out and explain about Matt? That was probably the simplest way of diverting Mike's interest, and it could be done without divulging all the details of her love life. Yet each time she had an opportunity to speak up, an inner reticence to lay open her private life to public speculation prevented her from doing so. Not even Charlie, who was a dear friend and whom she trusted completely, realized she was living in Matt's house. Thanks to her call forwarding service, calls placed to the Meadows phone now rang through to Matt's number, and nobody knew the difference.

Besides, she thought with dogged honesty, she wasn't altogether sure what title to give her relationship with Matt. Close friends? Lovers? Partners in an intimate liaison? Sexually compatible adults? . . . Emotionally involved man and woman headed for a permanent relationship?

On a wistful sigh, she stopped the direction of her thoughts. Either Matt would love her or not, and the end of the summer would tell. After rising from the bed, she padded into the bathroom to brush her teeth and comb out her hair. Then, back inside the bedroom, she turned back the covers of the bed, wondering how much longer Matt would work. She hoped not long. In less than three weeks she had acquired a need to sleep against his hard male length.

Snuggling inside the cool percale sheets, she yawned tiredly, drowsily seeking Matt's side of the bed, her movements reminding her that she still wore the "loud" towel. She started to remove it, then grinned sleepily, thoughts of other hands removing it sending her off into dreamland. . . .

A loud, thudding noise startled Katherine out of sleep, and she sat up, blinking against the lamplight, finding herself no longer alone. Matt was in the room, tossing a shoe toward the closet—much as a basketball player tosses a long shot toward the basket—grinning wide satisfaction when it struck the wall of the closet and bounded into place on the floor. Then he stripped off his shirt, wadded it into a tight ball, and aimed it in the same direction.

Lighter in weight, it missed the target by at least four feet, and he cursed softly, socks and belt going the way of the shirt, helter-skelter toward a target that defeated his aim.

Sleepily Katherine remonstrated with him. "Matt, you've made an unnecessary mess."

Mockingly he turned to her, bowing from the waist, saying tauntingly, "But it's my bedroom, Kat, my game, and I make all the rules." His finger pointed first to his broad chest and then to the trail of his clothes. "I like it that way. My way. If you want to play, you'll have to remember that."

His tormenting gaze stayed fixed on her bewildered face while he stepped out of his suit pants and deliberately kicked them toward the center of the floor. He nodded with a grim sort of pleasure as they landed haphazardly, the keys in the pocket clinking a soft, muffled protest.

Silent and slightly confused, Katherine watched him stride loosely to the bed. With a strange deliberation he fell onto his back beside her, his hands folded under his head. Around the mockery of his glance, he looked tired, his face taut and lined, and Katherine leaned over him, intending to bestow a commiserating kiss. But the whiskey on his breath was strong, and she drew back, more surprised than disturbed.

Quietly she said, "You've been drinking."

"Not a lot. Just enough to smooth the rough edges, so don't scold, Katherine. I don't need a mother." There was a harsh, jeering quality to his voice that suggested not all rough edges had been smoothed, and his eyes collided directly with hers, bright but not with amusement.

Thinking him overworked and perhaps frustrated because the work hadn't gone well, she once again bent toward him, whispering, "I fell asleep waiting for you." Her soft, inviting kiss was met by unresponsive lips, and again she moved back, eyeing him with concern. "What's wrong?"

And his horrible grin surfaced, mocking green eyes sweeping her towel-draped length with slow insolence. "I must have a headache."

"Do you need some aspirin?" Confusion shone from her eyes, and then a wariness that had her edging farther away.

"No, Kat," he answered, and there was deadly coldness in his flat voice and an icy brilliance in his gaze. After a slight pause he said tonelessly, "No, I don't need anything."

Wariness became dismayed comprehension, and she gasped, pulling to a kneeling position beside him. He was saying he didn't need her, and he was saying it with cold deliberation. The times she had been subjected to his taunts—both gentle and aggressive—were countless. But this was different. This was a dark side of Matt she didn't understand. He was aiming to wound.

Her voice shaky with the effort, she managed to ask, "Is this a permanent condition?"

"Funny you should ask that." He grinned again, then confided with lazy insolence, "I've been deliberating on that very thing for the past hour or so. A greedy man would see the summer through. A wise man would know when to cut his losses. It's kind of a toss-up. I'm a wise, greedy man."

"You're serious, aren't you?" Her heart was hammering the strangest pattern, seemingly trying to leave her body through her throat.

"Yes. Honestly serious but honestly undecided." The edge in his voice underlined his choice of words. "You can appreciate honesty, can't you, Katherine? As I remember it, an honest relationship was one of your prerequisites."

Katherine felt the blood slowly drain from her face.

211

Matt was mockingly voicing the desire that he wanted out of their arrangement, and all she could think was: *Less than three weeks! How extraordinary! Three months now sounds like forever!* Shivering under the cold surveillance of those clear green eyes, she drew a deep breath, made her voice calm, with no sign of the pain she felt. "In all this honesty, have you come up with an honest reason?"

"Just *one*?" he said tauntingly, heavily stressing the singular.

Her eyes closed, and she wondered why she wasn't breaking apart. Surely a thousand different pieces of herself should be shattering all across the bed. Inside she felt oddly disjointed, her heart, her mind, her soul separating into different entities, each screaming a violent protest that she neither voiced nor showed. Her fingers clenched and unclenched across the tops of her thighs, and when she felt him take one of her hands in his, she couldn't find the strength to pull it away. She slowly opened her eyes and stared at him, wondering if her heart had ruled not only her head but her eyesight as well. How could she ever have imagined hints of caring and warmth in those cold, remorseless eyes?

Matt shrugged almost imperceptibly, his voice an arid whisper. "I decided to knock off work shortly after you came to the den. I heard you talking on the phone. I heard you say among other things I was just a neighbor."

Her body absolutely unmoving, his words beat against her, seeking entrance into her conscious mind, and when they found it, a measure of comprehension swept through her. Her rigid shoulders sloped downward in the aftermath of relief. She found her voice, dry and thready. "I can explain, Matt."

"I'm sure you can, Kat. Business, right? And you want to keep me under wraps?" The undercurrent of laughter in his voice was a dark tide of contempt, and even knowing herself innocent of his veiled charges, she felt herself shudder under its force. Matt saw the quiver that ran along her body and smiled, asking with deceptive mildness, "Is Mike a friend, too?"

Momentarily misunderstanding the innuendo of his last question, she answered honestly, but her voice was croaky with desperation. "A casual friend, yes, but it is business that—"

"Ahhh, very good, darlin'," he interrupted with heavy insinuation. "Hudson's called here four times this week because of business. Isn't it odd that he never states that business and that you agreed to see him without telling me?"

She flinched, as much from the damning skepticism in his voice as from the hand circling her wrist, his finger pressing punishingly into her erratically pulsing vein.

"Matt, you don't understand. I was going to tell you. Mike's going through a difficult time, and I haven't wanted to—"

"Completely lose another friend?" he interrupted tauntingly with an underlining note of savage sarcasm. "And you didn't want to tell him about me." He laughed without humor, deep in his throat.

"I don't believe in telling clients my personal business."

"Do you really expect me to believe that?"

"Were you taught to trust?" she cried, hurt that he could condemn her so easily. She tried to free herself of his grip on her wrist, wanting to get away from him, knowing he was beyond listening to any explanations she had to offer. For some reason Matt didn't want to believe her innocent of faithlessness.

His grip on her wrist firmed. His voice deepened, became thick. "You're not leaving without a proper farewell, Kat, so don't try."

It hurt to jerk her wrist free of his grasp, but she

213

managed it, twisting for the far side of the bed. Only he laughed again, dangerously, and lunged after her. Slowly, with inescapable force, he dragged her beneath him. Writhing, her breath coming in harsh gasps that hurt her lungs, she fought him as he grabbed the edge of the towel and stripped it from her.

"Matt, no!" she whispered, horrified by the dark desire she could feel in him, the need to control her with physical passion.

He took no notice. His hand tangling in her hair, he tipped her head back so he could watch her, the other moving sensually over her breasts. Torn by humiliation, she felt her body's response to the light touch even as she stared in foreboding at the icy threat in his eyes.

"Matt, don't do this," she implored raggedly. "Don't . . . not like this."

He laughed again, softly, a finger trailing from her throat to her breast and then down to her stomach. "But you want me to do this, Katherine," he pointed out when her flesh quivered in unwilling response.

"You don't want me! You have a headache!" she whispered frantically, and watched an odd grin touch his mouth.

Then his mouth captured hers, surprisingly gentle, plundering, effectively stilling any reprisal she might have considered. Low and thick against her throat, he murmured, "My headache's gone, darlin'. This way we've always been good together. This way might make the summer worthwhile. This way I trust you completely."

Sheer shock kept Katherine still. She should have known Matt wouldn't follow any predictable patterns to assuage his anger, and the subtle persuasion of his teeth against her flesh told her that her body would betray both her outraged emotions and her tumultuous mind. His punishment for her imagined sins would come in the form of her inability to bank the responses of her body. Three weeks had given him the knowledge of exactly how to master her resistance.

And hating him, loving him, despising herself, despairing of herself, Katherine felt her arms go around his waist to draw him nearer. . . .

When Katherine awakened, it was to a bright spill of daylight infiltrating the bedroom through a partially drawn drape. She was alone in the bed. Her head ached, her throat was touched with raspiness, and she gazed about the room with heavy-lidded eyes. The floor was free of the clutter of Matt's clothing from the night before. Other than the tangle of the bed sheets and the maze of her memories, there was nothing to suggest what had transpired during the night. The bedroom door was open, but there was not sight or sound of Matt.

Having pushed herself out of bed, she headed for the adjoining bathroom, where she locked the door quietly behind her. Her reflection in the oval gilt-edged mirror over one of the twin sinks wasn't a revelation. It represented how she felt. Her complexion was pallid, the honey tan washed away by a long tormenting night. Golden amber hair was a mass of disorder, accomplished first by long, impatient fingers threading through its length to secure a hold on her twisting head and then, later, by those same fingers carefully lifting its weighty mass away from her face to reveal her humiliated features. Her lips were swollen, and she touched them tenderly with the tip of her tongue, the action prompting the memory of other lips, hard and demanding, then coaxing and tormenting, forcing unwilling responses from her flesh. Her eyes, dark-rimmed and sunken, mirrored the turmoil of her thoughts. Matt hadn't made love to her with the vibrant warmth she had come to expect from him. He had skillfully controlled her. He had consummately spun her into a world of the senses while keeping himself coldly, emotionally aloof. . . .

After the first long, drugging kisses Matt's mouth played with hers, tormenting her, his tongue alternately piercing and teasing, his fingers threaded through her hair to control the frenzied movements of her head. His hands expertly moved over her, drawing her to the edge of sensual tolerance, bringing her body to arching eagerness against his. Unable to withstand the cold satisfaction her quivering response brought to his frozen green gaze, she closed her eyes, softly moaning her compliance and despair.

Cool and condemning, his whisper breathed against her closed eyelids. "Do you feel less involved with those treacherous eyes shut, Kat?"

Both her eyes and her mouth flew open to refute the charge, and immediately his lips bruised hers, smothering words and denials. So, silently, she fought against his dominance, twisting desperately in his arms; but the skill of his fingers soon brought her breasts to taut, aching need, then played along her thighs so that her whole body shook with a growing intensity, her flesh screaming for his possession, and she surged against him, breathless and no longer struggling. With slow deliberation, using all the expertise he possessed, Matt continued to stroke her body, playing her senses to a wild tempo of sensuality.

Against her throat he murmured derisively, "That's right, darlin', show me your capacity for friendship. Demonstrate your neighborly generosity."

The hard, sardonic taunting chilled her, and she voiced a croaky plea. "Matt, please, you misunderstood. I—"

His mouth closed over hers in a slow, arousing kiss, hushing the weak protest. He laughed softly at the corner of her mouth. "No, Katherine, you misunderstood. You thought your summer commitment wasn't a binding one. Even now you think I'll listen to lies and excuses."

"I'm not lying!" she cried feebly.

"Your body's not lying," he acknowledged, smiling when one nipple surged into the palm of his hand.

All her senses danced to the arousing tune of revenge he played on her flesh, and Katherine met his descending mouth with feverish need. Velvet-rough, his tongue licked the outline of her mouth, then trailed fire to her ear. Insidiously disquieting, his words followed its path. "Don't deny your enjoyment of this, my devious darlin', and I won't deny mine." The cold mockery of his voice left her in no doubt that Matt's enjoyment came from his total mastery of her, not from any warm emotional need.

And even as he came over her, offering physical assuagement for the torrent of passion he had created with his clever, capable hands, he continued to torment her. When she would have merged with his body, he held her flat to the mattress, laughing soft triumph when she writhed against his controlling, torturous restriction.

"What do you want of me, Matt?" she cried out, going still under the cold clarity of his wounding gaze.

Right before he took her into the final realms of sensual ecstasy, he answered, using words that racked her heart. "Nothing but tonight, Katherine. Don't worry. Tonight you're all mine, and as long as we both know that, it will be enough." And with mind-shattering slowness, his eyes never leaving her face, he eased himself down onto her body. . . .

Examining her shattered image in the bathroom mirror, Katherine inwardly contemplated her fragmented soul. In a dry whisper she repeated Matt's words from the night before. "Don't worry."

Oh, God! She had been his, all right, down to her very heartbeat, and he had known it, coldly reveling in the fact.

Even while her tortured soul had reached its nadir, her body had joined Matt's in willing consummation, frenetically moving to the cadence of desire he set. And no matter how she tried, she hadn't been able to close her ears to the low, mocking laugh that acknowledged her frenzied need.

In groaning self-despair Katherine turned away from the mirror. Her image was too vivid a reminder of her humiliation.

An hour later her appearance had undergone a skillful change. Dressed in slim white pants and an emerald silk blouse, blousoned and tied with a drawstring waist, she looked crisp and fresh. Once again her feet were bare, the search for casual shoes given up when she remembered her canvas pumps were next door in her own house. Her face was carefully made up to camouflage the lingering traces of tension, and her freshly washed and dried hair was brushed away from her face and held back by tortoiseshell combs, the style accenting the smooth line of her cheek and jaw. Only the sober, winter-storm gray of her eyes detracted from the springlike veneer of her appearance.

And those cold eyes reflected a decision made through a long night of taunts and physical demands and the humiliating destruction of her pride. Not once but over and over, Matt had taken her to the edge of desire and beyond, and although she had repeatedly tried to explain, he had never listened. He had been too intent on letting her know that their mutual desire was the only thing they shared, and she had finally given up, no longer voicing explanations, no longer holding on to hopes born during their weeks together.

A glance out the bedroom window told Katherine it was midday. The June sun was high in the sky, its warmth penetrating the glass and the patch of sunlit carpet her bare feet curled into.

Leaving the bedroom, she went in search of Matt. The honesty Matt didn't believe her capable of demanded that she tell him to his face that she was leaving, urging her to a quick scan of each room, only to be frustrated at every door. Matt was gone. There was nothing to explain his disappearance. The den gave the only clue that he had been in the house at all. On the coffee table next to the blueprints and cost lists from the night before was a coffee mug, and the morning-edition newspaper was strewn across the sofa and onto the floor.

His disappearance was too much for Katherine. The indignity of her position and a growing memory of how explicitly Matt had shown his lack of trust and caring combined to shadow out the lingering need to face him squarely and announce her departure. She became angry —gloriously, ramrod-stiff, and sparkling-gray-eyes angry. Meekly waiting around was not her forte, nor was the solving of mysteries. She would leave immediately. If Matt wanted to find her, he could easily do so. If he didn't, then he deserved no consideration, no explanations.

Back in the bedroom she made the bed and removed the traces of her occupancy from the bedroom and bathroom. She threw shoes and as many of her clothes as would fit inside her suitcase, removed her key ring from her purse before throwing the bag inside the case as well, and then locked the leather piece with an irritable flick of her fingers. After carrying the one piece of luggage to the front entrance, she sat it to the side before jerkily opening the door, a fiery flush of growing temper spread high across her cheeks.

The unexpected sight of two men on the doorstep shocked her speechless. Grinning with varying degrees of surprise and speculation, Rob Thompson and John Rogers unconsciously blocked her path from the house.

"Hi!" John spoke good-naturedly, his generous mouth

219

splitting widely across his plump face, interpreting Katherine's startled expression as one of surprise over their sudden appearance. "We didn't call first, but another sick car needs Matt's attention."

"Hello, Katherine." Rob greeted her with a bright, warm smile, his mellow voice curious, one red eyebrow raised in questioning. "Are we to be allowed in?"

Katherine was more than flustered. She was trapped. Just to storm past them, suitcase in hand, would be the fastest route to total humiliation she could find, but inviting them in might mean a slow, torturous road to that same place. Either way the men were going to know her position in Matt's life. Not really deciding on either path, she heard herself lamely stammer a welcome. "Yes . . . yes, of course, come in."

The two men stepped over the threshold, their gazes centered brightly on her, and Katherine told herself she was relieved. At least they hadn't noticed the suitcase by the door.

"Where's Matt?" John asked boisterously. "Lazing about on a sunny Saturday?"

"I don't know. I mean, I'm not sure exactly. He's . . . he's around somewhere," she told them haltingly. She was so concerned with thinking of ways to divert them out of the foyer that she couldn't concentrate on a proper excuse for Matt's absence.

"Were you going somewhere?" Rob asked, his glance inquisitive.

For a moment Katherine thought he was referring to the suitcase, and she paled. Then she realized he had noticed the key ring held tightly in her fingers, and she laughed shakily, saying, "Yes. I have to run an errand. Why don't the two of you go on into the den? I'm sure Matt will show up shortly."

"You're not letting that old pal of ours run you off, are

220

you, Katherine?" John asked jokingly. "We don't blame you for running, though, do we, Rob? That devil's disposition of Matt's has lost him a lot of friends."

Katherine winced at his unfortunate choice of words, vividly remembering the devil's disposition. Cold, laughing, tormenting. Neither man noticed her reaction, however, because the devil himself offered diversion at that moment.

"Rob? John? What brings you two over?"

Matt had approached on silent feet, but his voice spun Katherine quickly around, her face white, her gray eyes wide with shock. Where had he come from? She had searched the house from back to front only minutes before. His casual attire of tan twilled chino slacks and navy ribbed cotton pullover accented his long legs and massive chest, visually reminding her of his strength and of his power over her. She gulped back awareness and gazed at his face.

Matt was grimly taking in her appearance: the strained face drawn into lines of wariness; the fresh grooming; the bare feet; the keys clinking from the movement of her trembling fingers. A faint smile curled the hard line of his mouth. His narrowed gaze wandered slowly back to her face, his darkly green eyes filled with what the two onlookers obviously interpreted as possessive desire for a woman. Katherine's side vision caught the nudging elbows that quickly passed between Rob and John, while she accurately read the curl of Matt's lips as the suppressed anger it was, not the quirk of affectionate amusement it appeared from a farther distance. Alarm tripped up her spine in a fine tremor, but her eyes never dropped from his, outwardly showing none of the intimidation or tension she felt.

"We're here to demand a drink and some lunch, ol' buddy," Rob informed Matt with a rich chuckle, effectively bringing two locked and warring gazes back to the unexpected guests.

"And to get you under the hood of Maggie's Audi Quattro," John inserted, laughing heartily at Matt's accusing expression, thinking it was meant for himself and Rob. "It's a tradition, Katherine. Rob and I periodically bring something for Matt to play with. We were around in the days when Corvettes meant a lot to him, and we do our best to remind him what he's missing with those pickups he insists on driving."

Katherine had to smile. The two men were extremely likable, especially in their present mood of lighthearted raillery. Her quick look found the beginnings of a reluctant smile tugging at Matt's mouth as well.

"I'm a practical man," he told his friends, the lift of one dark eyebrow making it a challenging statement.

"But you've still got an eye for beauty, so don't try fooling us. We all know you're a closet sports car freak," Rob told him, grinning, and then added an ill-timed reminder: "If Katherine weren't leaving, she might learn your true personality."

With the reminder his eyes swept to her face, reading the defiant flush accurately before lowering to the keys in her hand. Coming back to her face, those eyes blazed angrily, until the open challenge of her features prompted a smile. His expression clearly mocked her foiled attempt to leave and at the same time, reminiscent of the night before, condemned her out of hand, while to Rob and John it merely looked lightly amused. What a masterpiece of acting, Katherine thought with grim humor, deciding silence needed to be replaced by firm action.

"Rob, John, I hope your sick car gets well," she managed to say pleasantly. Then a furtive glance told her a big body was edging closer, and she spoke in a flustered

222

rush. "My errand . . . I need to leave . . . come for coffee sometime. . . ."

She quickly turned toward the door, only to have long tanned fingers deftly pluck away the keys dangling loosely from her hand. Two dark brown loafers, size eleven and a half, planted themselves firmly in the path of her two slim bare feet. And with a sinking heart she watched the slow deliberation of his movement to pocket her keys.

"Give them back," she whispered.

But Matt shook his head in slow denial, his chin thrust forward at a belligerent angle. "No need, Katherine. I'll run the errand for you later. Right now"—he wrapped an arm about her waist, forcing her to his side—"I need your help in feeding these two idiots who claim to be friends."

As he turned from the open door, his gaze spotted the suitcase, and his fingers dug punishingly into her ribs. Their eyes met, and had gray ones not been frozen with winter sleet, green ones would have sizzled them with lightning-hot flashes of rage. As it was, sparks from that emerald fury fell burningly across her upturned features, and she flinched, not once but twice, feeling each accusation as if it had been burned into her flesh. It all happened in the space of seconds, but Katherine felt burned to ashes when Matt turned back to his friends.

His grin at Rob and John was teasing, and only Katherine felt the angry tension in his body. "All right, buddies, lunch first and then Maggie's Quattro."

Then he did something that to Katherine was positively unforgivable. As he nudged the opened door shut with his foot he also managed to give her suitcase a healthy shove that sent it spinning toward the foyer wall. Four pairs of eyes watched in varying degrees of interest as it teetered uncertainly and then thudded to a halt.

Facing Rob and John took courage. Acknowledging their awareness of what that suitcase meant took grit. A hard-won pride, battered and bruised though it was, gave her both, and she planted a strained smile on her face, saying with a casualness she was far from feeling, "I guess I've been elected as chef's helper."

The next few hours were spent entertaining Rob and John or, rather, being entertained by them, the two men full of humor and an easy camaraderie and a mystifying determination to ally themselves with Katherine. Over and over during the remainder of their stay they adroitly and unobtrusively gave her their attention and thereby a strange sort of mental support. She responded gratefully, glad for any excuse to be out from under Matt's watchful surveillance.

By early evening the wish for her keys was fiercely potent. Her smile was threatening to slip, and Matt's increasingly hard glances told her their delayed confrontation was yet to come. Why had she foolishly locked everything inside her suitcase? Access to her luggage, her house, her car—all were in Matt's pocket.

Amid boisterous jokes about leaving early so they wouldn't overstay their welcome, Rob and John finally took their leave at nine o'clock that evening. Matt and Katherine bade them smiling good-byes at the door, lingering in its lighted arch until Maggie's Audi, recently and expertly tuned by Matt, zoomed off into the night.

And then, as if that were an unspoken signal, the smiles faded from their faces, and Katherine twisted away from the possessive weight of his arm, hearing him close the door on a faint click of finality that echoed in her head and heart and spirit. Matt leaned back against the closed portal, released a heavy sigh, and fixed her with a stare that said the anger simmering under the surface of his control for the last few hours was about to erupt. His features set, his big body negligent but alert, he was like a lazy, menacing warrior, at ease for the moment but prepared to strike when necessary. And so damned dear to her in spite of all that had transpired between them. She wanted to raise a white flag and throw herself in his arms, beg him to let her explain, plead with him to say he regretted not trusting her.

"I'd like my keys now" was what she said, her voice cool and crisp, her chin tilted at a haughtily challenging angle.

"No!" was what he retorted, his voice equally crisp but not as cool, the jut of his chin reminding her that aggression was his byword.

No other word was spoken, each combatant silently taking the measure of the other, until Matt abruptly moved away from the door and took a step in her direction. Without hesitation she wisely turned and fled, not liking the glint of determination she saw in his eyes. She brought herself to a halt inside the den, going to the back of a chair, not knowing whether to be alarmed or relieved when he followed her but made no effort to overtake her. They both knew he could have grabbed her before she left the entrance foyer had he wanted to. She watched him warily. He might not have grabbed her as soon as they were alone, but it seemed the intention was stamped into every line of his unyielding length.

"I'm not afraid of you!" she spat out defiantly, inwardly wincing at her choice of words. The fear came from her inability to combat her response to him. If he decided to stage a repeat of the night before, she couldn't stop him.

"I'd like to believe that," he muttered heavily. "Relax, Kat, and sit down. We have some talking to do."

Katherine skirted the chair, her eyes never leaving his face as she sat on its edge, her rigid posture indicating her caution and lack of trust. Matt seated himself in a chair facing her, his elbows on his knees and his hands hanging loosely between the spread of his legs. His scrutiny of her was narrowed and somehow piercing.

"Katherine, we'll start with what happened last night. It needs to be out in the open." There was an unmistakable note of conciliation in the deep voice, but as Matt searched her stony expression, his manner hardened. "Look, Kat, we've stumbled into some problems, and it's partly my fault. I accept that. What I don't accept is your attempt to run out on me today."

Partly his fault! Meaning I'm still the "devious darlin'" *I was during the night?* She was silently seething. *That's* *right, buster! Throw all the blame! Forget your own despic-* *able behavior! Or try!* She said nothing.

Matt read the silent fury in her eyes and answered it with a visible bristling. His head snapped to a taut angle, the muscles in his wide shoulders bunching into tense knots.

"You're not leaving!" he gritted coldly. "If I have to tie you to my side, you're not leaving!"

The hard voice and narrowed green eyes offered a threat, and Katherine responded with a stiff little jerk. Her hands grasped a fierce hold on each arm of the chair, her fingernails digging sharply into the soft velvet fabric. Inwardly trembling with anger, she offered a cool, goading, careless "Not until I've got my keys."

His snort of derisive laughter wasn't amused. "Looks like you'll be staying awhile."

"Like hell!" Katherine retorted succinctly.

"Dammit, woman, don't push your luck!" Matt roared suddenly, his own hands clenching into fists on the bunched muscles of his thighs. "I'm trying hard to work this out with you, but your attitude is—"

"Hurt! Angry!" she supplied in a wavering shout. "I don't understand your behavior last night! I don't understand why you wouldn't listen to me!"

226

Matt surged forward in his chair, and for a moment Katherine thought he would reach out those long arms and pluck her from her perch in the opposite chair. His features were contorted into fierce lines, his eyes and mouth narrowed in hard synchronization. But with visible restraint he shook off the kindling feeling possessing him and eyed her steadily.

"Katherine, I'm listening now. If you'll settle down, maybe we can get this straightened out so we'll both understand." The words were peaceful, but his voice held a belligerent edge.

Her nod of agreement was a stiff downward jerk of her head, her slender neck refusing to bend. "What is it *you* don't understand?"

"Mike Hudson. I promised fidelity, but I also expect it. You'll have to quit seeing him. And you'll also have to stop encouraging John and Rob."

Her eyes widened unbelievably and then closed to block out the sight of him—tense, angry, accusing. Dear God! He never let up! Now not only the specter of Mike Hudson was between them but also a shadowy suspicion of his two friends. He had vowed trust, respect, caring. He was delivering nothing.

"That's the way it's got to be, Kat!" he gritted insistently.

"For months you've accused me of jumping to wrong conclusions, yet your own suspicions keep tumbling forth." The pause was significant. She was remembering their first week together and the day he'd left for Paraguay, his strange watchfulness when he relayed her calls from Mike and Sara Gullidge. She was remembering the night he'd returned and she had come in late, his anger because she wasn't home. She was remembering the day they'd had lunch and wound up at home making love and his withdrawal after Mike's call, his strange comment about her hot line and getting burned. How odd that she had never correlated the incidents and realized he suspected her of being faithless. Her head rested against the back of the chair, her eyes blinking furiously to fight frustration and defeat. Then, more to herself than to him, she whispered with bittersweet irony, "You've never trusted me. You're not listening now."

For a moment Matt was quiet, and then his voice came to her, just as hard as before. "Are you telling me there's nothing between you and Hudson? Or that you didn't have John and Rob eating out of your hands today?"

"I didn't do anything today but respond to your friends' pleasantness!" she retorted, stung by the accusation into sitting straighter in the chair. "And I can't control Mike's behavior. I'm helping him find a house, and I'm sympathetic in the face of his loneliness; but I'm not involved with him, not on any intimate level. I tried to tell you this last night, but you didn't want to believe me. You only wanted to control me. I've done nothing to betray our relationship, Matt. You did that. You decided not to trust me because trust implies more than physical involvement."

Incredibly she hit a nerve with that last statement. His big body jerked as if he'd received a blow to the stomach. And for just a second his eyes were relaying a message of shock or anguish before the lids came down to veil his thoughts.

"I need a drink," he muttered, rising from the chair to walk with a curiously unsteady gait to the bar. Once there, he downed a double whiskey, neat, before turning back to face her. "Why were you trying to leave?"

Katherine was out of her chair like a shot, then behind it, clutching the back as if it were a lifeline to sanity. If she'd had anything substantially weighty within her grasp, she wouldn't have hesitated tossing it at his dark single-minded head.

"You take the cake, do you know that?" she cried so hoarsely that she had to take two deep breaths in order to speak more coherently. "Why was I leaving? Why do you think? You put me through hell last night and then disappeared this morning without a word. What did you expect me to do? Wait around for you to come back with more anger, more distrust, more cold retaliation? I didn't ask to move in with you! I didn't force you into this arrangement!" Her voice broke, and she whispered desperately, "Why don't you just let me leave?"

"Because I want to work this out!" he barked, his gaze noting the heavy rise and fall of green silk across her breasts and then the agitated flush in her cheeks.

"Do you, Matt? On what terms?" she asked hollowly, a shade distrustfully.

"The terms we agreed on!" Matt thundered, surging angrily forward to tower above her. "Your terms! You wanted honesty! I'm honestly trying, damn you! I'm not running out on the relationship at the first sign of trouble!"

Hating his blind, accusing attitude, Katherine eyed him truculently and then mocked him in an unwise whisper. "No, you're creating the trouble."

Too caught up in her own wrath to heed the white-hot proportions of his, Katherine compounded her clever retort by making an equally clever move. With a disdainful toss of her blond head, she turned her back on him and walked to the glass door leading to the patio, intending to open it for a breath of fresh air. *Insufferable idiot! His pride was touched on the raw because he'd sacrificed himself to a summer commitment and his choice of a partner wasn't thrilled down to her toes by his noble gesture!* Her hand reached for the door clasp.

Matt was big, but he was also quiet. Angrily, purposely

quiet. His hand was on the door clasp before hers, and when she turned sharply around, another big palm flew up to hit the wall by her head with a reverberating crack. For a moment Katherine thought he had hit her, the resounding echo of his palm connecting with the wall ringing in her ears. Then common sense told her she was unscathed —but not out of harm's reach. The sheer size of Matt up close was intimidating, and leaning as he was over her, she was conscious mainly of the harsh rise and fall of his muscled chest. Her eyes swept to his face, her head tilted back to see the darkening of his eyes. The sudden dryness in her mouth had her swallowing twice on the alarm blocking her throat.

"This is one time I'm not letting you run away" was his soft warning, issued in a voice as tough as tempered steel.

"What do you want, Matt? Your full three months?" she asked archly. But her eyes were wary, and a nervous pulse throbbed at her temple.

"I want *you*," he retorted harshly, his dark head jerking down threateningly close, but his next words were just a whisper, almost a caress. "One misunderstanding shouldn't overshadow what we've shared."

"What have we shared? Trust? Respect? Caring? What have we shared except your bed?" The questions came steadily, but her heart was pounding so loudly she wondered that Matt didn't hear it.

A funny light entered his eyes so close to her own. "Maybe more than you realize," he murmured, his lips a heartbeat from hers. "Doesn't our sexual compatibility tell you that much? That part is good, Kat. Very, very good."

Katherine didn't flinch away from him, but she nervously moistened her lips, her eyes pleading for understanding. "Not last night, Matt. Not without tenderness and caring. I can't jump right back in your bed. Not now. I need time."

"Forget last night, Kat," Matt muttered, the warmth of his breath heating her face.

His nearness was suffocating Katherine's ability to stay calm and rational. It was appalling, humiliating, to realize she wanted to throw her arms around his neck and beg him to love her, plead with him to let her stay forever. *But not on his terms!* Not with his controlling her very heartbeat without the smallest consideration for her feelings. Not once, in all his arguments about wanting her and trying to work out the problems in their relationship, had he said he was sorry. *Words again.* She wanted words. She needed words. The jerky, negative shake of her head was a last-ditch effort to regain control of her life.

Her throat hurt with the effort to speak. "I'd like my keys, Matt."

Matt slowly levered himself away from the wall and stood looking down at her, his expression unreadable. His entire body was stiff with tension, and his hand dipped slowly into his pants pocket.

Seemingly composed, Katherine watched him steadily, fighting back the urge to slump in exhaustion against the glass door at her back. As Matt's hand came out of his pocket, she breathed shallowly, and her hand came up, palm extended. When the cold metal hit her flesh, her fingers closed round the keys, and instead of feeling victorious, she felt oddly vanquished.

CHAPTER ELEVEN

Defensively Katherine eyed the occupant of the small pet carrier. Unblinking amber-green eyes returned the perusal, then cut hopefully toward the kitchen corner, seeking a familiar basket.

"It was only for a few hours each way, Mari. I know you hate the damned thing, but I couldn't drive all the way to Big Spring and back with you prowling over every inch of the station wagon." Stretching to relieve the kinks that several hours behind the wheel of her Chevy had produced, she then stooped to the cat's level, patiently explaining, "The delay in Abilene was unforeseen, so quit eyeing me so accusingly. It was either buy the tires there or face the possibility of not making it home at all. The man at the service station said we were lucky to have just the one blowout considering the condition of those miserable tires."

He'd also muttered some snide epithets about women drivers and their inability to take care of automobiles that had had Katherine seething impotently while new tires were jacked into place on the Chevy. It was only much later, on the long stretch of highway between Abilene and Fort Worth, that Katherine remembered another mechanic's reminder of the lack of tread on her tires and grudgingly admitted there was more than a hint of truth in what the chauvinist mechanic in Abilene had said. Tires had been her last consideration when she'd made the trip to the Meadowses' farm.

The tabby mewed plaintively, peering through the bars of her carrier. She looked for all the world like an innocent prisoner pleading for reprieve from a death row sentence.

With a softly laughing "Okay, okay! You've completely won my sympathies! One pardon coming up!" Katherine released the catch on the pet carrier.

In a flurry of gold and white fur, the prisoner was free, leaping gracefully out of her jail and going immediately to a familiar, beckoning niche. Within seconds Marigold was purring contentedly, nestled comfortably into the green cushion of her corner basket.

"I could do with the same fate, you little beast. All my problems solved by a nice, cozy bed," Katherine commented smilingly, and then frowned ferociously, knowing a nice, cozy bed was where her problems had started. One such bed, with its big, inflexible bedmate, had brought her to her present levels of heartache and discontent and loneliness.

The need to unload her station wagon took her outside. She removed her suitcase, and the boxes containing Martha's jars of homemade preserves and garden vegetables, and a portable cooler which held Peter's contribution to her larder of farm-grown goodies. Breakfast sausage, ham steaks, and inch-thick pork chops were packaged and ready for her freezer, a generous allotment of one of the half dozen hogs her father-in-law raised and fattened for market.

As she carried each item into her house, her eyes strayed to the gray-bricked residence next door. The driveway was empty, and although it was after dark, not a single light shone from the windows. The Clinton house had been empty for the last five days. Matt had left, presumably for East Texas and his bridge, four days after her departure from his house. Several times during those four days she had caught brief glimpses of him, at a distance as they left for work and then returned to their respective houses. Once they had spoken, although their short conversation hadn't been all that communicative. Just very, very disturbing, and it inevitably had aided in her decision to make her Fourth of July excursion to the Meadowses' farm.

Determinedly Katherine cast aside memories of that brief encounter and headed for her kitchen, a box of laden jars clutched in front of her, a frown marring her features.

Finding space in her pantry and freezer for all her homegrown bounty took a few minutes, and Katherine smiled as she worked, remembering Peter's parting admonishment. Hugging her good-bye, he'd scolded mildly, "Kathy, you used to be as round and rosy as Laurel! Now you make good use of the meats and Martha's jellies and vegetables. Come Thanksgiving, I want to feel flesh when I hug you, not these breakable bones." And to that Martha had added a poignant remonstrance, unknowingly double-edged. "Barry used to write home about his beautiful sunshine. He said her head was crowned by golden rays and her eyes held radiant sparkles. That's what I want to see Thanksgiving. Those radiant sparkles back in your eyes. Whatever's worrying you . . . well, you take care of it, Kathy. Peter and I will help if you need us."

Kathy. Over the three-day weekend her in-laws had called her the affectionate "Kathy" many times. It was the name Barry and his parents had always used, and to Katherine just as familiar as the "Mom" and "Mother" her son and daughter called her. But the missing sparkles in her eyes came from wanting to hear, needing to hear, a husky "Kat" or a caressing "darlin' " or, perhaps more accurately, from the evocative echo of those names resounding in her thoughts.

Methodically continuing her unpacking, Katherine experienced a fierce, hopeless need. The one time Matt had spoken to her since she'd moved back home, his voice had been neither husky nor caressing, but very deep and curiously taut, matching perfectly his grimly set features. Their meeting had been accidental, both of them retrieving morning-edition newspapers tossed almost side by side in the stretch of dew-laden grass between their two houses. From a distance of less than six feet, Matt had stared at her soberly and stated bluntly, "You left several of your things at my place. I'll bring them over tonight."

Having already committed herself to the rescheduled appointment with Mike Hudson, she'd responded quietly, "I won't be here tonight." And although she hadn't explained why she wouldn't be home, she had seen the knowledge written into Matt's hardening expression.

There had been a long silence, fraught with growing tension, before Matt spoke, a hint of roughness in his voice. "Okay, Widow Meadows, have it your way again. I'll give you more time, more space. I just hope my patience doesn't wear thin before your need for retaliation gives out." And with that he had stalked rigidly away, leaving her staring helplessly after him.

At first she had been appalled and hurt to think Matt was interpreting their separation as her need for retaliation. Only later did she recall his reference to his patience wearing thin and realized it could be an ultimatum. It was his way of telling her to come back to him on his terms or to tell him a final good-bye. Now she was remembering other words: "Have it your way again."

Her way? Again? When had it ever been her way? She had wanted his love and settled for his lovemaking. She had needed his trust and respect and received his suspicion and doubt. She had hoped for his commitment to her and accepted his offer of a summer affair. Her way had been crushed under the force of Matt's way all along. Bound helplessly by her love of him, she had allowed him to set all the rules and terms of their relationship, and he had done so dominantly, boldly, with a ruthless disregard for her needs.

The last jar found a resting place inside the pantry, and Katherine inspected the neat rows of vegetables and condiments. Her trip to the Meadowses' farm might not have accomplished a lessening of her need of Matt, but it had certainly improved her food supplies. Her stomach would be fed, and fed well, thanks to her in-laws' generosity. Now if only she wasn't suffering an acute case of emotional starvation . . .

Three evenings later Katherine was ruefully eyeing the remains of her dinner. A thick vegetable pie, laden with cheese and surrounded by a golden crust, had sounded like meager fare when she'd arrived home late and hungry. Now she wished her growling stomach hadn't ruled her sensible head. She had cooked too much. She hoped Marigold wouldn't be too replete from her nocturnal snack of insects to appreciate a healthy vitamin-enriched portion of vegetables in creamy mushroom sauce. Maybe if she sprinkled generous bits of chicken or tuna over the top . . . On second thought, maybe she would freeze the leftovers for another meal for herself. The cat was notoriously picky about her food.

The phone rang while her hands were immersed in dishwater, and Katherine grabbed the receiver with slippery fingers and cradled it under her chin, the cord stretched over her shoulder, as she turned back to the sink.

Her "Hello" was muffled, her chin more than her mouth over the receiver.

"Katherine?"

Just her name, spoken in a deep, quiet voice, but it was

enough. Disastrously so. The plate in her hand slipped from suddenly nerveless fingers and plopped back into the dishwater. A generous spray of soapy water doused her face and chest, and she gasped, almost missing Matt's "Are you there?"

After wiping her hands down the sides of her robe, she quickly fixed the receiver closer to her ear and said breathlessly, "Yes. Yes, I'm here."

"How are you?"

Hurting. Lonely. Still loving you. She made her voice neutral, saying, "Fine, Matt."

"You were away last weekend. I tried to call."

"I drove to West Texas to visit my children and their grandparents. Laurel and Timmy said to tell you hi." *And were just full of none too subtle inquiries about our relationship. The poor darlings still hear wedding bells.*

"They're good kids. Look, Kat, I need to . . ."

Long moments passed in which Katherine wondered desperately what he needed. To see her? To tell her he understood her motivations for leaving him? To explain that he was sorry for his lack of trust? Hopeful speculations whirled helter-skelter in her head and were abruptly shattered when he resumed speaking, a hard edge to his voice. "The cat. I called to let you know the cat was in my backyard. I put her over the fence."

Quietly, subdued, she said, "Thank you," and then was appalled to hear herself add expectantly, "Was there . . ." before the words were abruptly checked on a sane, stabilizing breath. *Was there anything else? Don't be a fool, Katherine! Twelve days of near silence indicate the man is not pining in need of you!*

"Was there what?"

The sharpness of his tone startled her. *Yes—what?* God, she didn't know. A glance at the counter by the sink, gave her inspiration, and in a nervous rush she asked, "Was

237

there any chance I left my watch at your house? I can't seem to find it." *Liar! It's right here on the counter, and your nose is growing longer!*

His long silence made her wonder if he'd seen through her feeble excuse. Then, roughly and with a brutal disregard for her feelings, he said, "I'll look for it in the bedroom. That's where you lost a lot of things, including your reluctance and your misgivings. If I remember right, when you lost your clothes, you lost all doubts and objections."

The reminder was acute and unnecessary, and Katherine gasped, the pain of it hitting her fiercely in the stomach and spreading with vicious encompassment all through her body. The bedroom. That's where she'd lost the last of her good sense. Giving herself freely and passionately to a man who had no understanding of the emotions guiding her actions. Her voice wobbling with the effort, she said, "Thanks for seeing to Mari. Good-bye, Matt."

And heard his terse "Katherine, wait, I—" before she hung up the phone, wiping strangely salty soapsuds from her face.

Matt was on her doorstep as she left for work the next morning, and Katherine wasn't really surprised. For more than an hour after she'd hung up on him the evening before, the phone had rung continuously and imperatively. And when she'd finally unplugged it, it was only to suffer another thirty minutes of a forceful summons at her front door. She had answered neither, indulging in the longest shower in history to drown out the noise, half drowning herself in the process in a mixture of warm shower spray and hot tears.

He looked awful. Dressed for the office in a light beige suit, his body was as powerful and indestructible as always, but his face was drawn, haggardly depicting the same loss of sleep she had suffered. His eyes were sunken and darkly circled, and his mouth was set tautly . . . and determinedly.

"I brought your things, Katherine," he told her as soon as she opened the door, indicating a paper bag in his hand. "It's only clothing. I couldn't find your watch." Unexpectedly a dark tide of red washed under the bronze of his complexion, and he continued, managing to sound both discomfited and aggressive. "What I said about the bedroom was a mistake. I seem to be making a lot of those where you're concerned. I would have apologized last night, but you wouldn't answer either your phone or your door."

Her response was a jerky little nod as she reached for the bag. He didn't release it, however, and they faced each other across its width, each of them clutching a corner of brown paper bag, each of them studying the other. Lingering hurt put a defensive tilt to her chin, and a trace of vulnerability clouded the steady regard of her eyes. Remote anger, perhaps self-directed, filled his eyes, thoroughly scanning her features, and a direct challenge angled a belligerent thrust to a strong chin.

His voice clipped, Matt issued the challenge. "It's been thirteen days, Kat. How much longer?"

Her voice taut, Katherine answered with defensive clarity, "I'm not moving back in with you, Matt."

"You agreed to live with me during the summer. You're breaking that promise!" he charged.

"I wasn't the only one to break promises!" she countered.

"Are you determined never to trust me again?"

"Are you deciding finally to trust me?"

"Katherine, I can't wait indefinitely for you to come around!" Frustration colored his anger.

Hurt tinged hers. "I've been around! I've been on a

239

whole merry-go-round of your anger, your terms, your dominance!"

The emerald maelstrom in his eyes swirled threateningly above her cloud gray gaze and then dropped in abrupt, hard-won control. While Katherine watched, Matt's gaze fell to the paper bag they held between them, and unbelievably she saw the beginnings of something amazed and delighted touch his expression. The eyes coming back to her were brighter, bolder, slowly filling with an oblique relief.

"All right, you little fraud," he murmured on a soft expulsion of breath, releasing the bag so suddenly that she clutched it to her chest to keep from losing it. "Pride's a hell of a thing. I've struggled with mine long enough to know."

Before Katherine could fathom his sudden change of mood, his finger reached out to touch the back of her hand. Her fingers dug into brown paper, a small reaction to the trail being foraged across the bones and veins of her hand and then lingering caressingly at her wrist. The heat of his light touch was potent. Removing herself from his reach was impossible.

His triumphant yet curiously softened gaze locked to the uncertain flicker of hers, and he told her huskily, "The next move's yours, Kat, but if it helps you to decide, then be assured that the recent struggle with my pride revolves around a stubborn, intractable widow. You say the word, darlin', and we'll end this farcical separation."

Then he was gone, loping across the lawns to his pick-up, his strides almost jaunty. As he backed out of the driveway, Katherine could still feel the burning heat on her wrist where his touch had lingered. She glanced down, half expecting to see a big red *M* for "Matt's" branded into her flesh. She saw, instead, what Matt had seen, what Matt couldn't have helped seeing—and interpreted correctly.

Brightly reflecting the morning sunlight, her watch brazenly circled her wrist, boldly announcing her lie of the night before, unfortunately and unwittingly giving Matt an insight into her true feelings.

Oh, damn!

The decision was difficult, and when Katherine wakened early on a Sunday morning, two days later, she knew it was the only one she could make. It was as simple as pride and as complex as love. Their pride had kept them apart, making her suffer acute loneliness and Matt experience the thwarting of his desires. Was love, her love, enough to bring them back together? The evocative thought brought her hurriedly out of bed. It was time to find out. There were six weeks left before her children returned from Big Spring. Forty-two days in which to discover whether or not Ol' Dad's and Ol' Granddad's shining example of strong, independent manhood could learn to love. It wouldn't be easy, but she was eager to begin . . . again.

Showering and dressing were done in a rush, and within minutes she was in the kitchen, her freshly washed hair piled in a cool upsweep on the top of her head, a bright orange terry romper covering the gentle curves of her torso. A slender expanse of bare thighs and legs led down to slim, naked feet. Her smooth shoulders and arms gleamed a cool defiance to the sultry heat of the morning as she let Marigold out for her early wander through the flower beds.

From the freezer she extracted two ham steaks, setting them to simmer in a covered skillet over a low-set burner. Coffee was soon bubbling in a glass stove top percolator. Katherine quickly put together a batter for pancakes, adding a generous measure of blackberry filling from Martha's gift of preserves.

It was barely seven thirty when she went to the phone and dialed Matt's number.

The greeting on the other end of the line was gruff and thick with sleep and would have been discouraging if Katherine hadn't remembered all the mornings in early June when that same tone had quickly become a warm bass rumble.

Calmly, in a voice as smooth as cream, she said, "I'm cooking breakfast. Have you eaten?"

A protracted silence had her heart lurching uncertainly and then pounding in furious relief when, slowly and distinctly, Matt answered, "No, and I've got a voracious appetite."

He abruptly hung up, and Katherine did the same, a smile curving her mouth. Matt had a voracious appetite. Great. Her smile became fierce with resolve. Perhaps he could handle the entire bill of fare, then, because she wasn't serving herself up a la carte. Not again. This time the part of her that fitted nicely in his arms was being offered only with the parts of her seeking entrance into his mind and heart and soul. No side dishes. No substitutions.

Within ten minutes the doorbell was ringing, and Katherine experienced a momentary panic, her fingers pressing into her throat to calm a wildly fluttering pulse. She had lost the last several encounters with Matt. She was nervous of the outcome of the forthcoming one.

Yet when she opened the door to him, her movements suggested only calm control and the expression on her face hinted merely of cool reserve. There was nothing about her untroubled mien to indicate that her composure was more than slightly regulated by the nervous pulses pounding at her temples.

Her guest was lounging on her doorstep, his hands braced on either side of the door, seemingly indolent. But his wide chest moved harshly with his breathing, the

242

cream pullover he wore defining his muscles with every inhalation of air. His hair was damp from a recent shower. A trickle of water edged down from his sideburn to the tendons in his neck and then disappeared inside the gleaming hair exposed by the opened throat of the shirt. Above the firm outline of his upper lip and again at the hard jut of his chin were two small cuts, and two tiny drops of blood glistened bright red in the morning sunlight.

Curbing her amazement at these evidences of his haste, Katherine observed quietly, "You're bleeding."

"New razor blade," Matt explained shortly, searching inside his pocket for a handkerchief. As he blotted away the minuscule flecks of blood, his voice muffled behind the handkerchief, he added, "I wanted to get over here before you changed your mind, so I shaved in a hurry."

Obliquely unsettled by his comment or perhaps by the hint of implied equivocation on her part, Katherine murmured a weak protest. "I wasn't going to change my mind. Your haste was unnecessary." Her gaze shifted meaningfully to the blood-dotted square of white linen in his hand.

Cramming the handkerchief into the hip pocket of his tan cords, Matt surveyed the mild agitation in her expression and went boldly forward into another blunder. Quizzically he gibed, "Are a couple of specks of blood going to make you sick?"

The frost of defensiveness entered her eyes while a faint line of arctic irritation firmed her soft mouth. Her voice bitingly sweet, she explained, "Splashes of blood make me sick; specks do not. And sometimes it's not blood but bloody-mindedness that I'm averse to."

A dark eyebrow went up in spurious surprise at her snappy retort, and the grooves around his mouth became more pronounced. But unsmiling, he regarded her steadily, and when he saw her fingers tighten around the doorknob, he quickly stepped over the threshold and into the foyer. A slight inclination of his head advised her to shut the door. When she only stared at him, with cool hauteur, he took matters out of her hands. A booted foot planted itself between a bare one and the door and then gave the wood panel a healthy nudge that had it swinging out of her grasp. It closed with a snappy little click, and she blinked in resentful surprise.

"You invited me, Kat, remember?"

Katherine backed one step away from the warning entering his eyes, realizing that Matt was deliberately using aggressive tactics to control the encounter . . . and her. Then she shook her head, slightly, reminding herself it was her home, her rules, her game. Matt was the visitor, not the host.

"Coffee's ready," she announced briskly, turning for the kitchen, adding over her shoulder in saccharine tones, "I hope you like ham steak and blackberry pancakes."

"Now why do I get the feeling I should meekly agree to any food selection, even if it's frozen solid and coated with arsenic?" came his sardonic murmur at her back.

Her slim, supple body went taut with annoyance. Oh, yes, that low-voiced taunt was definitely meant to needle! How many times in the past had she been the recipient of just such a maneuver? By putting her on the defensive, Matt managed to keep the upper hand in their confrontations. In the kitchen doorway she turned to favor him with a direct look, her eyes a cool and defiant shade of silver.

"If the menu doesn't suit you, I'm afraid you've come to the wrong place," she pointed out evenly, but the tilt of her chin echoed the challenge in her eyes.

She was answered in an unforeseen way, an annihilating, subversive way that threatened to crack the thin ice of her composure. With an unruly lurch of her senses Katherine watched Matt's mouth twist sensually, his eyes going over her in lustful regard. The menu she had referred to and the menu Matt was contemplating were not one and the same.

The elasticized bodice of her romper was given a hungry perusal, the bare curve of her thighs a ravenous study, and her gleaming shoulders were positively devoured by a consuming gaze. The knowledge that he was unscrupulously trying to shake her composure didn't halt her reaction. Against her will, her heart began to race madly. She nervously shifted from one bare foot to the other, appalled to feel her breasts going firm beneath the soft terry fabric of her romper, the nipples becoming pebble-hard and imperative.

A slow grin of wicked appreciation formed on his mouth, and with a provocative huskiness he murmured, "I've got no complaints with the menu. It's something I've been craving for over two weeks now."

Soft defenselessness parted her mouth. She had the insane urge to step closer to him, to press her body against the hard length of his. She wanted to kiss that grinning mouth, to forget all her resolutions about changing the tenor of their relationship to one involving more than physical compatibility.

In the foot or so of space separating them, the atmosphere suddenly crackled heavily with sexual tension. Matt's wicked appraisal of her softer parts became less a tactic to unsettle her and more an expression of his own longing and desire. His gaze burned into hers, then dropped disturbingly to her mouth. A muscle along his jaw rippled a crazy echo to the pulsebeat at her throat.

"Let me get you a cup of coffee," she breathed in a shallow effort to dispel the tension.

"Sounds good," he responded with a slurred intonation that betrayed arousal.

Automatically her gaze swept the length of his tan cords, and a hectic color tinged her cheeks when she surveyed the evidence of his quickened masculinity. Meeting his gaze, she was surprised to see anger mixed with passion.

"What did you expect? That little orange thing is a provocation!" he stated roughly, flicking a finger near the taut curve of her breast. "Did you wear it deliberately?"

"My choice of clothing was made with my comfort in mind, not your discomfort!" she said, flaring, not liking his implication that she had purposely set out to tease him. "If your libido is overcharged, don't blame it on me!"

As she turned jerkily away from him, she caught a fleeting flash of white as he grinned wolfishly, and she could cheerfully have strangled him. His swift changes from mockery to arousal to anger to amusement were unsettling and absolutely destructive to her self-possession. She had intended a nice, sane, adult conversation about their relationship, not this ridiculous sparring.

Foraging in the cabinet above her head, she grabbed two coffee mugs, tensing when two large hands planted themselves firmly against the counter on either side of her. The warmth of his potent masculinity heated her back, and she pressed into the counter to escape, her hipbones digging sharply into its edge. As she slammed the coffee mugs onto the counter, her mouth formed a quick demand that was never uttered. She issued a helpless gasp instead, the moist heat of his tongue flicking against her neck making her shiver convulsively.

"I've missed you, Kat," was breathed against her flesh, and she recognized the shading of warm amusement commingled with the husky desire. With maddening provocation his lips trailed to the slope of her shoulder, his teeth nibbling sensually. "I've missed seeing your back go all stiff with reserve when you're trying to keep me at a distance. I've missed hearing you spout frosty defiance when you disagree with me. And I've missed witnessing those occasional flare-ups of outrage when you think I've said something unforgivable." Sly and insidious, his tongue belied the amused tenor of his words, moving hotly to her neck, where he whispered evocatively, "Now turn around and kiss me good morning and stop trying to pretend we're strangers."

Responding to the husky timbre of his voice rather than the context of his words, Katherine half turned to face him before she caught herself. Her shoulder glanced off his chest, her hip off his muscled thigh. In an excess of self-reproach she chided the vulnerability that had her moving like a puppet on a string to the dexterous manipulations of the master puppeteer. Despite her body's response, this was not what she wanted. She wanted Matt to need her on more than a sexual level.

Glancing up at him askance, she tried to speak a protest. "Matt, I—"

His mouth swooped sideways and down, smothering her words with gentle ferocity, obliterating thoughts with a hunger and expertise that had her mouth moving in feverish urgency under his. His arms maneuvered her to a more satisfying position against his length and bound her close. His tongue flicked hotly against her lips and then boldly rediscovered her mouth, its urgent rhythmic penetration symbolic of the more intimate moments they had shared. The combined odors of minty toothpaste and spicy aftershave and warm male flesh filled her brain, and she was hard pressed to recall the aromas of freshly perked coffee and sizzling ham and the tangy sweetness of blackberries that constituted a saner world. When his hands swept to her buttocks, to press her tightly against his thighs, an unwelcome reason flooded back to her, and she twisted her mouth away, breathing unsteadily.

Her head fell weakly to his chest, and she didn't know if the thunderous beat at her ear was his heart or her own.

247

His lips brushed the top of her head and moved ardently to her temple, and the fingers at her chin said he would soon be sampling another taste of her mouth. She moved her head fretfully, denying him, her words muffled into his throat. "No. No more kisses. Please. Let's just eat breakfast."

For a moment he didn't speak, breathing raggedly, and then the soft hoarseness of his words, conveying both warm satisfaction and frustrated desire, told her, "Okay, darlin', breakfast first."

And breakfast it was, with Matt cast superbly in the role of warm, attentive guest and Katherine outwardly at ease as obliging hostess while inwardly a whole bundle of conflicting emotions. *Breakfast first.* She was all too aware what those simple words meant. Matt didn't realize how deeply concerned she was that they talk out their relationship and come to a new understanding. In typical male fashion he was assuming that her response to his embrace was a tacit announcement of total surrender. She wished it were that simple. She wanted his lovemaking. But *not,* she reminded herself fiercely, at the expense of her pride. *Not* when her soul demanded a more equal balance between lovemaking and love.

For the moment Katherine laid aside the conflict of her thoughts, listening with interest as Matt conveyed updated information on the road in Paraguay and the bridge in East Texas.

He told her wryly, "My eight-day stay in East Texas was gratifying from a business point of view. A lot of work can be done when a man channels frustration into energy." Then, before she could fully appreciate the implications of that statement, he conjured up a vague distrust by asking silkily, "Did you get Hudson's house problems straightened out?"

Refusing to be defensive, Katherine answered evenly,

her eyes direct and unequivocal, "He seems pleased with the house I showed him week before last. We've been back to view it twice since then. I imagine he'll have us drawing up a contract in the next few days."

The frown on his forehead indicated dissatisfaction with her response, but other than a tightening of his jaw as he chewed grindingly upon a tender morsel of ham, Matt didn't pursue the subject.

Moments later he was asking questions about her trip to Big Spring. He laughed deeply when she gave amused accounts of Tim's expertise with the tractor that had cost his grandfather two fence posts and Laurel's mistaken substitutions of salt for sugar that had ruined a whole batch of her grandmother's pear preserves.

Breakfast consumed, Matt sat back, giving Katherine a warm look. Magnanimously he stated, "That was the best meal I've eaten in two weeks, and to prove I'm a grateful guest, I'll do the dishes while you get your things together."

"What things?"

"Clothing, makeup, whatever you need. Or have you already packed?"

"No-o-o-o." She softly drew out the word, understanding. "No, I'm definitely not packed, Matt."

"Then hop to it, woman. I'm expecting a phone call from Paraguay within the next few minutes."

Taking the bull by the horns, Katherine told him clearly, "I won't be packing, so I can do the dishes if you're in a hurry to get home."

His eyes narrowed, became flintlike and determined. "All right, Kat, spit it out. You asked for time. I've given you fifteen days. Is it the business call? That won't take long, and then the rest of the day is ours."

"It's not the phone call." As she spoke, she rose from the table and took their used dishes to the sink. She turned

249

to face him and found his gaze fixed broodingly on her. She smiled sweetly, surprising him by asking, "Do you have a copy with you, Matt?"

"A copy? Of what?" He pushed back from the table and strode slowly toward her.

"I thought not," she murmured. "You didn't have one back in May either."

"What copy?" he repeated quietly, standing in front of her.

"You seem to think I've signed some sort of contract obligating me to spend the summer months in your house. I just wondered if you had a copy of the agreement."

"The agreement was oral, but you consented to it."

"A lot has changed since then, or hadn't you noticed?"

"I've noticed. But the changes weren't by my choice."

"But by your instigation."

"Will it satisfy your need for revenge if I say I regret my behavior that last night we were together?"

The hint of impatience in his words had her bristling. "An apology fifteen days after the fact? I don't want to hear anything not sincerely meant." With soft vehemence she stated, "And it's not revenge, Matt."

Stalking rigidly past him, she returned to the table. He came right behind her, grasping her upper arms, pulling her stiff body against him. When she strained against his controlling hands, harsh exasperation rose and fell at her back.

"Okay, okay, it's not revenge, but don't keep pulling away from me. That drives me nuts!" he muttered heavily, his arms caging her shoulders and breasts, holding her possessively close. Then, near her ear, his voice low and thickly intense, he said, "I'm sorry for what happened that night. I was wrong, and I realize that now; but it's over. Don't let that mistake ruin everything between us!"

"You're sorry for not trusting me?" she whispered. She

250

had waited fifteen days to hear these words, and she wanted to make sure they were clearly stated.

"Yes, and for what happened afterward."

"And you want to continue our relationship?"

"You must know how I feel about that!" he muttered, nuzzling emphatically into the side of her neck.

Her hands went to his forearms crossed in front of her and gently lifted them so she could turn. But when he would have drawn her to his chest, she braced her hands at his waist, keeping a distance between them.

"That's just it, Matt. I don't know how you feel about it," she told him quietly. Her heart hammered a faltering staccato when she clarified her remark. "I don't know how you feel about us."

His dark brows formed a wary line over his guarded emerald eyes. Slowly he said, "You should. I've shown you often enough."

She could see the watchfulness in his eyes, the hint of impatience, and didn't know whether to laugh or cry. Why couldn't he understand that she needed more than his lovemaking? Why couldn't he see beyond the limits of the bedroom? Choosing her words carefully, she said evenly, "I need more than a one-dimensional relationship. Compatibility and closeness don't have to be expressed only in the bedroom."

"Are you sure?" There was a caustic edge to his voice that said anger and exasperation were near the surface of his control. "We fared nicely those first weeks in June."

Pulling completely away from him, she said with controlled heat, "Sexual intimacy might be your only need, Matt, but my needs go further than that. Real intimacy, emotional intimacy, is more than knowing each other's bodies!" She swallowed painfully, wanting to add words of commitment but opting for a vague "Even temporary affairs require an essence of emotional involvement."

251

"And you want emotion without physical contact?" He didn't raise his voice, but the hard incredulity was there.

"You're twisting my words, Matt. I didn't suggest sex be excluded from our relationship. I merely pointed out that it isn't the *only* way two people can express their feelings."

"Name a better way!" he demanded tersely.

"Words, for a start!" she supplied heatedly, her hands clenching into tight fists at her hips. "What happened to your assertions of friendship and caring and enjoyment of my company? What is it with you, Matt? You have a superb command of the English language when you're jeering at love and romance and perfect relationships, but you can't find a single syllable to express what you feel!"

"I *feel* a hell of an urge to kiss *you* wordless, you bombastic little tormentor!" He raged suddenly, all semblance of control lost. His eyes wild with frustration, his big body exploded into movement, furiously pacing back and forth in front of her, arms and legs jerkily moving angrily.

And Katherine felt an untimely gurgle of laughter forming in her throat. Her hand flew to her neck, trying to soothe away the telltale quivers. It wasn't often Matt gave in to frustration, and the sight of him pacing so frenetically, following his less than eloquent verbal expression of his feelings, was unexpectedly humorous. Her teeth found her bottom lip, gnawing it desperately. She forcibly controlled a grin, and her eyes flickered rapidly, filling with the moisture of suppressed mirth. When Matt turned an accusing glare on her, her hand went to her diaphragm, urgently checking a convulsive tremor.

His hard, unbelieving green eyes pierced her, and Matt stated flatly, "You're laughing at me."

"No!" Katherine denied quickly, strangling on the word. Then a bubble of undisciplined mirth escaped, and she confessed helplessly, "Yes. Yes, I am, Matt. I'm sor-

252

ry." And immediately gave in to her imprudent sense of humor. Hugging herself, she bent almost double, peal after peal of unrestrained laughter spilling forth in outrageous delight. It was ridiculous, it was perhaps unwise, but it was also one of those crazy moments when she just couldn't help herself.

By the time her humor subsided to one last gasping chuckle she was out of breath and leaning heavily against the table. Her damp eyes had difficulty focusing, and her fingers wiped away the last traces of glee, the better to see six feet two inches of hard, unsmiling male standing not two feet six inches away. She gulped back a tiny sigh of well-being and straightened away from the table.

Fingers splayed on his hips, thumbs hooked through the belt loops of his cords, Matt was no longer in a state of frustration. What state he was in, Katherine wasn't certain. Although shimmering and alert, his green gaze boring into her was still incomprehensible, as was his toneless "You're full of surprises, Katherine."

"Comic relief." She excused herself flippantly and then swiftly sobered under his constrained regard. Shifting uncomfortably, she mumbled, "I'd better wash the dishes."

Edging warily past him, she went to the sink, where she turned on the faucet and added a generous splash of liquid detergent to the water. Matt followed. Slowly. Katherine was aware of the exact moment he reached her side, but a prickling of nervous caution kept her eyes studiously on the dishes. His shoulder brushed lightly against hers as he settled against the counter, facing the opposite direction from her. She ignored the contact, industriously swishing her fingers in the water to create a froth of bubbles.

The silence when she turned off the faucet was maddening. It tied her into knots. Breathing, heartbeats went into limbo. Wasn't he going to say anything? Chastise her for her laughter? Plow into her with one of his taunting assaults? A furtive, apprehensive glance from under the veil of her lashes found herself the subject of a soberly intense study. Was he angry? Disgusted? Annoyed? The silence lengthened. Katherine methodically ran a cloth over one plate, cleaning it, recleaning it. She could hear his breathing. Pregnant. Thick. Or were those her own shallow, nervous sighs that filled the air?

Matt spoke abruptly. "Tell me what kinds of words you want."

The tiny knot of tension that had tied itself to her heart unraveled. Those words he had just uttered were rebirth. Her blood began a life-giving flow, her pulse a quickening exhilaration. Matt was trying. Katherine silently rejoiced, abandoning the defensive posture she had assumed. Her head swiveled gracefully on her neck, and her eyes went directly to his, ready for action.

Quietly she murmured, "The words just express what you feel, Matt. I can't supply them for you."

His eyes searched hers relentlessly. "I want back in your life, Kat, but I'm not a poet. I can't come up with flowery speech."

"I don't expect poetry, just honest consideration. I'll give the same."

He straightened from the counter, his hands pushing through his hair, looking down at her with disturbed and disturbing eyes. "I do better when I'm holding you, saying love words."

"You mean lovemaking words," she corrected, frowning.

Matt shoved his hands forcefully inside the back pockets of his cords, and she knew it was to keep from grabbing her. She waited with inheld breath, hoping he would deny her clarification, and breathed shallow disappointment when his gaze drifted over her head and he sighed, muttering, "Yeah, lovemaking words."

Drying her hands on a towel, she stood in front of him, the space between them mere inches, incalculable heart-beats. Her heart shouted, *Matthew Clinton, I adore you! I'm absolutely crazy about you! How can that much love be unreciprocated?* What she said, her words solemn and huskily voiced, was "I care about you, Matt. I'll give the next six weeks as much effort as I'm asking of you."

"Why the limit of six weeks?" he demanded curiously.

Momentarily she showed her surprise that he didn't understand. Then she blurted, "That's when Timmy and Laurel come back home. Everything changes then."

"Does it?" A dark eyebrow rose infinitesimally.

"Yes, of course," she averred stoutly.

There was something challenging about the way he slowly folded his arms across his chest. He said coolly, "You're on."

For a moment Katherine waited expectantly to hear more. Then she realized he wasn't going to say anything else. Her gaze wavered, and she barely managed a bracing "Well, fine."

"I need to get home to answer the call from Paraguay. Sure you don't need help with the dishes?"

Mustering a smile, she answered brightly, "No, I can manage them."

He bent and kissed her forehead, murmured, "Thanks for breakfast," and was gone, striding out of the kitchen without a backward glance.

CHAPTER TWELVE

Katherine heard her front door open and shut and stood in stiff, unbelieving silence. For long minutes she was like a statue, unmoving, unthinking. Then her thoughts came so fast, so jumbled she couldn't make head or tail of them, knowing only that they were progressing quickly toward an explosive point. Matt was gone, and she still didn't know where she stood with him. She didn't know if he intended coming back. She didn't know, if he did come back, whether or not he would explain how he felt. A stiffening of hurt feelings, anger, and outrage had her thrusting her hands into the dishwater, vigorously scrubbing plates and coffee mugs and cutlery.

"You're on!" she mimicked acidly, succinctly summing up her thoughts. "How very verbose of you, Mr. Clinton!" She had wanted explicit phrases of caring and assurance and had received a cryptic challenge instead.

A handful of cutlery was slammed into the dish drainer. Plates and coffee mugs followed with the same consideration, viciously clinking against one another. A drippy cloth was slapped haphazardly over the stove and table. Pans were dropped heedlessly into the sink, causing a rolling wave of dishwater to slosh over the edge of the counter and splash onto the floor, spattering her bare toes and ankles. A fingernail snapped under the energetic scouring applied to a skillet. Her muttered, inexplicit cursing hummed about the kitchen and then resounded flatly against the walls. She rubbed a clean dishtowel, whipped out of a drawer, over the sparkling clean kitchen implements. Cabinet doors were banged open and shut. Pots and pans were clattered into their proper berths.

And the fine rage was abruptly curtailed by a mildly voiced "I see it didn't take you long to whip the kitchen into shape."

With a startled gasp Katherine whirled about, widened eyes finding the possessor of that deep, admiring voice propped idly against the doorjamb. A purring tabby was stretched languidly in his folded arms.

The flush of lingering temper spread high across her cheeks, Katherine croaked pointlessly, "You're not next door."

Matt deposited Marigold on the floor, grinning when the cat rubbed luxuriously against his legs before marching daintily to her corner basket. "My phone call took less than five minutes," he explained easily, his eyes roaming idly about the spotless kitchen, then settling on her with gleaming approval. "We're both fast workers."

How was it possible that more warmth could creep into her face? She wished she knew how long he'd been standing there, how much of her temper he had witnessed. Uncomfortable, she managed an agreeing "Yes."

His wicked green eyes acknowledged her discomfiture. Matt asked politely, "Have you made plans for the rest of the day?"

Her eyes darted away from him. Plans? This time the heat that surged into her face spread hotly throughout her body. Her original plans for the day weren't easily confessed. Loving and lovemaking were to have been the culmination of a new understanding between them, not this strange borderland between frustrated hopes and unexplained positions.

257

"I might work in the yard," she answered distantly.

"It's kinda hot outside today."

"Maybe I'll wash the car then. The red dust of West Texas is still on it."

"There's an idea."

His mild replies were nettling. Agitation grew instead of lessening, and she practically hissed, "The house could stand a good cleaning!"

"Might as well spend the energy some way," Matt agreed imperturbably.

Turning her back on him, Katherine slapped the dishtowel onto the counter, echoing tightly, "Might as well."

Her eyes searched the dining alcove, hoping to find something to distract her, calm her down. She felt as tense as a tightly coiled wire, all her nerves tautly wound. She tried reminding herself that she hadn't really expected Matt to succumb easily to all her plans and sighed disconsolately, knowing that deep down she had hoped just that. She heard approaching footsteps and sensed Matt standing behind her. Her eyes shut for a moment, and she drew a deep, curative breath. His arms came around her, and she felt his chest pressed against her back.

"Working alone gets a person all steamed up," he said, his low, growling voice muffled at her nape. His hands slipped upward, sensually surrounding her breasts.

"What?" she breathed, unable to think. His hands were doing wonderful, mind-shattering things, boldly pushing aside the elasticized bodice of her romper, gently crushing her breasts, his fingers kneading.

"Team effort lessens the strain. Let me help you," he offered, his voice a rough entreaty. He moved closer, and his thighs made contact with the gentle curve of her hips.

It was difficult to speak, but Katherine gave it her best effort, shallowly sighing. "I'm used to working alone."

His palms went to the sides of her breasts, and he raked

258

his fingers softly over the distended nipples. The breath at her shoulder was a warm whisper, and he purred silkily, "But it's better when it's done together."

A soft moan issued from her throat as his hands moved down her slender torso to her stomach. All tension left her. She felt helpless. "Yes, better," she whispered, then sighed tremulously. "You came back."

Matt turned her to face him, mocking huskily, "I came back. Don't I always?"

His eyes were filled with a significance she didn't understand, but his quick, hard kiss obliterated conjecture as he lifted her and carried her through the kitchen and into her bedroom. Carefully he lowered her to the bed, smoothing back the covers as he did so. He sat on the edge of the bed, his back to her, and peeled his shirt over his head. Boots and socks and belt quickly followed, but before he could stand to remove his cords, her slender arms circled his waist, her tender breasts pressing into his back, and he shuddered.

"I'm glad you came back," she breathed into his ear.

"So am I," he responded gruffly. He drew her arms more tightly about him, savoring the sweet, piercing contact at his back. His head was angled where she couldn't see his expression, and he said on a low note, "Kat, you're not the kind of woman a man sees only in the bedroom. You're . . ." His voice caught on a strangled laugh. "Considering where I've just carried you, that sounds ludicrous. What I'm trying to say is you're the kind of woman a man enjoys being around. You stir me, Katherine, in many ways. You give me pleasure even when you're laughing at my blunders or whipping around your kitchen in a fine rage."

His words crept around her heart, taking hold once more of what already belonged to him. Her breath caught, and she laid her head on his shoulder, after a moment whispering softly, "Matthew Clinton, you do have a way with you."

Her fingers curled into his chest hair, then moved down the hard, flat plane of his stomach. Unable to see the object of her task, her fingers gently fumbled. He groaned softly, and when the metal tab of his zipper hissed downward, she kissed his shoulder and moved back from him.

Kneeling in the center of the bed, her arms crossed over her breasts, Katherine watched him stand and step out of his clothing. His tall, muscled body was as she remembered from her lonely dreams, and his blatant power was a bold intoxicant to her senses. She felt spellbound.

The weight of his knee depressed the bed, and he knelt in front of her, extricating her arms from their covering position. Passionate urgency leaped from his darkened gaze, but maddening leisure controlled his movements. When he drew her hands to his mouth, the kiss he placed in each palm silently expressed the caring his words had implied. Then he placed her hands at his waist and cupped her face in his palms as he kissed her deeply, again and again.

"Your hair . . . take down your hair," he murmured against her cheek. And when she did, tossing the pins carelessly to the carpet, he buried his fingers in the loosened tresses, his kisses growing hotter, more urgent.

His unsteady hands eased the romper over her hips until it and her panties joined the pile of discarded clothing on the floor. Then Matt pressed her down into the mattress, hovering half above, half beside her to begin an onslaught of incredibly tender passion, his every move and word an expression of want.

"Do you have any idea, Katherine, what having you in my arms again means to me?" he asked thickly, tenderly cupping her breasts, his smoky gaze admiring the soft spill of creamy flesh in his palms.

Linking her hands behind his head, Katherine drew his mouth toward hers, her answer coming on a surrendering sigh. She tasted hunger and desire. She met it with her own.

Warm kisses, seeking kisses, rediscovering kisses ran her length. The moist heat of his mouth laved her flesh, courted her breasts, a velvet-rough tongue nudging, gently tugging at her nipples, drawing forth a puckering response from those sensitive peaks. A low sound of masculine satisfaction blended with her soft moan of pleasure.

His voice throbbed huskily at the curve of her throat. "The memory of this, Kat, kept me awake and aching for fifteen nights."

Her fingers delighted in the powerful structure of his shoulders. Remembering her own sleepless nights, she breathed with soft divertissement, "You make it sound like fifteen years."

"It felt like forever," Matt confessed with gruff insistence, his voice muffled in the valley between her breasts.

Along her thighs his fingers drew questing patterns, and she felt a warmth spread through her legs and into the very center of her being. Lovingly her fingers traced down the hardness of his sides, trailed provocatively over his lean hips, then clenched in gentle convulsion into the taut flesh of his buttocks when his teeth lightly nipped the soft hollow of her waist and then the silken expanse of her stomach.

She heard his voice, low and strained, whispering raspily, "You compel me, Kat." The heated arousal those urgent words betrayed was reasserted by the bold stroke of his arousal against her thigh.

His mouth burned upward to her breasts, again giving them his ardent attention, while his hand sought the soft flesh between her thighs, gently stroking. He discovered her pliant and ready for his caress, and he breathed

261

raggedly against her skin, "You feel so good to me, so right for me."

Urgently his mouth closed over hers, his lips burning, and under the deep, penetrating kiss she felt intoxicated. The potency of his kiss, his caress grew in the depths of her body,-showering sparks of excitement to the limits of her senses.

"I've needed you so, darlin' " was brushed over her lips. When her eyes melted to shimmering pewter, his gaze locked with hers, and he added with thick intensity, "You are the one substance I find I can't do without."

Her heart stopped for a moment, then quickened on a sweet, agonized beat. Not the avowal she yearned desperately to hear, but a beautiful avowal. Her eyes filled with the love she felt but couldn't voice, and for the moment she pretended to see the same message smoldering down on her from his smoky jade eyes. Under her hands his chest heaved on a low groan, and he came over her, lifting her hips to receive him.

The fusion of their bodies was a consuming, almost unbearable pleasure. She heard his breathing in her ear, the hoarse, whispered words of lovemaking. Their hearts beat wildly, caught together in a surging, expanding eddy of passion, consummated with a swirl of fire, a scalding rapture, and, as the shuddering of his body enveloped the tremors of hers, an incredible symmetry of souls.

Peaceful aeons later Matt raised his head from the damp hollow of her shoulder. Taking her face in his hands, he kissed her lingeringly.

"You're everything, Kat," he whispered feelingly.

Her soft answering murmur was almost a gurgle, expressing pleasure at his tribute and amusement at the male satisfaction lacing his tone. Her knuckles brushed lightly across the smug jut of his chin, and he grinned lazily, rolling away from her, stuffing pillows behind his shoulders. He drew her to his side, tucking her head under his chin, sighing expansively into her tangled hair.

Into the top of her head he asked slowly, "How'd I do?"

Surprise kept her silent for a moment. Then her fingers traced the line of hair that led down to his navel. There was only the tiniest hint of tart disapproval in her throaty, vamping, drawling "Ahhh, Mr. Clinton, your performance is a category in itself."

It was Matt's turn to go perfectly still, seemingly evaluating the sincerity of her words. Then he burst out laughing—a booming, deep-chested sound of genuine delight and amusement. Propping her elbows on his shaking chest, Katherine met the wicked pleasure of his gaze with suspicious eyes.

"Did you want a one to ten rating?"

"Darlin', I want and appreciate everything I can get from you," he drawled lazily, his fingers gently arranging love-mussed honeyed tresses behind her ears. "But I was asking if I'd met your new terms. Words—remember?"

"Oh." Her grin was sheepish. "I should have known Ol' Dad's and Ol' Granddad's pride 'n' joy wouldn't need a boost to his manly ego."

He grinned, but there was a curious glint in his eyes. "That's a strange way to put it."

"Didn't those two esteemed gentlemen teach you everything by which you mold your life-style? Independence and self-sufficiency? Strong convictions and iron-willed determination?" She smiled down at him, her finger tracing the outline of his mouth. "Stout avowals of realistic sentiments as opposed to sentimentality?"

"Is that how you see me?" His quizzical expression was difficult to read. She couldn't tell if he was pleased or displeased by her summation.

"That's how you are." She mocked him teasingly, de-

263

ciding to make light of it. "Your pride in your beliefs borders on arrogance."

Almost imperceptibly Matt's expression hardened, and it seemed to Katherine that her words had reinforced his beliefs. She held her breath, half expecting him to push her out of his arms and reassert his independence by leaving her. But after a tense, brooding moment a strange sparkle lit his eyes.

Dryly he remarked, "In need of no one, is that it?" And when she nodded wisely, he jeered softly, "My clever lover, your omniscience astounds me." He seemed on the verge of saying something more but limited himself to a restrained smile.

"I'm not omniscient," she objected on a mild grumble, wishing she did have the power to understand him completely. "There are many things that totally baffle me."

"Don't let it worry you, darlin'," he murmured consolingly, then added ambiguously, "A lot can happen in six weeks."

She wanted to say: *But what if, after six weeks pass, I find there's no chink in your armor of self-sufficiency? Will I be able just calmly to say good-bye to you?* She settled for an equivocal "Perhaps."

Matt grinned crookedly, changing the subject, reminding her, "You never did rate my word expression."

"We-l-l." She drew out the word, sending him a sly glance through half-closed lids before announcing pertly, "On a scale of prosaic to romantic, I'd have to give you an ardent and a half."

And then Katherine was dimpling around a quirking smile. Matt was looking immensely pleased with her response . . . and himself.

"A lot can happen in six weeks." Matt's words. Katherine's hopes.

Yet that first week Katherine saw no perceptible changes. True to form, the man she loved balked against the new restriction of separate roofs. When gentle coaxing and coercion couldn't get her to move back in his house, Matt tried a more direct approach, arguing impatiently, "How can you expect closeness when we're living apart? It's damned difficult to draw closer to someone you see only a few hours a week!"

"Matt, give it a chance," she pleaded softly. "We tried living together in June. I want the next few weeks to be better."

"Emotional compatibility. Physical separation. There's a contradiction there, Katherine," he said flatly. Then one dark eyebrow rose, and he asked jeeringly, "Are you sure you know what you want?"

Katherine was sure. She had five weeks left to find it.

The second week her intermittent lover boldly changed the status quo. He fell asleep beside her one night, the next morning murmuring teasingly about the mountain and Mohammed, his eyes filled with masculine contentment, his smile as innocent as a newborn babe's. By the end of the week several articles of his clothing had joined hers in the closet. His razor and shaving cream sat side by side with scented bath powder and moisturizing lotion in her bathroom, and a bottle of expensive whiskey, Matt's favorite label, found its way inside her kitchen cabinet. She didn't protest. Matt wanted more time with her. The thought was warming and optimistic.

The third and fourth weeks were both delightful and unsettling. Matt left for East Texas and stayed gone nine days. The morning he left Katherine found a note taped to the bathroom mirror: "You smile in your sleep, Kat, and the dimple's a temptation. There's also something lethal about a soft, clinging woman at six o'clock in the morning. A man could get hooked that way. I'll call you tomorrow night." When he called, Matt referred to his note, saying he was trying to maintain his rating. Remembering the "ardent and a half" she had given him for word expression, Katherine was doubly delighted. Not only had Matt hinted at a lasting relationship in his note, but he had done so deliberately.

Twice more he called during his absence, the second time only to chat for a moment before meeting some of his colleagues for dinner. The last phone call ended on an unsettling note. When Katherine asked when he was coming home, Matt retorted tauntingly, "Do you mean home to Fort Worth or home to you?" Recognizing the hard edge behind the mild taunt, she answered with a cool "Home from East Texas" and quickly found an excuse to end the phone call.

When he returned, the note Katherine cherished might just as well have been imagined. Obviously Matt had come home to Fort Worth, not to her. Other than brief daily calls to her office, Matt made himself scarce. He pleaded a heavy workload. He sounded tired. He also sounded oddly guarded. And Katherine could only wonder if he was regretting the whim that had made him write the note, if he was rueing the implications of permanency in its brief lines.

The fifth week found Katherine becoming anxious, and it showed in her fluctuation between edginess and quiet withdrawal. Time was running out, and there still had been no mention of love. In fact, their relationship seemed to be retrogressing instead of progressing. Matt was watchful and irritable rather than loverlike, and Katherine didn't know if her emotional state triggered his, or vice versa.

At one point their combined moods exploded into an argument, and Matt asked her roughly, "What do you want from this arrangement of ours, Kat? Just the superficial trappings of having a man at your beck and call for the summer?"

"No, of course not!" she denied vigorously, immediately bristling at the reminder of time limits. "I've told you what I—"

"Don't give me that bull about compatibility and closeness again! We see less of each other now than we did in June, and lately you're dissatisfied when we're together!"

"I'm sorry. I don't mean to be," she answered stiffly, unable to deny it, unwilling to explain why.

Disparagement claimed his expression, and he abruptly turned away from her, tossing derisively over his shoulder as he left the house, "That's the spirit, darlin'! Platitudes and evasion to the end!"

Two hours later he was back, his drawn features displaying the same torment and regret mirrored in her troubled gray eyes. When she offered a tentative "Matt, don't be angry. I—" he interrupted with a gruff, "Don't say another word," drawing her into his arms, muttering against her mouth, "We have one sure level of communication." As she met his passion with hers, Katherine silently and despairingly agreed with him.

The sixth week came in on the silent heels of the fifth. The words between them were limited and cautious, their time together articulated with subdued disquiet, enunciated with restrained turmoil. Even their physical communication was conducted with muted incoherence, passionate and intense, but vague in definition.

Katherine emptied herself of hope. The day before her children were due home, she bowed to the futility of dreams and began the process that would have her life rotating on its old, familiar axis once again. Plans of a life with Matt were put to rest. Six weeks had not brought the love and commitment she had yearned for. Matt had unbent only enough to become an intimate friend and more often an intimate stranger.

She methodically searched through her house for the traces of Matt's sporadic tenancy, placing each item, one by one, into a paper grocery sack—razor and can of shaving cream, a pair of jeans, two shirts, one tie, three socks, and one brass house key. The collection was small, bittersweet with memories. The task was short, made poignant by resolve.

She stared down at the paper bundle, and her eyes misted helplessly. Six weeks of her life fitted neatly inside one grocery sack. A summer of hopes packed away in less than fifteen minutes. Tears spotted against the porous sack, and she let them fall, allowing herself the final release of weeping.

Much later, dry-eyed, she determinedly took the bag and set it by the front door. She went to the kitchen, made coffee, blew her nose on a paper towel, and then dampened another one under the cold-water tap to blot her tear-stained face. She gave herself a bracing peptalk. She had taken a chance forty-one days ago, and it hadn't paid off. She had known the odds when she started out. There was no room for tears or feminine hysteria or recriminations. Matt had never misrepresented his beliefs, never lied, never promised more than he could deliver.

The coffee tasted bitter, and after the first tentative sips, she emptied it down the kitchen drain. She was rinsing the mug when the phone rang. It was Matt.

"Darlin', I just got in, and I'm starving. How does a late lunch of steak and salad sound?"

Like a fitting end, her mind whispered, his words triggering the recall of an afternoon in April. The loving had begun over a lunch of steak and salad, or at least that spring afternoon had seen unwilling attraction speeding swiftly into something more potent.

268

In a soft, subdued voice she murmured her thoughts. "Like a replay."

"Is that a yes or a no?" he inquired dryly.

"A yes."

"Get your scrawny little body over here then. I'll have the steaks started by the time you get here."

. . . Your scrawny little body turns me on . . .

In the bathroom Katherine made careful repairs to her makeup, camouflaging signs of recent tears. On a compulsive whim she changed into the faded jeans and chambray tunic she'd worn that day four months back, inspecting her appearance in the full-length mirror on her bedroom wall. Her features were tight, a little pale, and she pinched color into her cheeks, practicing a composed smile. Although softly curved, her body was straight and tall and slim. . . .

. . . You really should eat more . . . your ribs show . . .

On the way out of the house she grabbed the bag of Matt's belongings. Her bare feet sank into the sun-kissed grass as she made her way across the lawns.

. . . I've seen you barefoot more often than not . . .

Matt's house was unlocked, and Katherine entered without knocking, quietly setting the sack just inside the foyer before she made her way to the kitchen.

Matt was seasoning two steaks at the grill but turned when he heard her, smiling as he said, "Right on time," his eyes flickering as they took in her appearance.

Katherine's heart lurched as she noticed his attire. Jeans and boots and western shirt. Uncanny. She remembered the feel of those metal shirt snaps against her flesh. She was suddenly speechless.

. . . Lost your voice? Or was it your nerve, you bombastic little hypocrite? . . .

269

Her practiced smile fell into place, and she forced a bright, cheerful "Hi."

"The salad's your responsibility. Hop to it while I fetch the wine from the bar," he told her, pausing on his way out of the kitchen to plant a soft kiss on her mouth and murmur a low, satisfied "Mmmm."

Even wine.... *It's very good . . . try a little . . . it might increase your appetite . . .*

The beginning and the end. Vivid remembrance and stark reality drew comparisons as the meal progressed. The menu . . . their clothing . . . the locale . . . his smile, ironic at times, wide at others . . . green eyes, growing warm and dark as they appraised her . . . *I don't deny myself unnecessarily . . . When I see something beautiful and sleek and want it urgently . . .* Steak and wine were barely tasted. Katherine filled up on memories. Conversation was only sporadically joined. Her speaking voice was lost with her thoughts.

The end of the meal was heralded by a strange silence, and Katherine forced herself to sit calmly in her chair. The composure she had drawn around her like a cloak of defense had been stripped away by poignant remembrance. Words formed in her mind—bright, parting phrases—fading into unuttered speech under his determined green-eyed regard. Matt's gaze was fixed unwaveringly on her face, for how long she didn't know.

"I take it you weren't hungry." He broke the silence, his gaze shifting meaningfully to her barely touched plate.

"Not very," she admitted.

"And not talkative either."

"No, I guess not."

"But you do have something on your mind," Matt gibed softly.

"Yes." She swallowed heavily.

270

After a moment he inquired impatiently, "Do I keep guessing, or do you tell me?"

"I'll tell you." But her mouth, suddenly very dry, couldn't form the words. She sipped her wine, hoping it would liquefy her voice.

With silken precision Matt prompted her. "Could it have anything to do with that mysterious little bundle sitting on my foyer floor?"

Her fingers locked in a death grip around the stem of her glass, and she found enough voice to murmur, "Those are your things from my house."

"Are they really?" His response was very, very dry. "And right on time, too."

Her delicately arched eyebrows formed a puzzled line over her wary eyes. "What d'you mean?"

"Six weeks almost to the day," he murmured, sitting comfortably back in the big captain's chair, his arms folding across his chest in an attitude of waiting. His eyes were brilliant.

Her gray eyes fell before the accusation of his green ones, but her back straightened. She moved to the edge of her chair, unconsciously defensive. She said quietly, "Then you understand."

"Let's just say I've been expecting something like this for a while now."

"Have you?" she answered, faintly chary.

"Oh, yes, my darlin' lover. You're very precise and, in many ways, very predictable. Closeness and compatibility were allotted six weeks. Your generous time period is up."

Katherine's neck hurt from the strain of not bending under the lash of his soft contempt. Waveringly she said, "We agreed on the time, Matt."

"Did we?"

"You know we did. Even back in June, under the origi-

271

nal terms—your terms—we both knew our affair was a temporary one. You wanted it that way."

"And you? What did you want, Kat?" There was a waiting quality to his words that confused her.

"There's not much point in rehashing this, Matt," she said tightly.

"Not much point!" he grated harshly, his arms unfolding from his chest as he surged forward in his chair. His jaw was rigid with suppressed anger. "Why don't you quit hedging and give me the truth?"

"All right!" she said, flaring, her controlled façade broken by his hard scorn. "Your way and my way were never the same! You wanted—you got—an intimate friendship, without ties, without obligations! I wanted more! I *need* more!"

"Why don't you just say it?" He pressed her relentlessly, gritting the words.

"I wanted your love!" she all but shouted.

For a moment he was silent, and then his eyes lost some of their hardness, and he jeered softly, "Why didn't you ever say the word?"

. . . *Be reasonable, Katherine, be honest . . . your expectations are too high . . .*

With controlled patience she gritted, "It's difficult to discuss love with a man who doesn't believe in it." She slumped back in her chair, all anger gone. She was limp with emotional exhaustion, totally spent, the last few weeks of unanswered hopes and endless failures taking their toll. "Love won't change things between us. I may love you, Matt, but I won't be a part of an affair that goes on and on, with never a hope for more. I need more. I need permanence."

"You want commitment and marriage," he stated flatly, slumping back in his chair.

. . . *Your way is unrealistic . . .*

Katherine was near tears. She could feel them boiling behind her eyelids. Hot tears. Disappointed tears. Frustrated tears. She blinked them back. Furiously. She was not going to cry! Her eyes stared straight ahead, brimful but not overflowing.

A soft laugh came to her, sounding ludicrously out of place in the turmoil of her thoughts. It was followed by an amused "You know, darlin', for a woman with courage, you were cowardly about using a very simple word."

The accusation made her misty eyes sweep to his face. They widened at what they saw. Matt was grinning. Widely. From ear to ear. His eyes were bright and strangely contented, and with horrible dismay Katherine realized her confession had done exactly what she had always feared it would do. Matt was cheerfully contemplating the control of her life.

She stood so abruptly that her hip banged against the table. China and cutlery rattled, and with an uncertain topple her wineglass fell onto its side. Bright red liquid spilled a circular puddle, slowly elongating to form a rivulet that flowed to the table's edge. Momentarily mesmerized, Katherine watched its cascading descent to the tiled floor. What finally penetrated her spellbound haze she didn't know. Perhaps Matt's husky entreaty of her name. Perhaps her own soft moan of agitation.

She whirled away from the table. Only to fall into the same trap she'd fallen into on an afternoon in April. As she came abreast of his chair, Matt hooked her waist and hauled her down onto his lap. She fought him feebly, automatically. The strength to fight with force was lost in despair. She managed one or two flailing blows that connected with his unflinching chest and glanced off his strong chin. Then Matt easily brought her hands behind her, and she went still. When he adjusted her closer to his chest, she crumpled, burrowing her face into the warm

273

hollow of his throat. She was trembling uncontrollably, strangely dry-eyed, silent, and frustrated. His warm lips moved over her face, soothing the tension. Quiet, comforting words were whispered hoarsely in their wake. It was a long time before the content of those words penetrated her turmoiled brain.

Clearing her throat to speak, she whispered, "You what?"

"You heard me" was his low, satisfied purr.

Finding herself less restrained, Katherine jerkily sat up, balancing on his knees. His hands at her waist kept her from toppling to the floor. Her cheeks were pale, slowly flushing with heat. Her hair was disheveled, rioting about her face. Her eyes were circles, silver and unbelieving.

"Tell me again," she demanded croakily.

"I love you, Katherine," he stated slowly and distinctly. His smile was wide and complacent. "Your way is my way."

For a moment she made no response at all. Then four months of waiting, a summer of heartache, and six weeks of hopes made her hard, tight fist land right in the center of his stomach. She whispered furiously, "Well, it took you long enough to get it right!"

Matt's harsh expulsion of breath said he hadn't expected the blow. The eyes meeting hers were stunned, but the hands at her waist held on tightly, bringing her up to his mouth. He muttered an exasperated "Dammit, Kat, you'd try the patience of a saint!" right before his mouth closed over hers.

When she could think again, Katherine found her arms around his shoulders, her face buried in his neck. She sighed happily, whispering, "You're not a saint."

His low, wicked laughter was nuzzled into the top of her head. "No, that I'm not."

He pushed enough space between them so that his

274

fingers could trace the neckline of her tunic. His eyes traced the smooth lines of her face, lingering on the delicate angles, the soft hollows. His expression sobered, and he said huskily, "I want to marry you, Katherine. I want you with me always. I want you, and those kids of yours, and that cat. I want a home with you."

She hugged him tightly, echoing another acceptance of another proposal by saying fervently, "You're on!"

He laughed again, saying incredulously, "Hey, what is this? I lay my heart at your feet, and you give a two-word acceptance?"

There was a hint of vulnerability in his expression that Katherine had never seen. It reminded her that Matt, too, was in need of words—reassuring words. She hugged him again, smiling into his eyes, saying, "I've loved you forever, you tormenting man. And you know I want the same things you do. I always have." Her reward came when his eyes slowly filled with a growing conviction.

With a touch of his familiar mockery Matt said contemplatively, "I never thought I'd be admitting to love and forever, but eventually a man has to conclude that the wanting and needing and jealousy and possessiveness add up to something stronger than the desire to bed a scrawny little widow." Her smiling mouth drew his undivided attention, and his lips saluted the dimple in her cheek. Huskily he offered, "That's a deadly combination, lady. Gray eyes, skinny ribs, bare feet, and a dimple. I was lost from the first meeting and didn't even know it."

"Me, too," Katherine confessed happily, kissing his chin, and then his eyes, and finally his mouth, which had been her undoing. Her fingers undid snaps, teasing inside his shirt, causing him to shiver. She smiled even as her thoughts took another turn. "Matt? I've just thought of something."

"What's that, darlin'?" He sounded distracted, his

275

hands drawing the tunic over her head, his eyes delighting in what he uncovered.

"My house. Your house. We won't need both of them," she explained, losing her breath when his hand gently grazed across her breasts. Trying to keep her mind on her explanation, she gasped thoughtfully, "We could sell mine, I guess."

His hands were at her waist, unsnapping, unzipping, and he abruptly stood, lifting her with him. Into her hair he breathed, "Either way. I don't care. I know an excellent realtor." As he strode from the kitchen, he added under his breath, feelingly, "No more separate roofs."

Katherine smiled at the last heartfelt statement and breathed sweetly in his ear, "We didn't really have separate roofs. You spent half the nights at my house."

"I guess so." He reflected frowningly. In his bedroom he stopped by the bed, letting her down on its edge. He took her face in his palms, saying seriously, "I wanted you to have your way six weeks ago. I thought if I did everything by your rules, you'd learn to trust me again."

"Did you?" she asked skeptically, helping him off with his shirt. "I got the impression you were trying to rearrange all my rules."

A smacking kiss landed on the pensive moue of her mouth before Matt moved away to shed the rest of his clothing. He grinned at her, saying, "I didn't like living apart or not having you by my side every night. That doesn't mean I didn't want you to have your way."

"Oh, I get it!" She slapped her forehead as if a brainstorm had suddenly hit, then sent him a sly glance, her smile sweetly adoring. "You wanted me to have my way only if you could try everything in your power to change it to your way! That was thoughtful of you, Matt. Very thoughtful and very generous. Noble, in fact."

Her sweet sarcasm was answered by his heavily resigned "Okay, my clever darlin', I admit to being a little impatient at times. I'm not perfect."

A *little* impatient? At *times?* She whispered admiringly, "And humble, too."

Then she was scrambling for the far side of the bed, laughing, because her humble lover was lunging for her, retaliation in his eyes. He snagged the hem of her jeans just as she was about to roll to the floor, and when she twisted, he managed to strip the loosened pants completely off her. The quick, unequal tussle ended with Katherine lying on her stomach, her face buried in the bedspread.

Lifting her head, she tried to look outraged; but her face was flushed with laughter, and her eyes were bright and sparkling. "That was subversive and unnecessary," she announced frigidly.

Matt grinned wickedly, admiring the sprawl of slender femininity on his bed. Pulling back the bedspread, he came down beside her. He drew her into his arms and melted her feigned outrage by saying, "I've fallen in love with an exasperating, stimulating, articulating widow who promises to make my life exhilarating." He kissed the tip of her nose, said, "How am I doing?" and then kissed her answer into silence.

His kisses continued on the same light vein and swiftly progressed into something sweeter, more urgent. In moments the shallow, uneven tenor of her breathing matched the raggedness of his. Katherine slid loving fingers down his sides to his hips and heard his voice, low and hoarse at her ear, requesting urgently, "Tell me again, Kat."

The words he wanted to hear came out on a sumptuous sigh. "I love you, Matt."

The discovery of shared love was savored, deliciously prolonged amid warm kisses, arousing caresses, and gazes full of quickening desire. As he hovered above her, Matt's love words fell over each feature of her face. Her heart

277

trembled, and she responded with similar murmurings. Their words blended, met with the union of their mouths, and heightened their desire for each other.

The warmth of breathed laughter, low and infinitely sexy, blew softly against her throat. "Love in the afternoon," he murmured, smiling against her skin. "I suppose after today it will be nighttime loving only—the price of respectability."

His reference was to the return of her children, and her eyes clouded with momentary uncertainty. She threaded her fingers through the crisp thickness of his hair, gently tugging to bring his face up to hers. Solemnly she asked, "Does that bother you?"

His lazy grin evened out, and he said deeply, "Nothing bothers me but the thought of not having you."

"Mmmm," she murmured, reassured, smiling again. She planted a soft kiss on his chin. "You've had me for a very long time."

"Somehow it didn't seem that way to me," he murmured ironically. A knuckle traced the soft hollow behind her ear, then trailed lazily down to the slope of her breast. "There have been moments when we've been close, but the part of you I wanted most—well, it always seemed beyond my reach." He grinned crookedly, his knuckle lightly grazing the peak of one soft breast. The sensual gleam that brightened his eyes said he appreciated the puckering response his knuckle had drawn forth. "All those references to time limits, darlin', nearly drove me crazy and completely destroyed my confidence," he told her with husky rebuke.

In delight Katherine laughed, never before having witnessed a lack of confidence in Matt. Even now his hurt, reproachful expression couldn't obliterate his innate self-assurance. Her hand lifted to his face, tracing the firm line of his mouth, the strong jaw, the aggressive chin. "You mean you never once thought you had me in the palm of your hand?"

Her caressing hand was brought to his mouth, an ardent kiss placed in the palm before he pressed it against his cheek. "It's debatable who was in whose palm."

"You never denied wanting nothing more than a summer affair," she pointed out on a soft gasp. Matt was creating havoc with her breathing, his finger and thumb gently rolling a nipple into acute arousal. Her hand was on his shoulder, sliding across to his spine, and she complained softly, "Matt, I can't think when you do that."

"I can't either," he admitted, and bent his mouth to taste the fruit of his labor, subjecting the peaks of both her breasts to the sensual wanderings of his tongue. Then, with a sharp groan, he laid his head against her breasts, grabbing her hands straying to more intimate territory over his body. His words were muffled, slurred with arousal, but firm for all that. "Katherine, *you* put the time limits on our relationship."

A small sting of resentment at the unjust accusation had her squirming to the side, forcing his head up so she could see his expression. Her eyes widened. He was perfectly serious.

With soft heat, she began, "Matt, from the beginning, you—"

"I'm not talking about the beginning," he interrupted patiently, bringing her back beneath him with consummate ease. There was a wicked glitter in his eyes, but his mouth was solemn. "Calm down, silver eyes, and listen to my explanation." The pause was long enough for the frost of defensiveness to fade from her eyes. "At the beginning, as you put it, I was laboring under the false belief that getting you in my bed would be enough to satisfy me. I thought it was all cut-and-dried. I'd have you, I'd surfeit myself with this sexy little body, and then I'd be at peace

279

again. But every time you insisted that a summer was all we had I found myself pricked by annoyance. It wasn't until that night in June when you left me that I realized why. And by then, I'd made some terrific mistakes with you." His heavy sigh was redolent of their trouble in June. His mouth covered hers in a warm kiss, erasing any lingering pain from that memory. "After that I figured my best bet was to stay on your good side and go along—nominally, at least—with all your new terms." A lopsided grin acknowledged his tendency toward impatience. "You were still spouting time limits, and I just hoped the six weeks would give you time to trust me, maybe to realize we had something permanent going."

"Oh," she whispered with quiet chagrin, realizing that from Matt's point of view she had been the one to set time limits. She ran her hands lightly across the muscled slopes of his shoulders. Remembering how often she had yearned to hear words of love from him, she chided him gently. "You could have tried three simple words. I wanted to hear them."

"Ahhh, words." He groaned feelingly, grimacing at the reminder. Then his eyes brightened, oblique amusement in their depths. Slowly, stressing each word with sincerity, he vowed, "I love you, darlin', and I'm determined to get the words right."

Smiling, she looped her hands behind his head and brought his mouth down to hers to share a warm kiss. "I've loved you forever, Matt. We've both been guilty of not saying enough."

A blazing fire leaped into his eyes before his mouth met hers again, the tenor of the kiss changing subtly, warmth becoming demand. She answered it, the stirring of her senses releasing a flood of passionate longing.

His touch, his kiss, the feel of his body burning against hers aroused her, as always, to a heated conflagration. The embers grew hotter and hotter at the wayward caress of his hands and the nuzzling of his mouth along the sensitive points of her body. When his warm palm settled between her thighs, a pulsing heat twisted her body into his caress.

"Do you know how much I need you?" His voice vibrated thickly against the curve of her breast. His male desire throbbed heatedly against her. "Do you?"

A soft moan came from her throat, giving him her answer. He continued to stroke her, and with every sighing breath, every quivering response, every reciprocated caress she implored him to need her more.

There were no more words. Sweet but unspoken excitement built as he shifted his weight, positioning himself between her thighs. Their bodies commingled, unifying into one. Indescribable, budding, splintering feeling expanded by leaps and bounds. Clasped tightly together, the thunderous beating of their hearts syncopated the wild, soaring rapture of their movements. Their lovemaking knew the infinite reaches of love, mushrooming into a torrent of ecstasy, dissolving in a flood of pleasure.

In the aftermath of repletion, inertia threatened to take its toll in the form of sleep. Katherine snuggled close against him, her back to his chest, and heard a soft "I love you, Kat," in the amber confusion of her hair. She smiled drowsily.

From a vent in the ceiling, the cooling whisper of central air flowed over their damp skin, and she shivered. She felt the sheet being drawn over their bodies, heard more murmurings, spoken quietly but with an underlying note of expectancy.

The chest at her back moved on a contented sigh . . . "I love the way you make me feel." A hand stroked her length, lingering over the swell of her hip, splaying across the flatness of her stomach. "I love the way *you* feel." Soft kisses fell to her hair, her nape, nuzzled into her shoulder. "I love the way you taste and smell."

Now that she was more alert, inkling thoughts drifted into her brain, became certainty, and had her turning slowly to face him. Her suspicious gray eyes met his glowing green ones.

"I love everything about you, darlin'," Matt told her solemnly. His fingers brushed the tangle of her hair away from her face; his eyes sparkled with barely subdued anticipation.

She hadn't imagined the eager expectation, Katherine realized with delighted amusement. Although tempered, it was stamped into every feature of his face, every line of his purring length. It beguiled her. She knew what he expected, and still it enticed her. Her smile began at the corners of her mouth, twitching them upward, and then spread into her eyes, making them sparkle.

Earnestly, delectably, she vowed, "You're very romantic, and I love you."

Blatant triumph claimed his features. The glow of emerald eyes became a victory bonfire. Exultation widened his mouth into a gleaming smile. His chest expanded on a preening show of self-congratulation.

Near her waiting mouth Matt murmured softly, "I love your rating system, too."

THE WILD ONE

by
MARIANNE HARVEY
bestselling author of *The Dark Horseman*
and *The Proud Hunter*

Proud, beautiful Judith—raised by her stern grandmother on the savage Cornish coast—boldly abandoned herself to one man and sought solace in the arms of another. But only one man could tame her, could match her fiery spirit, could fulfill the passionate promise of rapturous, timeless love.

A Dell Book $2.95   (19207-2)

A love forged by destiny—
A passion born of flame

FLAMES OF DESIRE

by Vanessa Royall

Selena MacPherson, a proud princess of ancient
Scotland, had never met a man who did not desire
her. From the moment she met Royce Campbell at
an Edinburgh ball, Selena knew the burning
ecstasy that was to seal her fate through all eternity.
She sought him on the high seas, in India, and
finally in a young America raging in the
birth-throes of freedom, where destiny was bound
to fulfill its promise. . . .

A DELL BOOK $2.95

SWEET WILD WIND

by Joyce Verrette

In the primeval forests of America, passion was born in the mystery of a stolen kiss.

A high-spirited beauty, daughter of the furrier to the French king, Aimee Dessaline had led a sheltered life. But on one fateful afternoon, her fate was sealed with a burning kiss. Vale's sun bronzed skin and buckskins proclaimed his Indian upbringing, but his words belied another heritage. Convinced that he was a spy, she vowed to forget him—this man they called Valjean d'Auvergne, Comte de la Tour.

But not even the glittering court at Versailles where Parisian royalty courted her favors, not even the perils of the war torn wilderness could still her impetuous heart.

A DELL BOOK   17634-4   ($3.95)

**The second volume in the
spectacular Heiress series**

The Cornish Heiress

by Roberta Gellis
bestselling author of
The English Heiress

Meg Devoran—by night the flame-haired smuggler, Red Meg.
Hunted and lusted after by many, she was loved by one man
alone...

Philip St. Eyre—his hunger for adventure led him on a
desperate mission into the heart of Napoleon's France.

From midnight trysts in secret smugglers' caves to wild
abandon in enemy lands, they pursued their entwined destinies
to the end—seizing ecstasy, unforgettable adventure—and
love.

A Dell Book   **$3.50**   **(11515-9)**